MAD RIVALS

LISA SUZANNE

MAD RIVALS
THE BRADLEY LEGACY BOOK 1
© 2025 LISA SUZANNE

All rights reserved. In accordance with the US Copyright Act of 1976, the scanning, uploading, and sharing of any part of this book without the permission of the publisher or author constitute unlawful piracy and theft of the author's intellectual property. No part of this book may be reproduced or transmitted in any form or by any means, electronic or mechanical, including photocopying, recording, or by any information storage and retrieval system without the written permission of the author, except where permitted by law and except for excerpts used in reviews. If you would like to use any words from this book other than for review purposes, prior written permission must be obtained from the publisher.

Published in the United States of America by Books by LS, LLC.

This book is a work of fiction. Any similarities to real people, living or dead, is purely coincidental. All characters and events in this work are figments of the author's imagination.

Cover Design by Qamber Designs.

ALSO BY LISA SUZANNE

FIND MORE AT
AUTHORLISASUZANNE.COM/BOOKS

DEDICATION

    Some authors write something riveting here that might lure in a reader just from the dedication. I started publishing in 2013, and my first book was dedicated to my husband. And the next. And a few more. Then we had our first child, and it was to both of them. Then we had another, and it was to the three of them. This is the 78th book I've published, and this one's for them, too.

    It's always for them. ♡

CHAPTER 1
MADDEN BRADLEY

I Can Get Good Food Anywhere

I didn't want this trade, but sometimes the things we don't want turn out to be the best thing for us.

That's been a theme my entire life, and I can only hope it holds true this time.

Alex Sheffield, one of the top reporters of league news, broke the story about ten minutes after Coach called me to break the news.

"Madden Bradley, popularly known as Mad Brad around the league, has been traded from Chicago to San Diego."

I haven't even wrapped my head around it yet when my phone starts to ring. It's only been a few minutes since the trade was announced, and my father is already calling.

"Hello," I answer formally instead of *hey, Dad, how ya doin'?*

"Madden, son. Congratulations on your trade, but you know I'll need you in Chicago this summer to continue our work together at Bradley Group."

I don't want the family business, but I'm the eldest son in the prestigious Bradley family.

It's my legacy to carry the company forward whether I want to or not.

Give it to Everleigh, third in line and the oldest daughter. She has a way better business sense than I do despite my undergraduate degree in business.

But no. It's mine.

I don't have much career left in me. Traded in the final year of my contract. The Bears didn't want me anymore. The Storm will likely let me ride out my final year on the bench and then I'll disappear into the void.

I know it's business. I know the truth of the matter is that the Bears didn't want to pay me. They have other problems there, too. Firing the coach midseason is usually a pretty good indicator of that, and they just hired the Eagles' offensive coordinator. He's cleaning house, starting with me.

I clear my throat. "I haven't figured anything out yet. I need to go to San Diego for a few days and get the lay of the land."

"So long as I have your assurance you'll be around to work with me," he says shortly.

No, Father. I won't be.

But the good news for him, I suppose, is that he also has an office in Dallas. And Vegas. And New York.

The list goes on.

But you don't become a magnate in commercial real estate development without taking risks and spreading out your assets, I guess.

"We'll figure out a compromise," I say instead of any of that.

I'm not quite ready to leave Chicago anyway. We're finally coming out of winter, though I'm expecting a spring blizzard since we usually get hit with something when we're not expecting it. The weather will turn to my favorite season that isn't football season, and I don't want to miss it.

My entire life is here in Chicago—my brothers in football, players who are no longer my teammates. A sea of women—some of whom I've hooked up with. My family and the Bradley Legacy.

It's all I fucking hear about.

Okay, so maybe San Diego isn't looking so bad.

It's a new pond in which to cast my line away from the spotlight cast on my family—or, rather, away from the spotlight our parents work so hard to put us in.

I can't say I'll miss that, though I'll miss that sense of family. Monday night dinners cooked by my parents' personal chef for the entire family—or at least those who can make it.

Charity events and activities in the only place I've ever called home.

And my own home—a penthouse in a skyscraper downtown. I glance around the place and walk over to the windows that look out over Navy Pier and Lake Michigan on one side and downtown on the other. I'm in the New Eastside, just north of Millennium Park. I run the Lakefront Trail along Lake Shore Drive daily when the weather allows.

I don't want to give it all up. I love this city. I bleed blue and orange, have my entire life, and now I'm just supposed to…wear black and silver? Just like that?

I head over to my liquor cabinet and grab the first bottle I see. I take a healthy chug of the amber liquid as I try to come to terms with the fact that a month from now, all this will be a distant memory.

* * *

"Nice to meet you. I'm Madden Bradley," I say, holding out a hand to shake Spencer Nash's. We've met on the field before, and this is absolutely a case of game respecting game. I'm a couple years his senior. I'd peg him around thirty-two or thirty-three, and at thirty-five, I'm practically ancient for a wide receiver.

But I'm not going to let that stop me from playing my ass off. I'm a competitor by nature, and there was a hole on this roster that was filled by me. I will do what it takes to prove that I belong here and that I deserve to be on that field when the games begin.

"Mad Brad!" Clayton Mack says, slapping me on the back. "Welcome to the Storm. Call me Clay. Or Clay Mack."

I just got here this afternoon, and Coach Brian Dell introduces me to the other receivers along with the coaches who are in the office today. He gives me a few minutes with the men who are now my teammates in the locker room when he has his own meeting to attend to.

"So what's good in this town?" I ask.

"The views," Spencer says. "The beach. The fans. My wife's winery."

"There's some good food if you find the right places," DJ Evans tells me. "I can help you out there."

"The women," Clay adds as he wiggles his eyebrows.

I raise a brow. "The women?"

I can get good food anywhere. Hell, I hail from Chicago, the home of good food.

And I guess I can find good women anywhere, too. But if my new buddy Clay has an inside track, I'm all ears.

"I'm married, and my wife is from Minnesota, so I can't really attest to that," Spencer says.

Clay elbows Spencer. "This guy is always talking about his wife like getting married is goals." He rolls his eyes.

"You're not a marriage guy?" I ask Clay.

He shrugs. "It's not for everyone."

I chuckle as I voice my earlier thought. "Finally someone who shares my values. Clay Mack and Mad Brad. Sounds like a lethal combination for this town." What I really mean is that I think I just found my San Diego best friend.

I guess time will tell.

CHAPTER 2
KENNEDY VAN BUREN

There's a Solution

I never should have closed my eyes.
 A twenty-seven-year-old woman in downtown Chicago should be smarter than that, and I am.
I'm just so damn tired.
 I took public transportation—the bus—this morning. It's a longer ride, but I can work or relax versus the stress of driving. And on my way home from work, I can read.
 Or I could, anyway, until someone lifted my Kindle.
 It was on the seat next to me when I closed my eyes, and now it's not.
 I rummage through my purse just in case I stuck it in there without remembering, and…
 Wait a second.
 I rummage some more.
 Dammit.
 Great. Just freaking great.
 My wallet is gone, too.
 There was a twenty-dollar bill in there—the one my best friend Clem gave me yesterday to pay for tonight's dinner, which I only now remember I was supposed to pick up on the way home. Apart from that, all I can think of that might have been

in there is the membership card for the gym I've been trying to cancel for months and my license. I use my phone to pay by credit card, so I took those out ages ago.

Oh, and that old photo of Clem and me from our freshman year in college.

Replacing my license will be a pain in the ass since I don't exactly have all the free time in the world to report this crime to the police and spend half a day waiting around at the DMV.

What an inconvenient way to make a bad day a little worse.

I glance around at the other passengers on the bus, and they're all wrapped up in their own little worlds. The thief probably lifted my shit and got off at the next stop with nobody here the wiser. I wouldn't be any wiser to it happening right beside me, either—especially not with my eyes closed.

This isn't the life I envisioned for myself when I took a stand against working for the family business.

I wanted to earn my own way. I wanted to experience the journey of making myself out of nothing. I stubbornly didn't want to rest on the silver spoon I've been fed with since the day I was born.

But this? Getting robbed because my meager paychecks can only afford half the rent in a shitty part of town that's a full hour-long bus ride away from work?

This isn't exactly the stand I was trying to make.

This is dangerous. I was robbed on public transportation today.

Clem and I don't go out for walks after dark.

We know it's dangerous, but we take the proper precautions. Or, we usually do. Closing my eyes on the bus isn't exactly a precaution, I guess.

Shit.

I blow out a breath as we approach my stop, and I stand and start moving toward the front of the bus. I usually get on and off without a word to the driver, but not today.

"My wallet and Kindle were stolen," I say.

The look he gives me makes it clear that there's nothing he could care less about.

"On this bus. Sometime between when I got on and now," I amend.

"Report it to the transit authority and the police." His voice is gruff. He isn't going to do anything about it, not that there's anything to do, but it would be nice to feel like he cared that someone stole something from another passenger on his bus.

He doesn't. He just wants me off the bus so he can continue on his route and get through his day.

It's all any of us are doing anymore. Survival. And you know what? I'm getting real fucking tired of it.

There's a solution. The little voice in the back of my mind is whispering to me.

I know there is, I snap.

Then take it.

I heave out a breath as I walk down the steps, and I trip as I make the transition from the bottom step of the bus to the curb.

My purse flies off my shoulder, and the contents go flying all over the sidewalk as my knee skids across the jagged, rough pavement. It rips a hole in my leggings, and blood is already starting to drip from the spot.

It hurts like fuck, and my cheeks burn with embarrassment that I fell like an idiot.

Nobody bends down to help me pick up my shit despite the fact that there are multiple people who got off at this stop and others waiting to get on. They step around the idiot on the ground instead.

They're surviving, too. They're just trying to get through the day.

I gather everything up and scurry along the four blocks back to the apartment as best I can with a wounded knee. It's not broken, but it's definitely in pain.

Kind of like my spirit.

This isn't the life I want, and as I walk through the front door and drop my purse with a dramatic thud by the door, Clem springs up from her spot on the couch. I'm blocked by a little half-wall, so she hasn't seen the wound yet.

"Oh, good! You're home," she calls. "Ready to get cooking?"

I burst into tears, and she rushes over to me. She spots the hole in my leggings, and her eyes grow wide.

"Oh my God, Kenny! What happened? Are you okay?"

"Someone robbed me on the bus and my wallet and Kindle are gone and I didn't have any money to get our stuff for dinner and then I fell and I hate my life," I wail at her, and she grabs me into a hug as she soothingly rubs my back.

"Shh, shh, it'll be okay," she says gently.

This isn't the first time she's taken care of me—or vice versa. We were assigned as roommates at Loyola our freshman year, and the quirky and fun Clementine Carter became my instant best friend.

We shared the same major—visual communications—and took most of our classes together throughout our four years.

We've lived together since we graduated—going on five years now—both of us determined to live in the city we love so much as we make our own path separate from our parents.

I did that by snagging a graphic design position right out of college. I hate it.

She did it by finding a job working retail. She hates it even more than me.

We've struggled for five entire years to make ends meet, but the events of today just made me realize one very important lesson.

I don't want to just make ends meet.

I'm sick of this life.

I need to change it, and I want Clem to come with me.

I never wanted to be handed the job my parents have reserved for me my entire life, but I think right now…it may be my only choice.

CHAPTER 3
KENNEDY VAN BUREN

Wild Nights with a Stand-Up Guy

"**A**re you happy?" I ask Clem after I've changed into sweats and cleaned up my knee. She poured us each a bowl of some off-brand Cheerios, and I guess that's dinner tonight.

She twists her lips. "Truth?"

"Always."

She shakes her head. "No. Not even a little."

"Me either," I admit.

"This isn't it. You know? This isn't what I want out of life," she says. "Slogging back and forth to a job that sucks with a long-ass commute and no time to get out and just have some fun. No time to meet hot guys and have a wild night of crazy sex. No time to do *anything*."

I nod. "Agree. I hate it here. I hate this apartment." I glance at the crack in the wall that we complained about two years ago that still hasn't been fixed. "I hate the commute. I hate my job. But I love you."

"I love you, too. And I love our pact to live together until one of us gets married, but if it's here…I just don't know how much longer I can do it."

I take a bite of my cereal, and then I clear my throat. "What if I have the solution, but it goes against everything we believe in?"

She focuses her gaze on the slats of the vertical blinds covering our patio doors that have never hung quite right. One is missing, so there's always a way for outsiders to peep inside at our shitty apartment.

"I'd trade my morals for a better situation any day of the week," she says.

I laugh, though the truth is that it's not really all that funny.

"My parents have a job waiting for me back home. One with a big paycheck and plenty of benefits."

Her brows crinkle. "Okay? Well, I'm happy you'll get out of this at least."

I shake my head. "I don't want it. You know that I've never wanted it. But I'll take it on the condition they hire you, too."

"Hire *me*?" she asks, her hand flying to her chest. "But what will I even do?"

I nod. "We're in this together, Carter. We'll find a place for you. And, you know, we'll only accept if we have somewhere closer to the office to live. We can't live way down here and commute all the way up there."

She nods slowly. "I mean, obviously not. But what's your proposed solution?"

"We move in with my parents until we can save enough to get on our feet and afford a place of our own."

She twists her lips and wrinkles her nose. "I don't know about that."

We both hear our neighbors starting up at the same time.

The walls are thin.

"Oh, Michael, yes, yes, yes!" Katie moans, and good Lord, if I never hear Katie moaning over Michael again, I might actually get some sleep.

Clem sighs as her eyes meet mine, and it's like the porno going on next door is the straw that breaks the camel's back. "Make the call."

I head into my bedroom because I know, I *know*, that my mother will say something cruel about Clem, and I don't want her to overhear it.

"Kennedy, darling, how lovely to hear from you," my mother answers.

We've never really been all that close. To be honest, I was raised by a series of nannies more than by my own mother. But she's still the woman who gave birth to me, and I suppose I don't call home as often as I should.

When I was a pre-teen and learned where babies came from, I often wondered if I was an accident. When I hit my late teens, I finally realized that I wasn't.

Only…now I believe I was meant to be a boy—or that's what they were hoping for, anyway. I'm not, just one more disappointment in a long line of them, but regardless, I'm the sole heiress to Van Buren Construction.

I don't want it. I've never wanted it. But it'll be mine anyway.

And *that* is why this call is so goddamn hard to make.

"Mother, hello. Is Father with you?"

"He's still at the office. Is there something I can help you with?"

I draw in a deep breath and bite my lip, schooling myself as I come up with the words that'll hit exactly where I need them to without getting too detailed. I take the easy cop-out rather than getting into the details of Katie and Michael and the bus and my stolen wallet. "You were both right. Please say the offer to work for VBC is still open?" I beg.

"Darling, of course. You know you always have a place here. After all, this will all be yours someday."

I can picture her holding up a hand like those models on *The Price Is Right* as she indicates the entire house, its contents, and the business.

"Right. Well, with that in mind, I have a condition." It's just as well that I have a condition since their love for me was always conditional as well.

"What is it, pray tell?"

"That you hire Clementine, too," I blurt. "And that we can stay at the house until we save up enough to get our own place."

She sighs heavily. "You've always been the type to take in strays," she murmurs.

"Forget it," I mutter.

"No, no." She pauses, and then she says, "Fine."

"I don't want to hear another word about her," I warn.

"I will do my very best. It's just that we trust you to care for what we've built, Kennedy. You know our reluctance to hand it over to a stranger."

"She isn't a stranger," I protest. "She's the best friend I've ever had, and you aren't handing anything over to her."

"You know how work and money can come between friendships," she says a bit haughtily, and no, actually I don't.

I know that *my parents* had issues with people *they* used to call friends, but their life isn't mine, and Clem would never betray me.

"You'll get to know her, and you will love her," I say. "I'm so sorry, but it's the only way I'll do this."

"I already said fine once," she says curtly. "When can we expect you?"

I glance around the meager bedroom. There's really not a whole lot to pack up to get the fuck out of here.

And I'm not really all that sure my boss will even care if I don't give him two weeks' notice. He'll find someone to fill the position within twenty-four hours.

Same with Clem's job.

"Tomorrow."

"Fine. I'll have Edith make up your room and the guest room down the hall from you."

"Thanks, Mom," I say. I almost *never* call her Mom. It's too soft, but this moment seems to call for it.

"You're welcome. I just hope your father doesn't blow a gasket when he hears what I've agreed to."

"He won't," I say with confidence. I may not be all that close to either of my parents, but my father at least made attempts to bond with me over the years. He'd take me into the office and introduce me to the staff, or he'd show me what he was working on. He'd train me on the basics of what he does with the idea in mind that someday I'd be doing it.

My mother would sweep in and act like I was a nuisance. She worked with him for years and years until she retired last year to spend more time with her "charity work."

I've never seen that woman lift a damn finger.

Katie next door finally hits her orgasm, and they'll be quiet for at least a half hour before they start going at it again.

And now that I'm changing my life around, is it really too much to ask for me to find someone to have the same kind of wild nights Katie has? Can I find a Michael of my own? Only…not *Michael*-Michael. I stay out of it, but I swear I heard someone who wasn't Katie over there moaning his name a few weekends ago when she was out of town.

Just some wild nights with a stand-up kind of guy.

And a job that, if I'm going to hate it, at least pays well.

And a nice place to live that isn't my parents' house.

Is that too much to ask?

* * *

What a difference forty-eight hours makes.

It turns out my boss wasn't too happy with no notice, and maybe I should've been more careful about burning bridges, but if I'm going to work for my family business, it's not like I need the reference.

I'm sitting on the couch at my mom's favorite spa in Chicago with my feet perched on an ottoman across from me. Clem is beside me, and we're in thick bathrobes with slippers on our feet, face masks on our faces, and our hair held back from our faces by terrycloth headbands. I'm drinking tea and munching on an assortment of mixed nuts as Clem chews on some dried fruit that was on the snack bar.

This is the life.

My father felt bad for us as he welcomed us back into the house yesterday, and he told us to take the rest of the week to get adjusted—including *adjustments* here at the spa. Massages, facials, saunas, he got us the works, and it's honestly the best welcome home gift I could've imagined.

And yet…

It comes with conditions, just like everything always does in the Van Buren household. He's only doing this because he wants me to see how much better it is to live in their house and work in their office than it was to venture out on the scary streets of Chicago by myself.

Cue the eyeroll.

But the princess in me isn't exactly going to turn down this sort of relaxation. Clem and I both deserve it after the less-than-ideal work and living situations we endured over the last few years in the name of independence.

Fuck independence. I'll take these spa treatments and a cozy queen-size bed with a fluffy blanket any day of the week over the twin mattress I had at the apartment.

"Why didn't we give in to this ages ago?" she asks.

I giggle, though in truth, the answer is less funny and more complicated. I didn't want to give up my independence, sure, and I was being stubborn. I wanted to pursue my own passions rather than my dad's.

But it was more than that. It was about me finding my own way without the pressure of the Van Buren name. It was about earning respect from people because of a job well done instead of a last name.

It was about proving myself—and proving *to* myself that I could do it.

It was about not giving up.

And instead, it was a failure. *I* am a failure.

Granted, the Swedish massage helped wrestle those feelings to the back of my mind, but once the glow of relaxation wears off, those feelings will rise right back to the surface.

In the back of my mind, I can't help but think that there must be something I can do with my love of graphic design. There are plenty of graphics involved in the field of real estate development, from branding and logos to property visualizations and sales pitches.

But my father already invited me on a bid walk tomorrow, and I haven't had the chance yet to discuss with him what my role will be at VBC.

Inviting me on a bid walk makes it pretty damn clear to me what *he* wants my role to be, though.

We'll walk a property tomorrow with the other contractors putting in bids to develop the client's land. It's a huge deal, and my dad wants me there to watch the process. He had me do it during my internship before my senior year of college—the time in my life when I decided I wanted to pave my own path.

But things have changed. Life threw me some curveballs, and maybe this is where I'm meant to be after all. Definitely here at this spa, anyway.

CHAPTER 4

MADDEN BRADLEY

Half Plus a Few

I laugh as I shake my head at Clay. Between the two of us, we've gotten upwards of fifteen numbers tonight, but I won't use any of them.

Not tonight, anyway. I've got a late morning flight back to Chicago tomorrow, and the last thing I want to do is worry about how to tell some girl I'll never see again thanks for the night.

Still, the attention is nice. It's welcome, even. It makes me feel like I'm going to fit into this city okay even though Chicago has been my town since the day I was born.

I'm drunker than I've been in a while, so even if I wanted to use one of the numbers I got tonight, I probably wouldn't be able to focus enough to dial it.

I call it a night, and my thirty-five years come screaming loudly at me as I wake in the morning.

Fuck.

I can't do liquor like I could when I was in my twenties. Mornings like this are a reminder that I'm halfway through my thirties. I'm closer to forty than thirty. I'm nearing my midlife crisis. Is this where I get a little red sports car and find a woman half my age to mess around with?

Well…maybe not *half* my age. Maybe half plus a few years.

I push the thought out as I sit up. I'm a little queasy, and my head feels like someone sliced it open with a machete. Ibuprofen doesn't touch it. A steamy shower does little to help any of it. A greasy breakfast used to be the hangover cure. At thirty-five, well, it's not anymore.

I find some Pedialyte at the airport and chug it, and that seems to help the pounding in my head a little.

I sleep the entire way home, and when the plane touches down in Chicago, it feels like I'm home again. San Diego was nice. It was good. It was great, actually, meeting my teammates and the coaches, getting to know the city, looking at various places to live. Making friends. Taking numbers. Eating at DJ's favorite places. The dude loves to eat.

But it doesn't feel like home. Yet.

Maybe because it's *not* home yet. It will be once I get out there and make this thing more permanent, but I don't really need to worry about that until July. I'll have weeks here and there where I need to be out there, and it would probably serve me well to move sooner than later, but more than likely I'll spend the majority of this offseason keeping my dad off my back right here in the Windy City.

Ironically, that means spending more time with him…something I'm not really looking forward to.

But he beckoned me home with some big business deal he wants me to be there for, so I booked a flight to keep him happy.

Part of me would rather stay in San Diego. I'd rather go out another night with Clay. Maybe not feel so rushed and take some time to enjoy the ladies.

But that wasn't what life had in store for me.

I stand near my windows overlooking the lake. I stand here a lot—right here in this very spot. I should put a chair here, but this feels like the place where I do my best thinking. What'll I do when I don't have this view anymore?

I saw a place in San Diego that looked out over the beach. Maybe that'll replace this view.

I suppose I don't *have* to sell this place. Between the trust I got when I was twenty-five and my paychecks, I probably have enough to keep this place and rent a place in San Diego for the next year. Who knows what'll come next? It doesn't make much sense to put down roots out there if I'm only going to come back here to run the business.

My phone starts to ring, and I see it's my dad calling.

"Hello," I answer.

"Madden, it's your father. I'll need you at the office in the morning by nine. Our meeting is at nine thirty, and I'll expect you in a suit and ready to ask questions. I'll be shadowing you to see how you handle things."

Great. Just fucking great. So this is a test from my dad when I'm still hungover as fuck, and I'm not even sure I want this business.

I draw in a deep breath and let it out slowly, and then I head over to my computer to get some research done ahead of tomorrow's big meeting.

* * *

Sure enough, when my alarm blasts the next morning…I'm still hungover.

Fuck. It's been a long time since I drank enough for a two-day hangover, but here we are.

I take my morning run along the Lakefront Trail, and when I get home, I crack some eggs into a pan and toss a few slices of bacon into the skillet. I make some toast and slather it with jelly, and I dig in a few minutes later. The breakfast seems to awaken my senses, but I could use some strong coffee to really get me through the day. While I'm eating, I look up what drink at Starbucks has the most caffeine in it, and after my shower, I suit up as Dad requested. I spend little time on my hair, and I'm ready with plenty of time to spare.

I decide to walk to the office. It's only a little over a mile, and while these shoes aren't the best for walking, I need the exercise and fresh air. It's a rare gorgeous day for this city where it's not too cold, not too humid, and not raining, so I'll take it.

I place a mobile order for whatever it was that was recommended on my walk over, and I stop short when I see the line at Starbucks snaking out of the building.

Honestly, I will never understand why people don't just get the app. The line is *always* like this, and I assume it'll be another ten minutes before my drink is ready. I glance at my watch.

I still have plenty of time to wait and get to the office by nine.

It's a five-minute walk from here, and if it's not ready, then I'll just abandon it and fight this hangover off so I can impress my father with the research I did ahead of this meeting.

Order in process, the app informs me.

Thank God…something's finally going my way.

CHAPTER 5
KENNEDY VAN BUREN

Grande Iced Brown Sugar Oat Milk Shaken Espresso

I stare at my clothes as I try to figure out what to wear, and ultimately I go with my interview outfit—a knee-length black dress with a collar that buttons down to the belt and, of course, pockets, because what good is a dress without pockets?

I pair it with some demure black heels, and I glance in the mirror. I look professional and savvy and ready to stand quietly by my father's side while he asks the important questions.

To that end, I decide to hit up Starbucks before I head into the office.

Clem went straight in since she has to fill out the paperwork with HR. I didn't need to since I've been on the payroll since I was fourteen—and before that, my parents would just pay me under the table.

I guess working for Mom and Dad won't be all bad.

And Clem's got a good start as a junior assistant to the sales department. We won't get to see each other too often at the office, but eventually I'm hoping I can move her to be my assistant.

I place my mobile order after I park in the parking garage, and I head to the Starbucks just down the block from the skyscraper in the Loop where my dad's office is located.

I'm glad I went with my professional heels and not the Louboutins with the red bottoms. Those are gorgeous, and they're my favorite…but the heel gets stuck in every crack on the sidewalk, and I likely would've fallen ten times by now.

When I arrive, I spot the line out the door to order coffee. People and their caffeine addictions.

Not that I'm any better. Thank God for the app.

I manage to wrestle my way inside, but it's crowded and chaotic as I make my way toward the mobile pickup area.

I check for my name.

No *Kennedy* tags sitting in the mobile pickup, so I cross my arms over my chest and wait.

Someone bumps into me—surely by accident, so I'm not really offended—and I glance over in that direction only to be met with possibly the most gorgeous man I've ever seen.

Our eyes lock, my hazel ones with his dark brown, and a little tingle of something races down my spine as my stomach flips.

Holy hell, he's hot.

Wavy, dark hair that's definitely styled with some sort of pomade but still looks natural. A bit of scruff on his jaw to give him that bad boy edge. He's wearing a suit, but a quick glance tells me he most definitely works out and he's hiding a powerful, gorgeous body beneath that suit.

There's something familiar about him, but I can't quite put my finger on what it is.

Is this the kind of guy who works in these parts? Because, my God, I've been missing out. I could've been working here the last five years and met him and maybe we'd already be married with a kid or two…

He cuts into those fantasies with, "Sorry about that." His voice is deep, sexy, and a bit commanding as his hand comes up to my arm to steady me.

Oh my God, he's touching me.

My brain seems to short-circuit as I focus on the fact that his hand is currently branding my skin with heat, and I really want to look over at said hand to see if there's a gold band encircling his ring finger, but I can't seem to tear my eyes away from his.

"Are you okay?" he asks, prompting my brain to try to figure out how to collect itself.

I nod as I blink. "Totally."

Totally? Really, Kennedy?

I clear my throat awkwardly.

"This location is always like this," he mutters.

"Do you come here a lot?" I ask.

He lifts a shoulder. "Not a lot. Just when I head into the office."

"Do you work from home?" I ask, suddenly wanting to know everything I can about this man.

He twists his lips, and I get the sudden, overwhelming vision of what those lips would feel like dragging along my skin. Across my stomach. Down to my hip. Along my thigh. Into my—

"Something like that," he says. "What about you? I've never seen you in here."

I raise a brow. "You say that like you were looking for me."

He raises one back. "Maybe I was." He leans in. "Trust me, with all these assholes in suits, it's refreshing to find someone who looks like you in here."

"Like me?" I ask, my hand flying to my chest as heat rushes into my cheeks.

I'm positive I'm as red as a tomato, but there's not much I can do about that.

"Like you don't know you're gorgeous." His eyes flick from mine down my frame, and my pulse races. "But you didn't answer my question. Do you work nearby?"

Jeez. This guy. He just called me gorgeous, and I'm still buzzing from that, but he's trying to have a conversation, and he flew over it like it wasn't any big deal when I don't know if a man this hot has ever even entered my orbit, let alone complimented me the way he just did.

I need a minute here.

And caffeine.

It's why I'm here, after all. Not to bump into Hottie McHotface.

I know he asked a question, but I can't remember the answer. Or the question. Or my own name.

"Mobile grande iced brown sugar oat milk shaken espresso," the barista yells, and that seems to snap the trance I'm in.

We both move for the counter at the same time, and we both reach for the cup at the same time.

Our fingers touch as we each lay claim to the same drink, and then the barista clarifies things for us.

"For Bradley."

Aha! I have a name. Bradley.

And the fact that he orders the same thing as me at Starbucks.

"Are you Kennedy?" the barista asks, and I stare at her blankly. Is that my name? I'm not really sure.

She gives me a strange look, and I think I nod as she says, "Yours is up next."

"Guess I got my order in seconds before you, Kennedy," Bradley says with a grin, and he holds up his espresso.

I know it's a popular drink—maybe the *most* popular drink at Starbucks, and it's loaded with caffeine, which is why we're here in the first place. But we ordered the *same drink*. That has to mean something.

"Guess you did, Bradley." I flash him a smile, and I'm not sure why my banter isn't bantering this morning, but he really does something to my brain.

"Well, I better get to the office," he finally says, and it could just be me projecting my wants onto him, but I swear I hear a bit of reluctance in his tone.

"Me too. Enjoy your grande iced brown sugar oat milk shaken espresso," I say. Why do I say it with finality, like this is goodbye? I should leave a door open or exchange numbers or…*something*.

He holds up his coffee. "You too." He smiles one last time at me, and since he didn't ask for my number, I suppose I'm left to assume he's taken.

Of course he's taken. He's friggin' gorgeous. That smile he gave me was one of those panty-droppers. You know, the kind that would make *any* woman strip naked just for a shot.

But this is a hell of a way to start my first day at the office, and maybe with any luck at all, I'll run into him again.

I guess I'll be stopping at Starbucks every morning going forward into forever at this exact time just for that potential chance.

I walk back to my dad's office building with shaky knees as I try to brush off that encounter.

It should be a simple task, but the truth is that I haven't had a hot guy look in my direction in far, *far* too long. Not that he looked in my direction as anything more than apologetic after bumping into me, but damn...I looked at him with more than just irritation that he bumped into me.

As Clem would say, it's getting dusty down there, and I need something other than my little magical electronic helper to breathe some life into that territory.

A hot guy like Bradley the grande iced brown sugar oat milk shaken espresso guy.

It's been too long. Far too long. So long I'm pretty sure I forgot how to do it.

The truth is, I've never been in a serious relationship.

The boys in high school were just that...boys in high school. I lost my virginity my freshman year of college, and it wasn't really anything to write home about. Not that you'd write home about losing your virginity...

Jeez. This guy really jumbled me up this morning. He called me gorgeous.

Me.

Gorgeous.

I have to shake it off. I have a meeting to get to, and I need to at least act like I know what the hell I'm doing at this bid walk.

I sigh with hearts in my eyes as I step onto the elevator, suck in some deep breaths on the ride up, and meet my dad in his office. He glances at his watch and raises a brow like I'm late, but I'm not.

Well, that stern look pretty much pushes hot Bradley right out of my mind. I need to focus. *Pull it together, Van Buren!*

He told me to be here at nine, and I have an entire eight minutes to spare. He taught me to arrive early or not to show up at all, and I took that to heart.

I push aside the annoyance I feel. I can't get worked up every time he glances at his watch and gives me a stern glance. I remind myself that he's my boss here, not Dad…not that Dad would give me fewer stern glances, to be honest.

He fills me in on what we're going to be doing at the bid walk. I might be a little rusty, but it's not my first time. I scribble down some notes to make it look like I'm listening, and then we head down to the car waiting out front for us to take us to the site.

CHAPTER 6
MADDEN BRADLEY

You'll Handle It

I suck down my iced coffee as I think about the woman at the coffee shop. She was so…unassuming. She seemed like she might've recognized me, but then she called me by my last name—the name I keep in my app since *Madden* tends to get me recognized more than *Bradley* does.

Madden is a unique name. My parents apparently liked unique names since each of my six younger siblings also have fairly uncommon names. But Bradley? That name has saved me more than once.

I toss the empty cup in the trash as I press the button to call the elevator, and I'm silently berating myself for not getting her number. She just seemed like she was in a hurry to get out of there, and I suppose I was, too.

I'll allow myself time to think about her later, but for now, I need to focus. And that becomes even more important as I step into my father's office.

"Madden, I'll need you to handle this meeting without me. I've got structural issues on the Bernhardt site, and I need to make a site visit immediately." He pushes a tablet across his desk. "I don't have anyone to spare to send with you. All the information you'll need is on the tablet. I'm sorry for the short notice, but you'll handle it. You must, as this is your time to show off the Bradley Legacy."

He doesn't even allow me to respond. No time to brag about all the research I did for this meeting.

Just *you'll handle it*. As if there's any other option such as me *not* handling it.

He stands, buttons his suit jacket, and stalks out of his office.

Well, fuck.

I guess I'm up.

It's a half-hour drive to the site from the office, and I take one of the company cars that comes with a driver so I can use that time to assess my father's notes and research. They have several multi-use facilities throughout Chicagoland, but this site is the largest plot of land they've acquired.

If I'm taking over this company after I retire, these are the types of projects I want to work on. As much as I've pushed back against wanting this thing handed to me, the truth is that I've always loved to build.

It started with Lego sets when I was a kid, and it turned into 3D printing when I got a little older. Those hobbies were pushed by the wayside when I discovered my love of football, but my body can only take so many more hits before it's done. That time hasn't come quite yet, and I suppose going on this bid walk is good experience for what comes after the game.

Though honestly, if a year off to travel came after the game, I wouldn't say no to that.

I blow out a breath as we approach the site. It's a huge plot of land, and the client is looking to hire developers who can create a town square with everything in one space. I'm more well-versed in commercial development than residential, but we have plenty of staff members who excel in all the different aspects the client is looking for.

My driver pulls to a stop, and I spot other suits on a dirt lot not too far away. I get out of the car and head toward them, tablet in hand. I'm not the first to arrive, but as a car pulls in behind mine, I'm not the last, either.

I make my way over toward the group of men, and I stand near the back of the group. It's not a huge group, maybe eight or so others representing four or five companies aside from Bradley Group. A few of the men are chatting, and I don't recognize anyone here—not that I would. I don't exactly spend a lot of time in these circles.

I hear footsteps approaching, and I assume it's whoever got out of the car behind mine. I'm about to glance behind me when one of the guys in front of me turns around and makes eye contact with me. "Madden Bradley," he says, and there's a tinge of malice in his tone. "I'd heard you might show up here today. Where's your old man?"

"On an emergency site visit. Do I know you?" I ask.

"No, but I know you. I grew up near Green Bay." He gives me a sympathetic look like it was a curse that I played for his team's rival. "Good thing you're out of Chicago, man. Maybe now I can root for you."

I raise my brows. I don't really give a fuck who this prick cheers for. "Don't put that curse on me."

I say it lightheartedly, but I mean it with venom.

He chuckles, and for the first time, I wonder whether I'll get any sort of advantage because of my name. Will this company choose Bradley as their developer simply because of the advantages of being associated with my family?

The prestigious Bradleys produced seven children. Four football players turned pro. The black sheep baseball player turned pro. And, lest we forget, two sisters with successes of their own.

If I'm here, that means others of us could show up at any given moment. They won't, but nobody here needs to know that. The client may be a football fan, or maybe a baseball fan, and why wouldn't he hire the family that has the pull and connections to give him the experiences of his dreams?

Speaking of the client, he starts talking. "I think that's everyone," he says, looking around at the group gathered. "Welcome, everyone. I'm Simon Sterling of SCS Enterprises, and our company is excited for this mixed multi-use project. In a moment, we'll walk through the site to help familiarize you with it and the scope of what we'd like to do here. We have visions of this very space becoming a town square offering residences, office spaces, retail, restaurants, entertainment, and parks. At the end of our tour of the land, we'll be fielding any questions you might have. Let's begin."

The group starts to move, and the developer who arrived behind me steps into place beside me.

I glance over, and I find an older gentleman beside me, and on the other side of him, I spot some fine-looking legs in heels that make absolutely no sense for a bid walk when we're literally walking on dirt.

Still, I glance up from the legs at my competition and see a beautifully fitted tight black dress that seems familiar, but then it's a woman's dress, and I've peeled plenty of black ones from bodies in my lifetime.

My eyes keep traveling up, and even though this woman is wearing sunglasses, my breath seems to catch in my throat.

I recognize her.

Holy shit.

It's the woman from this morning. The one from Starbucks who flirted before I bolted.

Maybe we didn't exchange numbers there, but life has a funny way of swooping in to give me exactly what I need.

And maybe what I need is *her*.

She must feel my eyes on her because she turns to look past the old dude, and her eyes land on me.

Her mouth forms a round O shape as she gasps a little, naturally sending a message straight to my cock, and her delicate hand that battled against mine for an iced coffee this morning comes up to her chest in surprise.

"Bradley?" she asks, repeating the name she heard as it was read from my cup this morning.

"Kennedy, good to see you again."

"You two know each other?" the old guy asks, and she seems to snap out of some trance as she glances at him.

"No. I mean, not really," she says, sort of stuttering, and it's really goddamn cute.

"We've met," I say a little slyly and a lot more salaciously than entirely necessary.

Simon starts to say something up front, which cuts our conversation short, but it suddenly dawns on me that we're in a competition for the same thing here.

She works for another developer. A competing company.

I'm not about to let *anybody* win against me. Not even a woman as gorgeous as her.

CHAPTER 7
KENNEDY VAN BUREN

He's All Man

Okay, first things first, choosing heels was a dumb fucking decision for a bid walk where we're walking on undeveloped land.

But second...Bradley is *here*? And he's bidding on this same project?

How am I supposed to function properly when I can't even seem to think straight with him around? It's a valid question, honestly.

I'm trying to listen to Simon as he explains his vision. "We currently have twelve acres and are working on purchasing neighboring land for future expansion, so please consider the different phases of this project in your bids." He points out different areas and what his vision is for them, and I'm trying to listen but having an incredibly hard time since I can barely walk on this uneven dirt, and I'm still shook over seeing the hot iced coffee guy.

"Literally this morning at Starbucks," I say a little more haughtily than I intend to.

"Mm," my dad murmurs, and it feels like he doesn't really believe me.

Well, it's the truth.

"And we meet again," he says, and he's so calm and collected over there, so cool, while I'm a sweaty mess who keeps stumbling on divots in the dirt.

It's weird having this conversation with him across my father. He's almost flirting with me, and I want him to flirt more, but he's also my business rival. We're here to bid on the same project, and I can't let hormones come between what I'm here to do.

Not when this is my first project with my father. Not when he said he's shadowing me today. I may not have wanted this job, but I took it anyway, and hell if I'm not going to see it through.

Especially now that there's a competition at stake.

I'm nothing if not competitive.

We don't get a chance to say anything else to one another, though the insinuation is heavy in the air.

My father explained to me on the ride here how important it is to ask questions at the end to show how interested we are in the project, so I go first.

"Can you clarify the size of the lot?" I ask.

Bradley, who is now standing beside me close enough that I can smell his cologne that's causing my brain to misfire, snorts. "That information was in the RFP," he mutters, referring to the initial request for proposals.

Right. Of course it was.

But I don't like being made to look stupid and incompetent, which is exactly what he just did.

"Twelve acres," Simon says.

Bradley asks the next question. "You mentioned commercial and residential. In your phase one vision, is that combined into one building or separate facilities?"

"A great question indeed, and that's one we haven't definitively concluded just yet. We wanted to take a look at the different proposals before we made that decision."

Others ask questions, and I can't find the nerve to ask another one. I don't really have any, anyway. I just asked the first one to please my father, and the coffee guy obliterated my confidence with his snort and snarky comment.

He may be hot, and I may want to ride his lap while we're both naked, but he's kind of a jerk.

My dad unloads on me once we get back into the car.

"Under no circumstances are you to get involved with the Bradley family," he says.

Um…excuse me? And also…what? "The Bradley *family*?" I ask. I thought his *name* was Bradley.

"Mm," he murmurs. "The boy at the bid walk, that's Madden. The eldest."

Wait a minute.

First of all, he's *all* man, decidedly not a boy.

But also…

"Madden Bradley?" I ask. Holy shit. It *was* him. That's why he looked kind of familiar to me. He's a fucking football god around these parts. He was out of his element in a suit and tie, and that must have been why I didn't piece together who he was.

"Thomas Bradley has been a thorn in my side for over three decades, Kennedy. We simply cannot be associated with them."

"Why?" I breathe, suddenly wanting to know everything about the family.

He shakes his head a little as if to say that's the end of that discussion, but I need more.

"If you're going to put me on this project, don't you think I need to know everything I can about the competition?" I ask.

He sighs as he eyes me warily. "You know how work can come between friendships," he says, nearly echoing my mother's words from just the other day. "That's what happened."

"Details?" I ask.

He glances out the window. "Thomas and I attended the same college. He was a few years ahead of me, but we were on the football team together. We were the same major, so even though I was younger than him, he mentored me. We talked about opening a firm together someday. And then something changed. He was injured off the field and could no longer play, and he seemed to form a resentment toward anybody who could. We lost touch only to find ourselves competing for a bid several years later, once your mother and I started VBC. The former friends might've teamed up on the efforts, and instead, he went behind my back and did something to win that bid. I don't know what it was, but here's what I do know. He's been slimy and underhanded ever since, and every goddamned time I go up against him, he wins."

I may not be the world's most perfect daughter. I may not be all that close to my parents.

But I refuse to sit back and let some slimy, underhanded asshole take this project out from under us.

"What can we do?" I ask.

"Nothing," he says, and he glances over at me. "But I like the passion in your voice."

"Why don't you fight?"

"Thomas Bradley has the kind of connections you just don't fight against, Kennedy. Trust me. So if I lose this project to him, it wasn't meant to be." His phone starts to ring as he finishes his sentence, and he takes the call, effectively ending the conversation.

Okay, fine. My dad won't fight Thomas Bradley.

But that doesn't mean I can't fight his son.

CHAPTER 8

MADDEN BRADLEY

Tight, Black Pants

I arrive solo at the SCS offices two weeks after the bid walk.

In the last two weeks, I flew to San Diego to get in some more workouts with my new teammates and find a place to live. I still haven't settled on anything, so I'll have to go back again sooner rather than later.

The caffeine queen lady boss babe from Starbucks and the subsequent bid walk has only snaked her way into my thoughts hourly over the last week—down from half-hourly the first week, something I'm counting as a win.

I'm not sure why I can't get her out of my head.

There was something electric in the air when I think back to our connection. Maybe it was the way she was a little flustered when I looked at her, or maybe it was in the way she didn't seem to know who the hell I was. I liked that about her.

I was out of place in a suit in the middle of Starbucks. I'm fairly well-known around these parts, but I look different in a suit with my hair neatly styled than I do in a jersey and pads with eye black and helmet hair. Admittedly, it's harder to recognize me when I'm not in my element.

I was only in San Diego a few days, and I've spent the rest of my time at my father's Chicago office. My future office.

I've gone to Starbucks each morning on the off-chance I might run into her again, but I haven't.

I have enough resources to procure her number, but I have this sneaking suspicion our paths will cross again—like today, for example. Besides, it would feel strange to call her out of the blue. I've thought about what I'd say if I did it, and every time, I just sound like a creep.

No, I need to let things happen the natural way.

I told my father I could handle this on my own. I'm not entirely sure that's true, but I wanted the chance to see *her* again without my dad being a cockblock.

I found out after the fact that the man Kennedy was with was her father. From the sounds of things, he and my father are business rivals, but Thomas Bradley has met few people who haven't eventually become his rival, and none that he hasn't won against. It's quite the record, really.

I'm not terribly surprised to see the woman standing in the lobby chatting up the receptionist as I pull open the door, but I *am* glad to see she's here. I sort of assumed SCS would invite all the developers back to let everyone else down gently since obviously my company submitted the best proposal. I say that with confidence, by the way—not arrogance.

She's wearing black pants with a green shirt that accentuates the blonde of her hair, which is hanging in loose waves just past her shoulders. Her back is to me, but it's unmistakably her, and my eyes fall to her ass. It's cupped perfectly in those tight, black pants, and I salivate as I try not to openly stare.

Tight, black pants just do it for me.

And on her?

Damn.

That's one hell of a nice ass.

One I could sink my teeth into.

One I could spend all night caressing just before I bend her over and slide inside.

Fuck.

Great. Now I need to attend this meeting with a fucking erection caused by the woman who will be sitting beside me. I draw in a breath.

She glances toward the door when she sees the glint of the light reflecting off the glass as I open it. Her eyes meet mine, and she glares.

She *glares* at me. What the fuck did I do to earn her ire? We had a nice little flirt, and now this?

And furthermore, while I'm not surprised she's here, I *am* surprised when the receptionist welcomes just the two of us back to Simon's office. Kennedy follows her, and I follow Kennedy. We're both silent on the walk back, though I'm tempted to say *something*.

"Welcome, Ms. Van Buren, Mr. Bradley," Simon says, and he shakes each of our hands across the desk. He nods at the chairs, and we both take a seat. "Both of your bids were incredibly impressive, and you each had a unique take on how to make our vision come to life," he begins. He glances up at both of us. "As you can both see, you're the only two we've invited back, and there's a reason why." He pauses dramatically, and I'm tempted to inject some humor into the moment. I refrain.

Barely.

"Because the scope of the project is so large and we appreciated pieces from each of your bids, we've decided to split the project," he says.

My stomach twists as my heart drops somewhere down there. This was *my* project.

My father expected me to win the bid. Granted, he didn't have me *draft* the bid, but he did have me handle the walk, and he did have me oversee and approve the bid before we sent it to SCS.

He's going to hand me my ass, and it's likely well deserved.

I'm about to interrupt to ask whether we can negotiate this so we can get the full scope of the project when Simon continues.

"Van Buren will cover all residentials, and Bradley will oversee the commercial. We feel this is the best use of our resources and will also yield the timeliest method to break ground. There will, of course, be challenges to this, and we will need you to work together on all stages of the project together from master planning to infrastructure to branding and marketing."

Wait a minute.

We will need you to work together.

The gorgeous business rival glaring at me is about to become my business partner. Well, sort of. I have no clue if she's going to oversee the project on her end, but I'll sure as fuck be overseeing it on mine.

Except, you know, I have that whole *football* thing where I'll have to head to San Diego in a few months for training camp. Plus workouts in April, OTAs in May, and mandatory minicamp in June.

But when I'm not in San Diego, you can bet your ass I'll be right here.

Right beside the caffeine queen.

She opens her mouth to say something—likely an objection to this plan—but I slide in first. "What a fantastic opportunity, Mr. Sterling. Thank you for awarding Bradley with even a portion of this incredible project."

She glances at me, and the side-eye is fierce as our eyes connect. She obviously thinks I'm an ass-kisser, which is fine since it's her ass I'll be kissing in the more literal sense as soon as fucking possible. I don't know what it is, but this fierce need to get her alone washes over me.

"Ms. Van Buren, I'd love to set up a time to start discussing the master plans," I say, turning to her. "Are you free after we wrap up here?" Say…my place? Naked?

Okay, Bradley, slow your roll.

She obviously isn't going to reject my request in front of the client, and furthermore, she's not going to make excuses by bringing up other clients. She purses her lips, and the little lines at the corners tell me she's not happy I'm cornering her.

"Yes, that would work," she grits out.

There's something so cute about the way she's angry with me, and as much fun as it is to push her buttons, I can't wait to get to the bottom of why she's suddenly so angry.

CHAPTER 9
KENNEDY VAN BUREN

Could You Give Me a Ride

Is he freaking kidding me?
 He's doing this on purpose. He knows he just cornered me. I can't say no in front of the client, but I sure as hell will give him a piece of my mind when we're alone.

I don't want to be alone with him.

I don't even want to be in this office with him. He smells too good. Looks too good. Flirts too good.

I think back to my father's words about the Bradley family. Under no circumstances am I to get involved with the Bradley family, which—fine. Okay. But what do I do now? SCS is forcing me to get involved with Bradley. We're going to partner on this project.

I could easily hand this off to someone else in the office. Kenneth or Sara come to mind.

But I don't *want* to hand this project off. I don't want Sara getting close to him. Not because I'm jealous, but because he's dangerous. He's handsome and manipulative, and that's a recipe for disaster.

I don't even know if I can handle him, but since my dad owns VBC, I have a better shot at it than Sara.

We wrap things up with Simon, and he walks us out to the lobby after going on and on about how excited he is to work on this with both of us and our teams.

I'm decidedly *not* excited about it. I don't particularly want to spend any more time with maddening Madden Bradley than is completely necessary, but apparently *necessary* just stepped up a few notches.

His car is waiting out front for him, and I'm the idiot who drove myself. I walk over toward my car, and he pauses by his car before he thinks twice and follows me.

I stop next to my little white Mercedes, and I glance over at him. "What?" I hiss.

He chuckles. "There's a Starbucks just around the corner. Want to walk and talk there?"

I sigh. "Fine."

"Give me a second." He strides over toward his driver and says something, and the driver pulls out of the parking lot as he walks back over toward me.

"Did you send your driver home?" I ask casually as we start walking toward the coffee place.

He lifts a shoulder. "Figured you could give me a ride back."

"You didn't even ask," I point out.

"Oh, right. Sorry. Could you give me a ride back to my office?"

"How do you know my office is anywhere near yours?" I demand.

"Because we were both on our way into the office when we met at Starbucks that morning, so I figure yours can't be too far from mine, and Victor—the driver—has other shit to get to," he says.

Okay, fine. Seems reasonable enough. Still, he doesn't know I'm going back there.

It doesn't matter.

I blow out a breath and pull my phone out to place my mobile order, and suddenly his big fingers are moving toward my arm, and he's encircling my wrist before I even know what hit me.

His skin is touching mine. If he shifted his fingers infinitesimally, he'd feel my fluttering pulse as it picks up the pace at his proximity.

I refuse to give in to that feeling.

So he's hot.

Big fucking deal.

I clear my throat as I fix a glare on him. "What are you doing?" I shake my arm from his grasp.

"I already ordered you one," he says, and I don't miss the hint of cockiness in his tone.

"So first you presume that I can drive you back to the office, then you presume to know my Starbucks order?" My voice is trembling with anger. God! The nerve of this guy.

"I *do* know your Starbucks order, but it was the other way around. I ordered in the elevator on the way down. Then I dismissed Victor." His voice is warm and steady, and I hate him a little for it.

"Just because I ordered that *once* doesn't mean it's what I always order," I point out.

"Okay," he says, and there's more than a hint of sarcasm there. "Then show me what you were about to order, caffeine queen."

My head whips over to him. "Caffeine queen?" I repeat.

He lifts a shoulder, and then we're at the door, so he pulls it open and nods for me to walk in first.

I know he's not a gentleman. He can certainly stop pretending like he is one.

"It's how I refer to you in my head," he says, his voice low as I walk past him into the shop.

Wait a second.

Did he just admit that he *thinks* about me? I give voice to that thought. "You think about me?"

He nods. "Yes. Mostly with irritation."

I purse my lips. "Well I don't think about you at all," I lie. I think about how maddening he is all the time.

I've studied his Instagram. I've scrolled through the images of him on the field. I've recalled his words the morning we met, back when he called me *gorgeous*.

I've recalled my father's words to stay away from him.

I think about him far more than I should.

He's a forbidden fruit, and I need to stay away. I *have* to stay away.

"Okay," he says on a chuckle as if he doesn't believe me, but whatever. I don't need him to believe me.

"Mobile for Bradley," the barista calls, and two grande iced coffees sit on the counter. Madden walks over to pick them up, and he hands one to me.

"My treat," he says.

"Thanks." I narrow my eyes at him, not sure what his motivation is here. Knowing he's got manipulation in his blood makes me nervous.

We find an open table near a window, and we sit across from each other with him facing the door.

"So you wanted to talk master planning?" I ask.

"Yeah," he says. "But obviously that was just a cover to get you here."

"Huh?" I squeak.

He chuckles. "I need to confer with my team before we can really start talking master planning."

"Yes, of course. So do I," I say, though truthfully I have not the first clue what I'm doing, and I'm frankly shocked my dad sent me here this morning solo. He trusts me maybe more than he should, but he reminded me that I'm a bright businesswoman before I left the office.

"Where's your old man?" he asks.

"Why do you care?"

"Just curious. He was with you last time but seemed to be letting you take the lead. Are you taking over the company?" He tips his coffee to his lips, and for fuck's sake, I've never been jealous of a coffee lid until this moment, but my eyes study the way his lips take on the side of that cup and suck in some of the liquid. It's downright pornographic.

"Eventually," I say.

"Me, too," he says, and his jaw clenches a little at that. "Do you want to take over VBC?"

I raise a brow. "I don't know you well enough to get into these sorts of details."

"Right. I'll take that as a no, then." He clears his throat and looks away, and I get the sense that he doesn't really want his father's company, either.

I don't ask about it, though. This outing was his idea, not mine. He treated me to coffee, and it sort of feels like a date. But I won't let it be one.

"Take it how you want. I don't really care," I say.

He looks surprised by my words. "Why are you angry with me?"

"I'm a diehard Bears fan," I say. "I'll never cheer for anyone else. Or for anyone that's not on my team." I smirk at him.

He clenches his jaw, and it works back and forth in a super sexy way for a few beats. Clearly he's affected by the trade, and my words just pushed a button. I'm interested to hear more. I don't push it, though. A friend might ask, and we're not friends. If anything, we're enemies.

Before he can respond to my clear jab that he's no longer with the team, I add, "Aside from the fact that I have to split this project with you? How about the history between our dads?"

His brows dip together, and I conclude that he hasn't heard the story.

"You should ask your father about it," I say, and I raise my brows pointedly as I press my lips together.

His eyes flick to my mouth for a beat, and he shrugs. "Their history has nothing to do with us. Go out to dinner with me."

I blow out a breath. I can't deny the way my stomach clenches at his question. A guy who looks like *him* is interested in *me*? And it's not just that. He's not just hot as fuck.

He's a professional athlete who could have anyone in the entire universe, but for some reason his attention has landed on me.

He appears to be smart—smart enough to lead his office in this bid, anyway.

He's the total package, and he's from the one family my father warned me away from.

I can't get involved with him, and especially not now. He's my competition in business, his father betrayed mine, and on top of it, we're going to have to work together at least to some degree since we've both been hired to work on this project.

"No," I finally say.

"Why the hell not?" he asked, his ego clearly bruised.

"You're not my type." I fold my arms across my chest.

"What if I wasn't asking you out on a date?"

My head feels a little dizzy that I assumed he was, and I'm not sure how to respond to that.

"Fine, I was," he mutters. "Then let's have a dinner meeting after we discuss the master planning with our teams."

"I don't think that's a good idea. I'm happy to meet you during the daylight hours in either my conference room or yours," I say.

"So you're heading up this project for VBC?" he asks.

Say no, Kennedy. Tell him no. Put somebody else in because you can't get tangled up with this guy.

"Yes."

Fuck.

CHAPTER 10

MADDEN BRADLEY

Game Fucking On

I watch carefully as she snags her lip between her teeth, and for as much as I know nothing about her, I know *women*. She's telling me everything I need to know with her body language.

She regrets saying that she'll be handling this project for VBC. She doesn't even appear to want to work for her father, and we share more in common than she'll admit—or than I'll admit this early in the game, to be honest.

So why is she taking on this project? My arrogance has the answer.

She'll get to work with me.

She's only pretending to hate me.

Though she did pique my curiosity with that line about the history between our fathers. I know nothing of it, but I did my best to school my reaction when she mentioned it.

I've tucked it into my pocket for later. I'll bring it up when he's reaming me out for not scoring the full project.

My ego took a hit when she said I'm not her type, but I don't buy it anyway.

"Great. I'm heading it up for Bradley, so it looks like we'll be spending a lot of time together. Do you have other projects?" I ask.

She glances away, and then she admits what I suspected. "No."

"Will you look at that," I say, feigning shock. "Neither do I."

She rolls her eyes. "Enough with the theatrics, Bradley. How are we going to do this?"

"Do what?"

"Work on this project together when I can't—" She cuts herself off.

Can't…what?

Can't stand me? Can't stop staring at my mouth? Can't stop wanting me?

All three?

"When you can't…" I prompt.

She sighs and shakes her head. "Look, full disclosure, I just started full-time with VBC. I've been around the company my whole life, and I know what I'm doing there, but I don't need you and your complications while I get my feet under me."

I force the sly smile off my lips, but my cock thickens at her assessment. I'm a complication to her, which only means one thing to me.

She's interested.

Well, so am I.

But she wants to play games? She wants to make me the enemy?

Fine. I'll play. There's nothing I love more in life than a good game. The competitive spirit is alive and well inside me, and it thrives on a good challenge.

I'll get her to admit how she really feels before next season starts. That's a guarantee.

And then I'll get her naked.

Game fucking on.

"I won't complicate matters for you," I say. "So allow me to be honest with you, too. My father expects me to take on Bradley when I retire. I've always loved to build, but whether I liked it or not never mattered. I'm the oldest of seven children, so the company will be mine someday."

Her brows rise a little, and she tilts her head with sympathy. "I'm in a similar boat, but can we back up a second? *Seven* children? Is your mom some sort of saint?"

I chuckle at the question. "Hardly. The nanny who raised us might be, though."

"If you don't want it, why can't it go to one of the others?"

I take a sip of my iced coffee before I field that one. "The Bradley Legacy is very important to my father. So important that, frankly, I'm sick of hearing about it," I mutter. "But I also think that he trusts me with it. Birth order comes with some inherent responsibilities that I've stepped up to, and I'm most likely to retire from the game first since I'm the oldest, so I'm the natural pick. I can choose whether to give my siblings responsibilities if I so choose once they retire, too, I suppose."

"The game?" she asks. "Your brothers play football, too?"

"Three of them do," I say. "One plays baseball, and the other two are female."

"Five boys and two girls?" She shakes her head. "What was that like growing up?"

"How many siblings do you have?" I ask instead of answering that question.

"None."

"You're an only child?"

She nods.

"What was that like?"

She chuckles. "Lonely."

"At times, it felt that way with six siblings, too."

"How?"

I lift a shoulder. "Just that feeling of being alone in a crowd."

She nods. "Are you close with them?"

"Some more than others."

"Can you fire off their names and ages off the top of your head?"

I laugh. "I can. Dex, thirty-three. Everleigh is thirty-two, and Ford is twenty-nine. Archer is twenty-eight, Liam is twenty-six, and baby Ivy completed our family as a surprise just twenty years ago."

"And you are?" she asks.

"Thirty-five."

Her brows shoot up.

"Geriatric, right?" I ask wryly.

"Well, kind of." Her neck is corded as she pulls a face as if to say *sorry*, even though I don't get the impression she actually is.

I chuckle. "I know it's impolite to ask, but what about you?"

"Twenty-seven."

It's my turn to be surprised as my own brows shoot up. "A baby," I murmur.

"Hardly," she says haughtily.

"And what were you doing before you started full-time at VBC?" I ask.

"Graphic design," she says, and I almost think she's about to give more to the story, but she stops. "So how's this going to work when you have to go play football?"

It's a valid question, and it's one I've put some thought into—though I have to rethink it now that SCS split the project rather than handing it all over to me. "I'll likely have someone else from the company step in when I'm not around, but all approvals will go through me."

That *someone else* will definitely be a female. No way in hell I'm giving some other guy the chance to work closely with Kennedy.

She drains the rest of her coffee. "Well, I should get back to the office. You ready?"

No, I'm not. I'm rather enjoying this chance to sit and chat with her.

It started to feel like we were moving beyond that enemy energy and even toward friendly territory, but as soon as she realized it, she stiffened up on me.

I nod, and I stand and finish what's left in my cup. We walk back toward her car, and I slide into the passenger seat.

Her car smells like her.

I noticed it the day I accidentally bumped into her that morning we met, and it's more powerful locked in this small space with her.

It's something coconutty and…full of joy or something. I'm not used to joyful scents. I'm used to locker rooms, to be honest.

It's making me want to smell more of it. It's making me want to run my nose along her skin as I breathe more of her in.

Fuck, I have got to get this under control.

These errant thoughts have to be because I haven't had sex in a few weeks. I should flip through my contacts and find somebody to satisfy that craving so I stop acting like a horny bastard around this woman.

I won't, though. Right now, she's the focus of my interest, and I'm at that beginning phase where I don't think anyone else will do.

As she starts the car, music comes blaring out of her speakers with Eminem and Rihanna's "Love the Way You Lie" on full blast.

"Shit, sorry," she says, clearly flustered as she moves to turn down the volume.

"It's a good tune," I say, turning it back up, and she laughs as she pulls into traffic.

When the song ends, a Megan Thee Stallion hit starts to play, and she turns off the radio altogether. Silence envelops us, and I break it by asking, "So you're an Eminem fan?"

"I like that song. What do you listen to?"

I shrug. "Everything. Whatever speaks to me. I like songs I can run to."

"What's on your pregame playlist?"

"Mostly rap. Some classic rock." These questions feel too personal, and I'm not sure why. It's like things just got intimate between us when it wasn't supposed to be that way.

She navigates to her parking garage, and it turns out her office is only a few blocks from mine. I walk with her toward the elevator, but she's going up and I'm going down.

It's strange. I'm not quite sure how to say goodbye.

I want to lean in for a hug. Maybe press my lips to her cheek.

But this is business professional, and she's already set a boundary telling me that she isn't interested in my complications. So I will respect that boundary.

As we're waiting, she glances at me. "Well, this has been fun," she says awkwardly.

I nod. "We'll need to touch base in the next few days about the project."

"Of course. Call the office, and we'll set something up."

I pull my wallet out and grab a business card. It's old school for football players to have business cards since everything is done via social media these days, but when I was a young player ready to take on sponsorships, I had about a thousand made. I've given out a little over a handful to actual potential sponsors over the course of my career, but I still keep them in my wallet since they make an easy way to give a woman my number.

"My personal number is on there," I say, handing it over to her. "Don't lose that. I don't want to have to change my number and order new cards."

She giggles as she flips it over in her hand, and then she grips it tightly. "I promise to use caution."

Her elevator arrives, and as the doors open, she says, "Well, bye."

I hold up a hand to wave, and I wish I wasn't so goddamn excited for the moment she decides to actually use the number on the card.

CHAPTER 11

Shouldn't Have Sent a Boy

The elevator is taking forever, so I end up hoofing it down the stairs.

I can't seem to figure out why I'm so enamored by this woman as I walk the couple blocks back toward my office.

Is it because she wants to play the game?

Is it because she's a challenge?

I'm inclined to think it's neither of those because I was enamored with her the moment I first saw her at Starbucks. She was neither a game nor a challenge back then.

Bumping into her was a way to open the door. It was crowded enough that it worked. Only…it didn't. She was flustered, and I wasn't myself, and it all spiraled before I got the chance to score her number.

And now she has mine, but whether or not she'll use it remains to be seen.

She'll have to…right? I suppose she could have her assistant call my office to arrange a meeting, but I'd rather hear from her.

When I get back to the office, I head toward my father's office. Darla, his assistant, greets me with a smile. "He's free if you'd like to head on in," she tells me, and I nod politely at her.

"How did it go with SCS?" he barks at me before I've even crossed the threshold into his office. "You were there a while, so I assume it's ours."

I draw in a deep breath through my nose, and I exhale with my words. "We were awarded the commercial half."

His lip curls with disapproval. It's not the first time he's looked upon me with that same sort of derision, but typically it's not because I lost half of a big deal for the company. "And the residential?"

"Went to Van Buren."

"Goddammit, Madden. You had one job," he hisses. "And to lose it to Van Buren?" He shakes his head as his lips tighten. "All the companies that put in bids, and it had to be his."

Oh, that reminds me... "What exactly is the history between the two of you?"

"That's not your business," he spits. "How did we lose this? I signed off on the proposal. There's just no way they could've found a better way."

"Well, they did."

"I'll talk to SCS. I knew I shouldn't have sent a boy to do a man's job." He grabs his phone, still sputtering with disgust.

I ignore the pang in my chest from his words. Now's not the time to dissect how they hurt.

Not when I have to stop him.

I can't let him do this.

He may be a cutthroat businessman, but I'm not.

I'm a football player first and foremost.

And I'm attracted to the woman I want to work with on this thing. If he calls and gets his way, he's going to blow my shot.

It's a stupid reason to stop him from making the call. But, admittedly, it's not the *whole* reason.

The truth is...I don't want to handle this project alone. I'm still learning, and I have an entire team behind me to help make this a success. But only having to deal with the commercial side—the side I actually *like*—is a bit of a relief.

Not that I'd ever admit that to Thomas Bradley. But it's the truth. I didn't want to have to deal with residential. That's not my specialty. I didn't build *apartment complexes* or *houses* out of Lego bricks. I built fire stations and truck stops. I built from the Lego City brand, and before it was rebranded to that, from the Lego Town sets.

"Before you make that call, can I ask you a question?" I ask, scrambling to figure out what the hell I'm going to say but also knowing I need some answers.

He narrows his eyes at me, but he sets his phone down without dialing it. "What?"

"Is Van Buren your enemy?"

He looks uncomfortable at my question, and I'm even more curious to hear the answer. "You could say that."

I shouldn't do this. I should stop myself. I should choose the road of less manipulation.

But I don't.

"Then don't you want to keep your enemy close?" I ask.

He tilts his head before he leans on his elbows and steeples his fingers in front of his mouth.

I continue before he can come up with a reason why this is a bad idea. Trust me, I already know all of them.

"What about getting someone on the inside to see how their process works? Think of all we could do with that. Get me in there, and I can work my magic. I'll get access to their client list, their best project managers—hell, their best janitors. Whatever you want from the top down. And it's not just that. We'll have to master plan together, and all the infrastructure and zoning will be us. They'll have their tiny residential corner, and we'll get credit on the rest."

He eyes me a little warily, and for a beat I'm worried I've overstepped.

And then he says the words every kid craves hearing from his father. "I'm so proud of you."

They're the words I wanted. I just don't want them under these circumstances. Not in the context of lies and manipulation.

I have no real intention of taking VBC down. I'm just trying to use the language I know he speaks.

"Okay," he says with a short nod. "Let's do this. Let's see how it goes, and let's see what you bring me from VBC."

Shit.

I went too far.

And now he's going to be sitting by, waiting for answers.

"Okay. But I need to know what went down between you," I say.

"We've known each other since we were in college. He was a couple years under me, and we were the same major. When he got out into the field, he learned real quick that this business is harsh. That's all you need to know."

This business is harsh. Yeah, no shit. Well…that told me exactly nothing.

I'm left to come to my own conclusions, and my immediate thought is that my father did something to teach him that lesson.

I nod, and I stand to turn to walk away.

"Remember the family legacy, Madden." His voice is a cold reminder.

I nod once.

I'm so goddamn sick of hearing about the family legacy, but he's looking at me to be the one to shoulder the burden simply because I had the inconvenience of being born before the rest of my siblings.

It's a lot of pressure squarely on my shoulders. I'm still not even sure I want all this, but here I am anyway. The obedient boy seeking his father's approval.

I'd like to get to the bottom of what happened between him and Van Buren, but it feels like all will be revealed in due time. Right now, I have a commercial development project to manage.

And a raging boner that hasn't gotten any relief since long before I sat at a coffee table across from the daughter of my father's enemy.

* * *

A few days later, I'm walking up to ring the doorbell at my parents' rather stately mansion in Lincoln Park. My sister Ivy, the baby of the Bradley clan, answers the door, and she rushes into my arms for a hug.

"How's my biggest bro?" she asks as she pulls back and ushers me inside.

"Real excited to be here," I say dryly.

"Then you and me should just sneak out and grab dinner together. The oldest and the youngest—it could be a thing, you know."

I chuckle as I realize how very much I've developed my own life and haven't always been a very good big brother. "Let's plan on dinner soon."

"I want to come see you when you're in San Diego, so maybe next time you're out there I can fly out to meet you."

I think for a second how dangerous it would be to introduce my twenty-year-old sister to the likes of Clay Mack, but she didn't ask for the intros, so I won't be making them. "You got it," I say instead.

Liam, the youngest Bradley boy and currently a backup quarterback for Pittsburgh, is already at the table, and so is Ford, the sibling right in the middle of the pack and current tight end for Tampa Bay.

"Hey, the old man is here!" Liam says from his spot at the table, and Ford laughs.

I clench my jaw as I wait for more barbs about my age, but Ford doesn't offer any. They both stand and give me a hug.

"Your jersey on clearance yet?" Ford asks, and I roll my eyes at him.

I don't bother with an answer to that. I was traded, so the answer is probably yes. "Anyone else coming tonight?"

"Everleigh said she'll be here," Ford says. The two of them have always been close.

"I think Dex is in Vegas, and Archer's playing tonight," Liam adds as I sit in the chair that was assigned to me at a young age.

That covers it. Really, five of seven is pretty good considering we're all grown adults with lives of our own.

Everleigh walks in a moment later, and we all stand to hug her as well. She sits, and our parents walk into the room at that moment and take their seats rather formally at opposite ends of the table, reserving greetings for when we're all seated.

I always wondered what it would be like to have been born to parents that showed affection once in a while, but the Bradley family ain't it. To be hugged by our mother when we show up at her house for dinner would be nice. To get a handshake from our father rather than the usual sneers or reproaches might solve some of our underlying issues.

But it's never been that way, so why would it start now?

At least I'm semi-close with my siblings.

Once we're all seated, Greta, one of the housekeepers, tips a bottle of wine over our glasses. My mother holds hers in the air once we've all been served, and she says, "To the legacy."

We all repeat her words, but honestly, what legacy is this? Family first has been drilled into us since infancy, but what kind of family is it when they don't even seem to care that we're here? It's all for show, and it always has been.

Yet I continue to show up. I continue to act as they've trained me. I continue to strive for their words of affirmation. Despite all that, I do enjoy the chance to catch up with my brothers and sisters.

After we're served our main dish of filet mignon with black truffle butter, Ivy asks what everyone has been up to.

Everleigh has been working long hours in her position as a personal brand strategist for celebrities. Ford has been enjoying the beaches near Tampa in his time off, and he's here in Chicago catching up with friends before he heads back to Tampa. Liam has been living here with Mom and Dad in the offseason and spending long hours working out to keep up his stamina for next season. Ivy is still in college, and she's splitting time between her apartment on campus and here with our parents.

Unlike Liam and Ivy, I was never that way. Once I moved out of this house, I stayed the fuck out except for Monday night dinners when I could make it.

"I can tell you what Madden has been up to," our father says, and I sit up a little straighter, though I likely should brace myself for what I already know is coming. "Giving away half our business to the competition."

"Oh, Madden," my mother clucks with disappointment.

I sink back down against my chair. One single comment from our father is enough to keep me quiet the rest of the meal.

After the meal, Ford, Everleigh, and I escape to the front porch. The two of them sit in two of the Adirondack chairs, but I perch on the railing instead.

"Can I ask you what Dad meant by his comment?" Ford asks.

"I want to know, too. You shut down after that, Mad," Everleigh says.

I shake my head with a bit of disgust. "I was basically the spokesperson for a Bradley proposal on a town square development, and we were awarded commercial while another company won residential. He approved the plans, yet he blames me since I was the one who went to the meeting."

"He's always been hardest on you," Everleigh says. "How are you feeling about this season and what comes next?"

I lift a shoulder. "I need to get to San Diego to get a feel for it, you know? I might have better insight. They may not even sign me to a second year. Who knows? They could force me into retirement, and then I get to work for Dad." I roll my eyes.

"If you don't want it, just walk away," Ford says—as if it's as simple as that.

"Then who gets it? Dex?" I ask.

They both laugh as if it's the most ridiculous thing they've heard.

"I don't want it," Everleigh says. She's next in line.

"I still have a few years left in me on the field," Ford says. "Arch won't touch it, and Liam and Ivy are a long way off from being able to manage a Fortune 500 company."

"We all are," I say. "That's why Dad put in a team to support whichever one of us is the next CEO of Bradley. And I guess out of the seven of us, I'm the most logical choice. I'm the oldest. I'll probably retire first. I actually *like* real estate development." I press my lips together. "But damn if that dude doesn't make me feel totally incompetent."

"You're not," Everleigh says. "And he does that to all of us. You just are the lucky one who gets to bear the brunt of it since Bradley Group is going to you."

"Thanks," I say, feeling a bit of solidarity with my sister over all of it.

We chat a while longer out on the porch, and I think about inviting the two of them to dinner sometime, too.

But just like so many of the best-laid plans, the idea moves to the back burner in favor of workouts, work, and staying busy.

Still, I'm hoping I can make my siblings more of a priority going forward.

CHAPTER 12
KENNEDY VAN BUREN

Tiger & Mule

Me: *Can you meet tomorrow morning to*
  I stare at my draft. To what? To kiss me? To bend me over the conference table? To...
I backspace.
Me: *Tomorrow morning, 9:00. Conference room B at VBC.*
Too bitchy.
I delete that, too.
I decide to text Clem instead since we've barely talked since we started working even though we live in the same house.
Me: *How's VBC treating you?*
Her reply doesn't come right away. I know I need to get in touch with Madden's office. We have a ton of project planning to do together up front. Part of our bid had sustainability and environmental goals, and from the start I need to make sure we're on the same page there. Then there's the timeline and utilities—something vital to the planning stage because if we're off on our timelines, construction could be delayed.
It just feels like there's so much to do, and my dad gave me a laundry list of where to start.

straight in. After coffee yesterday, I have a feeling that's exactly what Madden is doing, and I'm not going to sit back while he one-ups me. I'm going to put in the work and learn this shit so I look informed and prepared for every meeting we have.

I'm placating my dad as I assure him I know what I'm doing. He wasn't pleased that we're going to be partnering with Bradley on this, but he *was* pleased that our enemy didn't win the entire bid over us.

Ultimately I chicken out on texting him, and I have my dad's assistant, who's working a dual role right now as my assistant, call his office to arrange the meeting.

Tomorrow morning at nine. Conference room B.

Clem writes me back a little before lunchtime.

Clem: *Going great! Wanna do lunch together in fifteen minutes?*
Me: *Yes! Meet you by the elevators!*

I'm excited to do lunch with Clem. We've been working here for a couple weeks together, and we've only done this twice before so far.

It's always a much-needed break from my day when I get to laugh over lunch with my best friend.

She's waiting there for me when I approach, and she's looking all cute in a flowery dress, jean jacket, and large-framed glasses.

"We need to do this more often," I declare.

She nods and offers a smile. "Now that the first paycheck is in, I absolutely agree."

We both laugh as we walk down to the sandwich shop on the corner, still early enough to hopefully miss the lunchtime rush. Lucky for us, there's no line. We place our orders, and Clem excuses herself to the restroom while I wait for our sandwiches.

I'm in la-la-land as I think about what I'm going to wear Friday morning to my meeting with the hot football star I hate when a deep voice rasps low beside me.

"Couldn't rack up the nerve to call me yourself?"

Chills race down my spine as my body seems to physically react to his proximity.

I whirl on him, practically knocking into him but instead stopping myself with my hands on his very firm, very broad, very sexy chest. "What are you doing here?" I ask.

Seriously, Kennedy? *What are you doing here*? Could I not have come up with at least a semi-intelligent response? Clearly no.

I'm flustered, and I forcibly remove my hands from his chest. His hard, firm, expansive chest.

Jesus.

"I'm grabbing lunch, which I assume you're doing. No?" He smirks at me. The bastard freaking *smirks*.

"I am, and I'm here with someone." I'm not sure why I make it sound ambiguous. I'm here with my best friend.

"Mm. I came alone." His words drip with sex, and I don't even know why.

God, what is wrong with me?

I fold my arms across my chest. "Well, enjoy your solo lunch, then."

"Maybe I could join you. A working lunch," he suggests.

I hate how thrills light up my spine at the offer. "No thanks. I'm good."

I'm in no way *good*.

"Are you here on a date?" he asks.

"Not that it's any of your business, no." I tap my pointer finger on the opposite bicep. "I'm here with my best friend, and we have a lot to discuss."

"Like that hot football player you're partnering with on the SCS project?" he asks.

"Make no mistake, Bradley. We are *not* partners, nor will we ever be," I snarl.

He holds up both hands in surrender. "Easy, tiger," he says.

I glare at him. "Tiger? You're making up pet names for me now?"

He chuckles as if he gets a rise out of ticking me off. He's damn good at it, that's for sure. "It wasn't a pet name when it slipped out, but it does seem to fit."

"Okay, then, mule."

His brows dip. "Mule?"

"Yeah, you know. Like an ass." I raise a pointed brow as I purse my lips, and boom! I finally got in a jab when I seem to turn into jelly around this man.

He laughs.

The bastard *laughs*.

This is not going well, and I'm only saved from more of this misery when the lady at the counter calls my order number.

"Excuse me," I say, needing to move past him to get to the counter, but he doesn't budge. I huff out a breath and squeeze my way past him, and my ass happens to rub along his body as I move.

And holy. Freaking. Shit.

Is that a banana in his pocket, or is he as affected by these random run-ins as I am?

Is he *turned on* by this banter we can't seem to escape?

I gasp a little and turn to look at him, and when our eyes meet, there's a definite heat there. And he's smirking again—or maybe still.

The more I interact with him, the more I want to slap that smirk right off his hot face. Why does he have to be so hot and also so completely off-limits at the same time?

Because just to be totally clear, he *is* off-limits. Not only are we working together on this project, but he's also my family's sworn enemy, which means that even though I'm not really all that close to my father, he's *my* enemy, too.

His dad did something that cost my dad business, and *that* affects me. It's my future company for better or worse, and who knows what sorts of irreversible damage Thomas Bradley did to VBC.

That is why we can't get involved.

No matter how hot his stupid face is.

I turn and spot Clem grabbing a table, and I take the sandwiches over to join her, not giving Madden a second look on my way by.

"Hottie alert in line," she murmurs when I sit and pass her the sandwich. "Thanks."

I glance over and know who she's talking about, and *great*, just *great*, he sees us both ogling him from our table. "Warn a girl when the dude's looking straight at us," I mutter.

She giggles. "But how hot, am I right? He must be…what, like six-four?"

"Six-three," I say, and then my hand flies to my stupid mouth.

"Kennedy Jayne Van Buren, how in the hell do you know that?" she demands, pausing in her pursuit to extract her sandwich from the brown paper bag it's wrapped in.

"That's Madden Bradley."

"The football player?" she asks, her eyes wide.

"And before you get any ideas, he's the heir to Bradley Group, and he's an asshole."

"He's still looking over here." She waves, and goddammit, why did I pick such a friendly, inviting person for my best friend? A bitch who glared across the room at him would've suited me better in this moment.

I shake my head at her. "Knock that off."

"There is *something* crackling in the air here. Talk to me, VB," she says, abbreviating my last name to two letters as she tends to do. It's either Kenny or VB, and she's always Clem or Carter. "Do you know him?"

"He bumped into me at Starbucks one morning, literally. The morning of the bid walk for SCS. We ordered the exact same thing. I was flustered and ran out of there because *look at him*, and then we ran into each other again at the bid walk. VBC was awarded the residential, and he was awarded the commercial."

"So now you get to work with that fine piece of dreamboat?" she asks, folding her hands and leaning her cheek on the back of them as she closes her eyes to feign dreaminess.

"Mm," I grunt. "Something like that. But my dad and his dad hate each other, and my dad already warned me off the entire family. So yes, we're working side by side, and yes, he's gorgeous, but it doesn't matter because he's the enemy."

"Don't you see?" she asks. "That makes it forbidden, which makes it even hotter."

I roll my eyes. "It is no such thing." I take a bite of my sandwich, and lettuce falls out everywhere. It's hanging out of my mouth and sitting on my chest, and wouldn't you know it? The mule chooses that moment to appear at our table.

"Need some help there, tiger?" he asks me.

Oh, Jesus. Now he's calling me by his new pet name for me.

Clem's wide eyes shift from him to me, and I see it all there as I glance up at her.

She wants this for me.

Well, too damn bad.

"I got it," I say thickly around the food in my mouth. I grab a napkin to clean up my mouth, and I brush the lettuce off my top. "Aren't you, like, a famous NFL star? Don't you have somewhere else to sit? Someone else to sit with?"

He shrugs. "I get recognized, but I don't care to sit with people I don't know." He pulls a chair from a nearby table and sets it on the side of ours so he'll be sitting right in between Clem and me. "Hi, Madden Bradley. Nice to meet you," he says, sticking his hand out toward my friend while he completely contradicts what he just said.

"You don't know us," I say.

"Correction, I don't know *your friend*." He says it with more than a hint of flirtation, and I know what he's doing here. He's trying to get a rise out of me. He's flirting with *my friend* right in front of me to see how I'll react.

"Oh, well, allow me to introduce you, then. Clementine Carter, this is Madden. Madden, Clem. Fair warning, Madden's an asshole, and Clem is as kind as they come, so back the hell off."

They both look at me in surprise, and okay, fine. Maybe that was a tad aggressive. But I stand by my words. I'm not backing down.

"Clementine," he says, ignoring me. "What an interesting name."

"It was my great-grandmother's name. My mom was very close to her," she says. "Madden is an interesting name, too."

"Named after John Madden. One of my father's favorite football figures."

"Did he ever play?" Clem asks, and I hate how easy conversation is for them when I feel like I've struggled through every sentence I've strung together with him.

Madden shakes his head. "College, yes. Pro, no. He was drafted and sustained an injury during training camp that ended his playing days."

"That's awful," Clem says.

I'm not sure why that piques my curiosity even more. Why would his parents choose to name him after someone who was injured and never even got to play? The man had quite an amazing career as a coach and broadcaster after that, so maybe that's why. Plus, you know, the video games.

I sit silently and take another bite of my sandwich, attempting to be a bit more ladylike this time.

"What about you? How much longer do you plan to play?" Clem asks.

He glances up and sort of freezes for a beat, and then he shrugs. "I've got one year left on my contract. We'll see how San Diego treats me."

I knew he was recently traded to San Diego, so he'll probably be moving there. Good. A little distance between us wouldn't hurt things. And I can use my status as a diehard Bears fan to push his buttons.

Though we do have some clients in California…

MAD RIVALS

I immediately push the thoughts out of my brain. I certainly don't want to leave this city I love so much for a place where literally the only person I know is Madden fucking Bradley.

His eyes sweep over to mine, and I can tell he's wondering what I'm thinking.

I'll never admit that deep down, I'm wondering how hard it would be to convince my dad that there's no time like the present to get a move on the San Diego market.

CHAPTER 13

KENNEDY VAN BUREN

You Think I'm Hot?

We're walking back to the office, and Madden is far behind in the rearview when Clem asks, "What the hell was that?"

"I'm sorry?" I say it like a question, asking what she's talking about.

"The heat between you and that man! Whew! It was enough to give me the sweats."

"That's just because you're wearing a sweater like it's twelve degrees outside, and today is sunny and seventy."

"I hate Chicago weather," she mutters. "I was freezing this morning when I chose my outfit, okay?"

I laugh.

"You're avoiding the question, ma'am," she points out.

"I know I am."

"So what's going on?" she presses.

"God, he's so fucking hot, isn't he?" I finally groan.

"Absolutely the most gorgeous man I've ever laid eyes on. And he clearly has the hots for you. You should've seen the way he was eyeballing your tits when you had lettuce all over them."

"Maybe he has a thing for lettuce," I mutter petulantly.

"Or maybe he has a thing for Kennedy. What's this about your dads? Can we sidestep that and get to the fuckening?"

"The fuckening?" I repeat.

"Yeah, like an awakening and a good fuck at the same time. A fuckening."

"How is this an awakening?" I ask, my brows dipping.

"Dude, sex with that guy would be a spiritual experience. Guaranteed."

I blow out a breath. Okay, so now Clem knows I'm dealing with a hot guy. But that doesn't change things. "He's such a jerk, though."

"Give me two examples," she says.

"Why two?"

"Because if you only have one, it could be an anomaly or a misread on your part. Two is stronger evidence."

"Um, okay, well, day one he purposely bumped into me," I say, though I have no idea if that's actually true. "And then he dismissed his driver and forced me to drive him back to his office."

She rolls her eyes. "He bumped into you for a conversation starter, and he invented a way to spend time with you despite your icy attitude. I don't know, babe. You know you're my ride or die, but I think maybe you're being the jerk in this situation."

"Ew, Clem!" I practically screech. "Don't you dare say that! You're supposed to be on my side."

"You know I am. Always. But I think you're dismissing this guy for silly reasons when you might be missing out on something amazing. A pro football player from a billionaire family like the Bradleys? Fuck the family feud. I say go for it. You're not even that close with your dad."

"I know, but this is business, too. I can't just go for it. I have to think about the future of VBC and all its employees. I can't get tangled up with a guy who has the power to destroy all of it. I can't trust him."

"Because you haven't given him a chance," she points out.

"And I won't. I can't." My voice gets a little shaky. "I already lost all the control I had over my life when I gave in and took this job, Clem. You know that better than anyone. I can't lose even more to a man who's considered a rival. I just have a lot to prove, and sleeping with the enemy just doesn't feel like the right first impression."

No matter how goddamn hot he is. No matter that he's a professional athlete who appears to be showing an interest in me.

She reaches over and squeezes my hand. "I know, babe. I'll drop it."

"Thanks," I whisper as emotion seems to claw at my chest.

I'm glad she understands. I'm glad she's going to drop it.

But it doesn't change the fact that her words hit where they were meant to. I'm not giving him a chance, and there's definitely something there between us.

Hate. I remind myself that it's hate that's between us.

I have to. I can't lose the last tiny shred of control I have left.

I spend the rest of the afternoon preparing for my meeting tomorrow with Madden. I assume he'll be bringing a team with him, so I pull together a quick meeting with the heads of zoning, infrastructure, utilities, traffic, sustainability, and safety. They're all aware of the project since they each contributed thoughts on the bid, and Dave, our head of zoning, is available to sit in on the meeting tomorrow.

I also tell the sales manager that I'd like Clem to sit in on the meeting.

It's just safer this way. It'll help to have backup. It'll help not to have to face him alone.

And then, purely because of his words to me that I didn't have the nerve to text him, I finally send him a text.

Me: *This is Kennedy Van Buren. My office looks forward to collaborating with you on the SCS project, and I'm just confirming our 9:00 meeting tomorrow at my office.*

His reply comes quickly.

Madden: *I wondered if you'd ever use the number I gave you, but I really thought you'd be more creative than a confirmation.*

I have no idea what to say to that, so I don't reply.

I decide to text Clem instead, but before I can, my dad pops his head into my office.

"I'm going to sit in on the Bradley meeting tomorrow," he says.

I nod and force myself to keep my cool. "Nine o'clock." I don't want him there. I get nervous enough around Madden. I don't need my dad there inspecting every single word coming out of my mouth when words cease to work the majority of the time when I'm around that man.

He flusters me, and I don't like it. It's why I wanted Clem there. Why I invited David.

But my father? No thanks.

My dad presses his lips together, and he doesn't say anything at all to the time of the meeting.

Why are men so weird?

I pick my phone up to text Clem.

Me: *Thank God you're coming to that meeting tomorrow. The hot football player and my dad are going to be in the same room, and I'm already sweating.*

I set my phone to the side to get some work done, and my phone dings a second later with a new text.

I pick it up, and butterflies take flight in my chest when I see who it's from.

But when I click on the text, those butterflies seem to straight up die as dread spreads all throughout their place.

Madden: *You think I'm hot?*

Oh. My. Motherfucker.

I glance up at the text I just sent, and sure enough, the text meant for Clem went to freaking *Madden*.

God, I'm an idiot. I thought I switched to her contact, but my dad flustered me, and I have a million things on my to-do list today, and shit, shit, shit.

I hold down the text to see if there's some way to unsend it, but it's too late. He's already read it. Hell, he's already *responded* to it. It doesn't matter if I unsend it or delete it. The words are in his head now, and I'm trying to figure out how to handle that.

Me: *That text wasn't meant for you.*

Madden: *But it was about me.*

Me: *I refuse to confirm that.*

Madden: *Are you meeting with other football players behind my back?*

Me: *If I was, it wouldn't be your business.*

Madden: *To be clear, I'm not meeting with other gorgeous real estate developers who appear to miss their former graphic design job.*

That's the second time he's called me gorgeous, and I sink back into my chair as I try to figure out how to reply—once again coming up blank, naturally.

Me: *Can we forget this happened?*

Madden: *Not a chance in hell, tiger. You called me hot. I'll never forget this moment.*

Me: *STOP WITH THE TIGER BUSINESS.*

Madden: *Then stop being all fierce and demanding.*

Me: *You are beyond annoying.*

Madden: *I aim to please.*

I can see he's going to have to get the last word, so I let him settle in there.

It doesn't work.

Madden: *You sure you can't squeeze in a dinner with me? For the sake of business, of course.*

Me: *I'm sure.*

Madden: *I want to know what happened between our fathers.*

I freeze at that.

It's out of left field and completely unexpected, but even if our fathers weren't enemies, it would be a terrible idea to get involved with him.

Me: *Then ask your father.*

Madden: *I did. I didn't get anything out of him. I need to know what you know.*

Me: *Not my story to tell.*

Madden: *Why do you hate me?*

This is getting deep for a text conversation with a man I hardly know, but maybe he communicates over text better than in person.

Me: *You're cocky, you're annoying, you think you know everything, you're a business rival. Do I need to go on?*

Madden: *You forgot one. You think I'm hot.*

Me: *See what I mean about annoying?*

Madden: *[smirk emoji]*

He even smirks over text. What is with this guy?

Me: *I need to get back to work. I have a big meeting I need to prepare for with a rival company.*

Madden: *I could help you, you know. Say…over dinner?*

Me: *In your dreams, mule.*

Madden: *See you in the morning, tiger.*

I roll my eyes even though a little smile plays at my lips. Wait a minute. No. No smiles. I slap that smile right off my face, and then I get back to work.

CHAPTER 14
MADDEN BRADLEY

She's Not My Type

I wasn't nervous when recruiters came to watch me play football in high school.

I wasn't nervous when I headed to the Combine.

I wasn't nervous for the draft, my first training camp, or the first time I took the field as an NFL player.

But this? This stupid fucking meeting…yeah. I'm a little nervous.

I don't want to fuck anything up, and I don't want to come off looking like I don't know what I'm doing. But I don't.

I still have no clue why my dad gave me this project. I guess it sort of just fell into my lap. He'd planned on going to the bid walk, had an emergency and couldn't attend, and let me handle it.

And here we are. Now the real work begins, and I assume today will be establishing timelines and planning out where and when our two companies will need to collaborate to ensure the smoothest possible build.

I'm out of my element here, and the irony of that strikes me as I walk into Starbucks to pick up two iced coffees. I have no clue if she has her own, but it can't hurt to walk into a meeting like this with a gift, right?

I pick them up and trek down the block to the VBC offices located up on a high floor in a skyscraper—just like the Bradley Group offices a few blocks the other way.

I take the elevator up, and I'm met with a receptionist when I walk in. I'm carrying two coffees, and the fancy laptop bag I bought two nights ago specifically for this occasion is slung over my shoulder.

"Good morning, I'm Madden Bradley here for a meeting with Kennedy Van Buren," I say to the attractive woman in her mid-twenties sitting behind the desk and eyeing me like I'm a piece of meat.

"Of course, Mr. Bradley. Right this way." She stands from her desk, and her sleek dark hair is pulled back in a high ponytail that still falls to the middle of her shoulder blades.

She's exactly my type, to be honest, but she's also…

Well, she's not Kennedy.

I have no idea why, but that's who I'm interested in right now.

And truthfully, she's *not* my type.

She's gorgeous, yes. Stunning, really.

Historically I've slept with more women with dark hair and dark eyes, but Kennedy has blonde hair and this interesting shade of eye color I still haven't quite identified. Hazel, maybe. Sometimes they seem to glow green at me, and other times they're an amber shade. I wonder what shade they turn when she's being fucked.

I draw in a deep breath as I do my best to ward off the impending hardening of my cock at the mere thought of that.

Jesus, I have got to pull myself together.

Ponytail leads me to a conference room where I immediately spot four people gathered: the CEO of this place, his daughter, her friend, and some dude who already looks bored.

I suppose it slipped my mind that her dad was going to be here. And whoever she was texting about me, which is likely the friend I've already met.

I was too focused on the word *hot* in that text to comprehend anything else it said.

"My apologies," I say, entering the room. "I only knew Kennedy's order." I set the iced coffee in front of her.

She's watching my every move like a hawk watches its prey, and she looks...*different* as my eyes meet hers.

Something is different with her hair. It's maybe wavier than usual. Her eye makeup is a little darker today, and she looks professional in a white shirt and skirt.

She looks prepared.

She looks like she put in some extra effort.

Was it for me?

She looks hot as all fuck.

"Thank you," she murmurs, and those interesting eyes of hers are golden today.

The four of them stand to shake my hand, and I tear my eyes from her as I introduce myself to each of the men. I learn the bored dude is Dave from zoning, and Kennedy thought it would be a good idea to have at least one of the department heads sit in on our initial meeting.

The meeting goes surprisingly well. She's prepared. I'm prepared. We establish a timeline, and her father, Dave, and Clem pretty much just sit back and listen.

It's just hard to concentrate when I can't stop staring at her hair. Or when her eyes meet mine and I forget what the fuck I was saying.

"I'll run this by my office and let you know if we anticipate any changes," I say as we wrap up the meeting.

She nods. "I'll do the same and get back to you via email by next Tuesday. If all goes well, hopefully we can get this timeline to SCS and get started on the permits in the next few weeks."

I stand and reach my hand across the table to shake hers, and she stands, too. She sets her hand in mine, and fuck it if fireworks don't start booming and crackling all around us.

Can her dad see those? Clem? Dave?

Can she?

Or is it just me?

I don't know what the fuck is happening, and I don't think I like it. But the more time I spend around this woman, the more one thing is clear.

There's heat between us.

And I've never ignored heat. It's too dangerous to ignore. It could lead to heatstroke, or fire, or worse.

Now I have to figure out how to get her to stop ignoring it, too.

I head back to the office and send the timeline to the rest of the team. I wrap up a few other loose ends, and then I head home.

I don't have anything planned tonight—a rare occurrence on a Friday night for me, but since I'm no longer playing in Chicago, the opportunities have already dwindled. Clubs and bars want local players, not traitors, which I've been called more than once since I signed the trade deal.

I didn't even have a choice, but people neither understand nor care.

I should've planned a trip to San Diego this weekend, but I didn't. I didn't know if the meeting would turn to shit today and I'd have to spend all weekend revising the timeline or what. Thankfully that's not what happened, but now I'm left on a Friday night with nothing to do.

I grab a beer from the fridge and turn on ESPN for some background noise, and then I open my phone and find myself navigating to her contact.

I read through our text messages from yesterday.

I can't help my smile at the one where she called me *hot*.

And then I stare at the bar where I'm supposed to draft my next message, and I think about what the hell I can say to open the door to try to get to know more about the mystery that is Kennedy Van Buren.

CHAPTER 15
KENNEDY VAN BUREN

New Message from Madden Bradley

My bedroom in my parents' house has a big bench built in under the window, and that's where Clem and I find ourselves after work on Friday evening. Dinner's done, and we grabbed a bottle of vodka to bring up to my room. Now we're sitting on opposite sides of the bench, feet up and resting on the side of each other's legs as we sip our drinks and stare out the window.

"How are you liking VBC so far?" I ask.

"Much better than that shit show I worked for before," she says. "And did I tell you about Lance?"

My eyes dart over to hers, and her cheeks are flushed—not from the vodka since we just started. "Lance?" I raise a suggestive brow.

"He's in the same department as me, and he's just, like, so *cute*. He's kinda dorky, and he's tall and skinny, and we've been sort of flirting. He gets all awkward, but then he hits me with this totally unexpected deep voice, and I just melt."

"Someone's smitten," I say with a smile.

"Yeah, you."

I roll my eyes. "You said you were dropping it."

"And I would if I really believed there was nothing there. But Kenny, he brought you your Starbucks order." She raises her brows pointedly. "That means something."

"It means he knows my order. That's it." I shrug.

She shakes her head. "Dudes don't remember shit like that."

"We have the same order. He's just playing a game. He's pretending to be interested so he can take what he wants and drop me in the end."

She pulls a face that clearly tells me she doesn't believe that for a second. "Do you really think that?"

Now that I've said it aloud, it's honestly what makes the most sense. I studied the photos of him online, and when he's been photographed with a date, it's almost always a tall, thin woman with long, dark hair.

I'm only five-foot-five, and my hair is decidedly blonde.

What if that *is* what he's doing? What if he's not interested at all in me, but he's acting like he is so he can steal valuable information from VBC? What if he's going to try to take on the entire project and steal residential out from under us?

We signed contracts. He can't do that.

But that doesn't mean he can't learn a few trade secrets or figure out where our weaknesses are so he can pounce later.

I finally blow out a breath as I lift a shoulder. "I just don't trust his intentions."

"Okay, say he's untrustworthy and he's just playing a game to take what he wants from you. Would it really be so bad to play the game with him? To take a few things of your own?" She wiggles her brows slyly.

"Are you suggesting I sleep with him?"

She shrugs without responding.

"How would that help things?" I ask.

She purses her lips. "Have you seen that ass of his? It's not gonna hurt things, bitch."

I laugh. "You're too much."

"I'm aware."

"So are you sleeping with Lance yet?"

"No!" She's nearly defensive, and that's my first clue that she already really likes him.

But now sex is on my brain, specifically sex with Madden, and I'm not sure how to get that out of my head. I don't *have* to let feelings get involved…but that doesn't make it a good idea.

I shake my head without any words as I shake that thought right out.

No.

It's a terrible idea.

Sex will always complicate things, and we have to work together. I can't.

No matter how much I want it.

Playing his game would be dangerous. I don't think I could have sex with someone as hot and intriguing as he is and keep my emotions out of it. Especially not when I started smiling just looking at his text messages yesterday.

I feel like I'm so screwed. Everything in me tells me we're supposed to be enemies. I'm supposed to be keeping him at arm's length.

And yet…every time I see him, he piques my interest just a little more.

Of course Clem had to bring up the fact that he brought me coffee. My exact order. Of course she recognized that.

Of course she's reading into it.

Clem narrows her eyes at me. "What are you thinking?"

She knows. She always knows.

My traitorous phone chooses that exact moment to let us all know I have a new message. It's sitting between us, and she grabs it before I can.

"New message from Madden Bradley," she reads, and she hands the phone over to me.

I press my lips together, ignoring the butterflies that seem to be gathering in my belly.

I snatch the phone from her hand. "I'm sure it's something about SCS."

I open the message, and it's definitely *not* related to work.

Madden: *Was there something different about your hair today?*

I flash the screen at Clem, and she reads it.

"My hair?" I say. "He's texting me on a Friday night to ask about *my hair*? Hell yes, there was something different about it. I put actual effort in. I wanted to *look* my best so I could *feel* my best for the meeting with the enemy."

"He's not the enemy," she mutters, but I don't even acknowledge that she spoke because I'm angry typing out a reply.

Me: *Why are you texting me at 8 p.m. on a Friday asking about my hair? Shouldn't you be out with your superstar buddies?*

Madden: *I was thinking about you.*

I hate that my stomach flips when I read that one.

I hate that the butterflies seem to be flapping up into my chest.

Me: *Why?*

Madden: *Because your hair looked different.*

Me: *I put a few curls in. Are we good now?*

Madden: *No.*

Me: *Why not?*

Madden: *Because you still haven't agreed to dinner.*

Me: *And I won't.*

"What are you rage texting to him?" Clem asks.

I scoot over a little so she can switch sides and sit beside me while I wait for him to reply.

Madden: *What about a drink, then?*

Me: *Why? So you can try to get on the inside with VBC?*

"Don't send that," Clem sputters.

"Why not? What do I have to lose by letting him know what I really think?"

"Suit yourself," she huffs, and she slips her own phone out of her pocket and moves back to the other side of the bench.

I'm shocked when my phone starts to ring and it's Madden Bradley calling me.

Calling me.

"Uh, Clem? We've got a nine-one-one situation here."

Her eyes move to mine as I flash her my screen.

"What are you waiting for? Answer it!" she screeches.

"Hello?" I say tentatively.

"Is that really what you think I'm doing?" he demands, cutting right to the chase.

I blow out a breath. "I don't really know what to think."

"What are you doing right now?"

"None of your business."

He chuckles. "That's the most Kennedy answer of all time. Come meet me for a drink."

"How do you know I'm not busy?" I ask, a little sass in my tone.

"Because you're texting me on a Friday night, and it's quiet at your house."

"How do you know I'm at my house?"

"Admittedly, it's an assumption," he says. "Would it be creepier if I said it's because I'm watching you?"

I can't help but bark out a laugh at that. "Definitely."

"I'm not, just for the record. So how about that drink?"

"I already have a drink in hand, but thanks."

"What does Kennedy Van Buren drink on a relaxing Friday night at home?"

"Tito's and soda with a lime." I take a sip as if it's proving a point even though he can't see me.

"In case you're wondering, I'm nursing a beer."

"I wasn't wondering."

He laughs. "Goddammit, Kennedy. I really like you."

"Why?"

He quiets on the other end of the line. "Do you really want me to answer that?" His voice is warm and husky when he poses the question, and it sends a shot directly to my vagina.

This is a terrible idea, but I can't seem to stop myself.

"I do."

"I noticed your hair was different. I know your Starbucks order. I know that you click your pen three times when you're making a point, and I wondered if it was for emphasis or just a nervous habit. I'm noticing things about you I've never really cared to look at before."

"What can I say? I'm fascinating," I say dryly.

He chuckles. "I can't argue that. But it's not just those things. You're fierce, and you're funny. You're blunt as hell and don't seem to give a fuck. It was your beauty that first caught my interest, but it's your personality that kept it."

I don't know what to say to that.

And even if I *did* know, I'm not sure I could possibly speak right now since my entire mouth just went completely dry.

"Can you at least tell me what your dad said about my family that made you hate me?" he asks.

"I don't hate you," I admit quietly. Especially not after what he just said. "I just don't trust you, and I don't think it's a good idea to get involved beyond what we have to do in the office."

"I get that," he says. "But can you let me try to prove you can trust me?"

I glance over at Clem, and I notice for the first time that she's studying me. She can probably hear every word he's said to me, and she's nodding at me. "Go for it," she mouths.

I sigh. She's no help. "Fine."

He pauses for a beat as if he can't believe I just said that. "Fine? Like…you'll meet me for a drink in, say…a half hour?"

A half hour? I'm supposed to make myself presentable and arrive at some unknown destination in *a half hour*?

Clem is nodding her head nearly violently.

"Fine," I say reluctantly. "Do you know Dot's Tavern?" It's just around the corner from my parents' house, so I can walk home.

"Yep. See you in a half hour," he says.

"Bye." I hang up before I change my mind.

Clem squeals. "You have a date with football star Madden Bradley?"

"It's not a date," I mutter.

It's totally a date, though, and I need to figure out what the hell to wear.

CHAPTER 16
MADDEN BRADLEY

Aligning Values

I drive to the bar and figure I can take an Uber home if I need to, and I head inside once I arrive. I don't see her, so I slip outside and wait near the door for her. I'm wearing a hat since I'm dressed down in jeans and a T-shirt, and I'm more likely to be recognized when I'm not in businessman mode, and I keep my head down as I wait for her.

I'm surprised when I see her approaching on foot, and I study her for a beat. She hasn't spotted me yet, and I'm not sure how I've lived in this city for my entire life and never run into her. If I had, out of the context of business, would things be any different?

Would she have given me a second glance if I had nothing to do with Bradley Group?

Somehow I think her dad still would've warned her off me, something that feels incredibly unfair to us both. We should be able to explore what we want without our fathers' mistakes hanging over us, and yet…she won't.

Which is highly unfortunate. My eyes fall to the way the jeans she's wearing hug against her body, and I imagine that body moving beneath me.

I blow out a breath as I try to collect myself, and I kick off from the wall to head over to meet her on the sidewalk.

"Did you do something different with your hair?" she teases, and I can't help it. I laugh. She's funny as hell, usually because she's being all demanding and uptight, but somehow being around her makes me feel this sense of joy that's been missing from my life.

Maybe it's the challenge, but maybe it isn't.

I lift the hat from my head, and she tilts her head and pretends to study me.

"Ah, yes. There he is," she says as I set the hat back into place.

"Less chance I'll be recognized in a hat," I say with a shrug, and I gently rest my hand on the small of her back to guide her toward the door.

She glances back at me as if she's surprised by my touch, and I know this isn't a date, but it's also not a business meeting.

It feels sort of like a drink between people who could become friends if we could plot a path to get past our father's mistakes.

But first, I need to know what those mistakes are.

It's a Friday night, so of course it's packed when we walk in, but I slip the hostess some cash, and she manages to find us a table. Kennedy orders a vodka soda, I order a beer, and it sort of feels like the two of us are just continuing our phone conversation here in person.

I lean in a little closer so she can hear me over the loud din of bar noise on a Friday night, and she leans in, too. The smell of coconuts is strong this close to her, and it's pulsing something unfamiliar down low in me.

Before I can open my mouth to speak, she says, "So how are you going to prove I can trust you?"

I chuckle at her forward question. "I don't really have a plan, to be honest. I guess I'll just be myself and hope for the best."

"Because that's worked so well for you so far?"

I shake my head. "Because I learned a long time ago that you get a hell of a lot further in life being yourself than by pretending."

"What taught you that lesson?"

I shrug, not sure I want to get into it, but if I'm going to earn her trust, I need to show her who I am.

"Back when I was in high school, my senior year, we won the state championship. I went to a party with people I didn't know, and I guess I was trying to prove something. I smoked some weed, not a big deal, but in hindsight, it could've cost me everything I'd been working toward. If the college I'd already committed to decided to slap me with a random drug test, I would've failed. It was in the morning when I woke up that I realized how stupid I'd been. I was trying to be the guy who fit in with everybody when I didn't even care about those people. I didn't even see most of them again. What did I care what they thought about me?"

She tilts her head as if my story affected her in some way. "Have you done any drugs since then?"

I press my lips together and shake my head as the server delivers our drinks. "Only prescribed or over-the-counter ones. You?"

She holds up her glass of vodka. "This is about as hard as I go."

Seems our values align there.

"I try to live a clean lifestyle. I have to in order to stay competitive on the field, but in the offseason, I don't mind kicking back with a beer or two on the weekend." I hold up my bottle, and she taps her glass to mine.

"My friend Clem and I have been known to share a bottle of vodka over a weekend, but that's about as crazy as it gets," she says with a smile.

"Clem. That's the girl from the office, right?" I ask, and she nods. "You two are close."

She twists her lips, and my eyes flick there. "Very. She's my best friend. We met our freshman year of college and have been inseparable since. We lived together after we graduated, worked these awful jobs in a terrible part of town, and quit together to start working for VBC."

"It feels like there's a blackmail story there," I say with a twinkle in my eye, and she giggles.

"My parents have always wanted me to come work for the company, and I told them I would if they hired Clem, too." She raises her eyebrows as if to say she got her way.

"Tell me more about your parents," I say, and I notice the caution even in my own tone.

"You first."

"Yeah, maybe that's not such a good idea." I chuckle, but then I continue anyway. "My father can be a dick, my mother can be totally absent, and somehow they got together at least seven times unless one of my siblings isn't my full-blooded sibling." I shrug as if it doesn't much matter to me either way. "The seven of us were essentially raised by a team of caretakers—nannies, cooks, and housekeepers. My parents were always at the office. Always traveling for work. Always attending charity balls." I take a long swig of beer before I press my lips together. "Your turn."

She tilts her head a little, and she takes a sip of her drink, too. I notice hers is almost empty, so I signal the server to bring us another round.

"Similar except for my parents getting together seven times. Just the once." She flashes a smirk. "Didn't need to try again after the first attempt was so successful. But they both spent their days at the office. They had the nanny bring me by, likely to parade me around and pretend like they were good parents. They put me to work as soon as they could." She's quiet for a beat, staring into her drink, and then she drains it. "Sometimes I think the only reason they had a kid was to have someone to pass the company to."

"Do you really believe that?"

She twists her lips a little, and then she nods. "Yeah, I do. And I don't know if I'm really that person."

I can't help but wonder how much vodka she had before she arrived and whether she'd be as honest about that with her supposed business rival if she hadn't had a few drinks first. I'm also wondering if she doesn't think she's the person to take over VBC because she doesn't want it or because she already thinks of herself as a failure.

She seems to have a pretty good handle on what she's doing despite only being there a short time. Maybe she *is* that person, and she just hasn't realized it yet.

Just as maybe I'm the right person for Bradley Group.

Instead of asking why she isn't that person—something I can relate to more than she knows—I ask something else that I'm wondering. "Then why are you working there? Why'd you leave a graphic design job for this?"

Her eyes dart to mine, and I know I've mentioned it before, but she seems surprised I remember that about her.

The server drops by our next round before she answers, and she helps herself to a generous swig first. "There were a lot of little reasons, to be honest. Clem and I wanted to prove our independence, and we did for five long years. We lived in a shitty apartment in a bad part of town working shitty jobs we both hated." Another sip of vodka. "We were both working the kinds of long hours where you don't even get to have a social life, and it sort of all came to a head. I closed my eyes on the train home, and someone stole my wallet and my Kindle, and then I fell getting off the bus, and—" She cuts herself off and sets her hand over her eyes for a beat, and then she closes her eyes.

"And?" I prompt. It's hard to imagine the sophisticated and smart Kennedy Van Buren as anything less than what's seated beside me.

"And I had no money to buy dinner, limped home with a bleeding knee to listen to my neighbor banging his girlfriend, looked at the cracks in my walls, and asked Clem if she was happy because I was sure the hell not."

"Was she?"

She shakes her head, and I can't help but reach across the table and circle my fingers around her wrist. I give it a squeeze, and I'm not sure why. Solidarity, maybe. Sympathy.

Her eyes fall to the place where my hand connects with her skin, and I study her face as she studies my hand.

Her eyes are rimmed in red, and she sniffles a little as she makes these rather surprising confessions.

"All I wanted was a little independence. I wanted to make it on my own. My parents said the door was always open if I wanted to return, and I knew I had the solution for both Clem and me. I know the business. I was raised there. I worked there until I left for college. It just took admitting that I failed to the two people I most wanted to succeed in front of."

"You didn't fail." My voice is soft and tender, and I'm not even sure where it came from.

Her eyes lift to mine, and I let go of my hold on her wrist.

"Babe, your wallet was stolen. You were in a dangerous situation. You got out of it. Why would you think that's a failure?" I ask.

Her brows dip together. "Did you just call me *babe*?"

My brows mirror hers as I think back. "Did I?"

"You did." Her eyes have gone from red-rimmed to slightly twinkling, and I get the distinct impression she *likes* that I called her that.

If I did, it slipped out.

But if it slipped out, it's because I'm starting to feel more and more like there's something here. There's enough between us that it feels appropriate to call her an endearment like *babe*. I just don't know if she's ready for it.

"Sorry. I meant to say *tiger*." My eyes twinkle back at her, and then I drain what's left in my second beer as I feel the intensity thicken between us. And I can't wait to take it to another level.

CHAPTER 17
KENNEDY VAN BUREN

I Want Him to Kiss Me

This entire night has been easier than I was expecting, and it's only leaving me confused.

We've covered a lot of topics, but we haven't gotten to the thing I know he wants to ask. He keeps ordering us another round, and I keep drinking, and I should really stop since my lips tend to get looser and looser the more the vodka flows, but I'm finding myself *enjoying* this evening.

He said his dad wouldn't tell him what went down between our fathers, and I don't honestly know all that much.

But it sort of feels like the next couple years of working on this project together will go a lot smoother if we can do it from a place of friendship rather than from that place of rivalry that I've been working from.

And I'm getting this strange sense from him that he's being genuine. He cares. He's not just here to get some insider info on me or my company.

It's like something is shifting between us, and I like it. Maybe it's the vodka, but maybe it's not. I'm tucking my dad's warning away, but I'm also an adult who can handle myself despite my recent failures proving otherwise.

I clear my throat after our server drops off our latest round of drinks, and I blurt, "Your dad did something underhanded to my dad. I don't know what it was, but they played football together, and they were close friends until your dad stopped playing. I guess they lost touch. Years later they were competing for bids, and your dad did something to win the bid over my dad, but he didn't say what. He made it sound like he'd do it again, and I asked what we could do to fight it, and he said that your dad has connections we can't fight against. I don't know what any of it means, but my dad warned me off your entire family."

He freezes at my words, and then he blinks as his brows dip close together as if he has no idea what I'm talking about. Maybe he does, but maybe he really doesn't. I'm still trying to gain my bearings around him and figure out whether or not he's trustworthy.

"Kinda makes you wonder what secrets he's keeping," I say absently, but I can tell Madden's wheels are turning now.

His jaw continues working back and forth as he stares into his beer bottle, and then he seems to snap out of it. "I'll get to the bottom of it."

"Well, I gave up the farm on my secrets about not really being sure if I want to run the family business. You go." I nod at him and punctuate my sentence with a sip of my drink.

He chuckles. "I'm thirty-five. I was traded in the last year of my contract from a place I loved and didn't want to leave." He shrugs. "If I don't have a stellar season, I'm basically fucked. And there are already several receivers on San Diego who can outrun me. I never asked to run the company when I retire, but it's always been my father's plan for me."

"What do *you* want?" I ask.

When he tilts his head as his eyes meet mine, I get the sense that nobody has ever asked him that before.

"I don't really know. I guess I never had to think about it because this was always the plan. I majored in construction management at Purdue and played football, and I guess I'm just biding time to fulfill a destiny that was always meant to be mine."

"Isn't that poetic?" I tease, but the truth is I hear the melancholy in his tone. "What about a family?" I ask, and I'd never get so personal with a business associate if it weren't for the vodka.

He lifts a shoulder. "Honestly, it's just another thing I pushed off until I was done playing. I guess I'll have a lot of decisions to make in the next few years."

"Is there anyone you'd, um…you know. Start a family with?"

His eyes move back to mine, and there's some heat in there as he seems to contemplate his answer. I shift under his scrutiny. Maybe I'm imagining the heat. It's only one interpretation. He could just as well be looking at me like I'm nuts for asking something so personal.

He surprises me by saying, "No. I've done a pretty good job of setting my personal life aside to focus on football."

"So you've never been in a serious relationship?" I ask, surprised both because he appears to be a pretty damn nice catch and because it's one more thing we share in common.

"How can I be when I'm committed to football?" he shoots back.

It's a valid point, but it also seems like that commitment is starting to fade as he stares down what's potentially his last year playing.

"What about you?" he asks.

I point to my own chest rather dumbly, and he nods encouragingly. "I've never really had anything serious, either. I don't have football as an excuse. I just never found anything worth hanging onto."

He flattens his lips for a beat, and he squints as he studies me. "Yeah, you look like one of those."

My brows pinch tightly together. "One of what?" I ask defensively.

"One of those women who won't settle for less than the best. The happily ever after with the perfect man who doesn't exist leading her to her storybook ending." He points his bottle at me. "Right?"

"Just because I haven't had a serious relationship doesn't mean I'm seeking perfection." Does it? Maybe Clem and I will need to dissect that later.

I don't know why I'm getting defensive. I guess Madden just brings that out in me.

He nods. "Okay."

"You don't believe me," I say.

"And you don't care what I believe."

I tilt my head a little in agreement. "True."

He chuckles, and I blow out a breath.

"I should get home," I say. I don't have a real need to, but I think we've probably shared enough secrets this evening.

I'm afraid if I stay longer—if I *drink* much longer—my lips will get even looser, and that's probably something I can't afford.

"Did you walk here?" he asks.

I nod. "I live close by."

"It's late to be walking by yourself. Let me walk you home. Or at least let me add a stop to my own Uber home."

I narrow my eyes at him, and I know he's just doing it to be nice. I relent as I nod, even though the thought of him walking me to my door fills me with both tingles and dread. "Okay. You can Uber me."

He pulls out his credit card to pay the tab, and I start to put up an argument.

He holds up a hand. "Stop. It's a business expense."

I narrow my eyes at him, but I hold up both hands in surrender anyway.

We head out front, and the cool evening air sends shivers down my spine.

"The car is four minutes away," he says, flashing his phone at me to show me the driver is en route to us, and I wander back toward the building and lean on the bricks several yards down from the door.

He steps into place and leans beside me, and he's just a fraction too close.

I make the mistake of drawing in a deep breath, and it's filled with him. It's warm and rich, a little spicy and heady, and it makes me think of sex. With him. Tonight.

It's off the table. I know it is. Still, I can't help but peek over at him, and when I do, I find his head angled down as he studies me. His eyes are heated and glow with need, and despite the way I should feel tentative, I don't.

I want him to kiss me.

I want to see if the passion is as strong as I imagine it will be.

It's like he senses what I'm thinking as he kicks off the wall and moves to stand directly in front of me. His eyes are hot on mine as something unspoken passes between us.

"Tonight was nice," he says softly.

I can't seem to come up with any sort of coherent response. "Yeah." It's a mumbled word that nearly rides the line of being a needy moan.

His eyes flick to my lips before they move back to my eyes, and I wonder if he does this with all his female business rivals or if this is a first for him the way it is for me. Are we even still rivals after tonight? It's hard to tell. My father doesn't want me going near him, and yet his head is starting to lower, and all I can think about is his lips connecting with mine.

I'm a little drunk, I think. Sober Kennedy would stop this train, but right now, I can't. I can't look away from his gorgeous face as it moves closer to mine.

I can't push away the body that takes a step closer. Well, I *can*. I don't want to.

All I can think about is his lips, his hands, his body as it closes the space between us until I'm consumed by him.

His body presses to mine, pushing me back into the brick wall of the building, and my breath catches in my throat as one of his hands moves toward my hips and the other slides around my neck.

He's touching me, and I grip onto his biceps to steady myself. I'm still pressed against the wall, yet it feels like I'll fall to the ground if I don't hold onto him.

I tilt my chin up, anticipation and adrenaline running rampant through my chest as he moves until there are no more inches between us. My stomach flips as he leans down, and his nose brushes mine. It's a million sensations all at once. His scent overwhelming me. His touch pulsing a dull ache down low in my belly. The sound of cars rushing past down the street drowned out by the beating of my heart pounding in my ears.

And now it's time to find out how he tastes.

I close my eyes, and his lips connect with mine.

It's overwhelming.

It's explosive and hot, and when his fingers grip a little harder on my hips, a moan rises up out of my chest.

He takes the opportunity to open his mouth to mine at my moan, and his kiss is somehow both tender and aggressive at the same time. His tongue moves against mine with a skilled sort of confidence that tells me he must have many talents with that tongue.

I dive right in, too, meeting his tongue brush for brush as we attempt to navigate this new, unexpected connection together.

My God, this man can kiss. It's not just his firm lips or the way he's holding me. It's the way he's all-consuming in any room he walks into, the way he overwhelms me with simply how hot he is, the way we can bicker and banter and yet still somehow windup right here in this moment. It's that heat of hate lined on the backside of this passionate moment.

His fingertips dig into my hip as he shifts, and I feel his erection as it presses against my stomach. It's long and hard, and it's proof he wants me as much as I've been fighting against the fact that I want him, too.

This kiss is unlike any other I've ever encountered. There's passion there as we explore the attraction we've both felt, and it's making me want more with him. It's making me want to set aside whatever differences we had and take him into my bed.

I can't, obviously.

I live with my parents, one of whom expressly forbade this sort of thing.

But maybe we could go to his place?

Tingles explode in my chest at the thought.

He pulls back unexpectedly, and he leans his forehead to mine. "Fuck," he groans, his voice a hoarse, strangled rasp.

My chest tightens at his curse. He's kissing the enemy, and then he stopped. He didn't mean to kiss me at all.

I can't back up out of his embrace since he has me pinned to the wall, but shame and embarrassment fill me in equal measures at his single word that managed to ruin whatever this moment was.

Heat pricks behind my eyes, and I finally gather the courage to set both of my hands on his chest to push him away.

I touch my lips, and then I glare at him.

He looks epically confused at my glare. "What?" he asks.

"You know what," I hiss.

He tilts his head, but then he glances away from me and toward the black car that's idling at the curb. "Our ride is here."

"I'll just walk," I spit at him, and I move to walk away.

He grabs my arm, halting my progress. "Where the fuck are you going?"

"Home!" I yell at him. I'm crushed that he pulled away so abruptly when he must've realized what we were doing, and I hate that I feel that way.

"The car is here," he says, his voice an overly calm contrast to mine. "Why are you acting like this?"

Oh, now he wants me to relive the whole mortifying experience? I don't think so.

I rip my arm from his grasp, and I'm halfway between embarrassed and furious over this whole situation. I practically run to get away from him, my feet stomping with each clap against the pavement, and I never look back.

CHAPTER 18
MADDEN BRADLEY

It Never Came Up

What the fuck was that?

What the fuck is wrong with her?

Questions swirl around my head as I take the car home solo. I think about texting her, but she was angry. Angry I kissed her? The way she melted into me, the soft moans…no. It wasn't the kiss that made her fly off the handle.

It had to have been that she realized it was *me* she was kissing. Or she was drunker than I thought she was and she realized what the fuck she was doing.

I have no clue. I'm confused as fuck.

I wanted to keep kissing her, and I only pulled back because my phone buzzed to let me know our ride was here and waiting for us.

I was going to invite her back to my place. I guess I'm glad I didn't have to face that particular rejection.

I blow out a breath as the car pulls up to my building. I thank the driver, hand him a twenty instead of tipping in the app, and head upstairs as I try to shake off whatever the hell that was.

What now?

I turn back toward the car. "Are you able to take me somewhere else?" I ask the driver. He looks a bit unsure, and I pull out my wallet and pass him a hundred-dollar bill. "I'll make it worth your time."

He shrugs and nods as if to say, "Get in."

I give him the address, and ten minutes later, we're pulling up in front of my parents' house. "Wait here for me. I won't be more than a half hour, and I've got another hundred for you."

"You got it," he says, and I walk up to the front door.

It's late. I realize that. But I just had a very interesting conversation with someone, and I need to know more.

I ring the bell and bang on the front door at the same time, and the door opens a minute later.

"Madden," my father murmurs, a hint of surprise in his tone. He's wearing a bathrobe over his expensive silk pajamas, and he looks like someone I don't even know. "What are you doing here so late?"

"What secrets are you keeping where Van Buren is concerned?"

He presses his lips into a thin line. "It's complicated, Madden. I played college football with Van Buren. That's really the end of it."

"What happened?"

"It doesn't matter. As you know, I had to stop playing because of an off-the-field injury. But I did everything I could to ensure my sons had the opportunities I missed out on because of it." The way he says the words gives me chills.

I did everything I could. What *exactly* does that mean?

"So what happened with Van Buren?" I ask.

I raise my brows pointedly.

"We were friends. Years later we met in a business setting, and I won a bid over him. He was a sore loser, that's all." He's flippant, maybe overly so, and I get the sense that he's leaving something out of the story.

"What did you do?" I hiss.

He shakes his head. "I didn't do anything."

I don't believe a word out of his lying mouth. He's too poised, too sure of himself.

"While you're here, I have some news," he says.

I narrow my eyes at him, wondering what the fuck he's going to hit me with next.

"I found an office space in San Diego. We're expanding past Chicago, Vegas, and New York. You can work there on your days off when you're in San Diego, and you can run that office."

My brows dip. "What the fuck makes you think I want that? I'm not going to work there on my days off. I'm in San Diego to play football, not to run your company."

"Your company, Madden. The Bradley legacy."

I force myself not to roll my eyes at his terminology.

It doesn't matter if I'm in San Diego to play football. If Thomas Bradley wills it to be so, so it will be.

"Will you be in town next Saturday?" he asks.

I think through my calendar, and as far as I know, I'll be here. I think about asking why, but before I do, he says, "We've agreed to attend the Chicago Urban Renewal Fundraiser Gala next weekend, and you should be there. There will be great opportunities to network. We'll also bring Ford," he says.

At least I'll have someone to talk to at this event he's forcing me to attend.

"Fine," I mutter.

"Have your tux pressed before then, yes?"

How did I come here to confront my father and somehow end up in charge of an entirely new office while also agreeing to attend a charity ball next weekend?

I have no idea, but that's what he does. He changes the subject. He twists things until we have no choice but to agree.

And so I guess I'm going to a gala next weekend.

CHAPTER 19
KENNEDY VAN BUREN

Nowhere to Run

I don't want to be here.

I don't even have Clem with me.

I told her about the kiss with Madden when I got home that night. Eight days later, embarrassment still burns.

She said I misinterpreted his curse. She says he wouldn't have leaned his forehead to mine if he wanted to get away from me, and I guess her argument has legs.

"You weren't there." That was my flat reply. In the moment, it felt like he stopped because he realized what he was doing. And that didn't make me feel very good.

The past week was busy with work, and I forced it out of my head. Or, I tried to. I can't exactly forget about the hottest kiss of my life no matter how it ended, and given the fact that I need to communicate with his office fairly regularly since we have this project together, his name crosses my radar more often than it should.

God, why did he have to end it that way?

What a jerk.

He called me. The next day, my phone rang, and when I saw it was him, I was too mortified to answer, so I sent it to voicemail.

He didn't try again. I guess we'll cross paths at some point, and for now, I'm trying to put the whole stupid situation behind me. This was exactly why I knew it was a bad idea to get involved with him all along.

I get out of the car my dad ordered for us, and I make my red-carpet appearance with both my parents. I wish I had someone to bring along as my date, but I don't.

Instead, I'm here solo, and this gorgeous ballgown is just a total waste. It's a silky emerald green gown with sequined shoulder straps and a slit that leaves very little to the imagination. I had my hair and makeup done thanks to my mother, who insisted we get the works done ahead of this ball, and I feel like I'm glowing as I force a smile for the cameras along the red carpet.

This is a big event for the city, drawing huge celebrity names as well as local businesspeople that will be important connections for networking.

As I step off the red carpet and turn toward the ballroom, though, I spot him.

Madden Bradley.

He's standing just outside the ballroom doors.

I don't know why it never crossed my mind that he might be here tonight. Of course he should be here. It's a gala for the same community we're both a part of.

My chest tightens, and I feel like I can't breathe in this dress for a second.

He hasn't seen me yet. There's still time to run.

He's talking to another man who looks like him, and I wonder if he's one of the seven Bradley siblings.

An older gentleman and a woman who has the same dark hair as Madden stride over to them, and I gather these are his parents. The older man must be my father's nemesis, proven true when I see my father stiffen and hiss, "Bradley."

I blow out a breath. My parents instructed me to network tonight, and I assumed I'd be talking to people who might become future clients. I didn't brace myself for having to face my competition.

I was already uncomfortable with having to walk into a room full of strangers and try to make friends. But now I have to do it under Madden Bradley's scrutinizing gaze?

I'm not quite sure how I'm going to get through this night, but one thing is clear.

I need a fucking drink. Stat.

I stand on my mother's far side as we pass by the Bradley Group, and I don't dare make eye contact with a single one of them as I pretend I'm overly interested in walking into the ballroom.

I don't care about this ballroom. I don't much care about this event, to be honest. I just want the ground to swallow me up. I just want to go home, slip into pajama pants, and bury myself under my covers with a good book—on my Kindle app on my phone since I still haven't replaced my stolen Kindle.

I beeline for the bar and get a glass of wine. I should've opted for something stronger to hit the tipsy scale a little faster, but this *is* a professional event, and I suppose getting drunk is a poor choice. Besides, wine is my favorite. I only drink vodka when I want to numb or get tipsy.

I turn with my wine to find my parents again when I bump directly into a chest blocking my way.

"Nowhere to run," he says, and his eyes positively burn down on mine. He seems…angry? "You're stunning tonight, Kennedy. Did you do something different with your hair? And that dress…" He trails off as his eyes sweep down my form, and my body heats with each place his eyes land.

"Get out of my way," I demand, and he chuckles.

"Not without finding out why you're avoiding me."

"Are you serious, Madden? You want to do this now?"

"Well, no. I wanted to do it last Friday, but you ran scared." He nods at the bartender. "What's on tap?"

I move to escape him as he listens to his options, but he grabs onto my upper arm, halting me where I am. I'm not going to make a scene by ripping my arm away despite how tempted I am.

"Where the fuck do you think you're going?" he hisses, low enough that I'm the only one who hears his words over the loud din of gala music and chatter, and then to the bartender, he says with a much friendlier tone, "I'll try the Goose Island."

The bartender fulfills the request, and he drops my arm once he has his drink. He turns toward me, those eyes still burning down at me. "We need to talk."

"Not here."

"Then where?"

I contemplate what to tell him. I'd really like to just avoid him altogether, but he's not giving me that option.

"What do you want to talk about?" I ask.

"About why you got mad at me and ran off."

"Because, Madden," I practically spit at him. I lower my voice and lean in toward him so nobody overhears us. "Because you gave me the hottest kiss of my life and abruptly ended it like it was all some big mistake to you."

His jaw slackens. "Is that what you think?"

"It's what I know," I hiss. "Now if you'll excuse me." I move to walk away, but his words stop me.

"The car was there."

I turn around. "Huh?" I ask rather dumbly.

"The car was there, Kennedy. My phone buzzed to let me know, and maybe you've never taken an Uber, but if you don't get into the car, they drive away. I didn't end the kiss because of regret. The only regret I felt was that I had to end it."

It's my turn for a slackened jaw. "You…you don't regret it?"

He shakes his head as his eyes gleam at me. "Far from it. I was going to invite you back to my place, but you ran. Hatefully, might I add."

I clear my throat as I feel the heat creep into my cheeks. Oh, God. Now I'm mortified for a completely different reason.

Why does this man keep doing this to me?

I want him, but I still kind of hate him. And I'm supposed to be staying far away from him, not allowing myself to give in to his brand of temptation.

Yet, I find myself wanting another taste. I want to experience the feel of his heat as his body presses to mine. I want to feel his fingertips digging into my hip, his big hand sliding around my neck. Sliding into my panties. Sliding against my nipple.

Oh, God. He's staring at me. He just told me he was going to invite me back to his place that night.

I don't know what to say to him. I tip my glass to my lips to give myself something to do while I try to come up with something to say, and instead of drafting up a witty reply, my glass is empty and I need more wine.

I turn back to the bartender. "Another white wine," I say, and he nods. He fills a glass and passes it over to me, and I turn back toward Madden, who's smirking.

"Tell me that's for my benefit," he murmurs, and somehow that low voice of his seems to have this line directly to my vagina.

I hold up my glass without a word, and thankfully some man I don't recognize sidles up beside Madden.

"Madden Bradley, how the hell are ya?" the guy asks, and the two shake hands like they're old buddies.

I take the opportunity to slip away.

It's a bold reminder.

I can't do this with him. Not here, not tonight. Not at all.

I'm supposed to be networking, not letting the competition soak my panties with mere words.

Dammit.

I hate the hold this guy has on me. We hardly know each other, yet it feels like every moment we've spent together has brought us closer together. And every moment that's brought us closer has me seeing him in a different light.

I keep pushing this narrative that he's my enemy, but maybe he isn't.

Or maybe he is, and some hate sex would get him out of my head.

I'm still not totally sure I can trust him, but it's not exactly like he's proven I can't. What if I just…let go of whatever is holding me back and give this an actual chance?

Would that really be so bad?

Dinner hasn't been served yet. Cocktail hour is meant for networking, so I force my feet to move. I approach a woman I recognize as one of the hosts of tonight's event, and I start chatting her up about what a lovely event this is.

Eventually I lead the conversation to business only to find out she's already working with Bradley Group but is happy to keep VBC in mind.

Right.

And so the evening goes. Bradley Group is the clear dominator in this industry. I knew they were big, but I think my dad downplayed just how big. They've got their hand in nearly everything in this city and the surrounding metropolitan area, and it's actually quite surprising that Simon from SCS awarded us even a fraction of his project.

My mind is racing as to why that might be, and I remember my dad saying something about Thomas's connections.

For the briefest moment, I wonder if there's a way for me to access those connections for VBC's benefit. That's not really my style, though.

I'm talking to one of VBC's current clients about their experience with our company so far when I feel his gaze on me from across the room.

I glance up, and sure enough, he's having a conversation with someone, too, but his eyes are burning into me. Branding me.

From across the room.

I continue the conversation, my eyes not leaving Madden's, lingering there a little longer than they should. He glances away first, and I turn my attention back to the client.

It's not the only time that happens.

I don't get the chance to talk to him again before dinner, and I'm not sure whether to be grateful or disappointed in that fact. During dinner, he's at the table beside mine on the far side. We're facing each other, and his heated gaze meets and holds mine more times than I can count.

It feels like foreplay.

I'm so damn hot for him that I'm worried I'm leaving a wet spot on my dress. I knew I should've opted for black material.

After dinner, I excuse myself. I need a minute to collect myself. I need a minute away from his eyes. His scrutiny. Him.

But I can't escape him. I should've known better.

He's right behind me. "Walk to the far end of the hallway. There's a set of restrooms down there nobody's using."

I don't know why I listen to him, but I do.

I also don't know why he knows this information. Maybe because he's already been in there with someone else.

I wander down the hallway with other ballrooms, all the way to the furthest end away from our ballroom. These are vacant. Quiet. It's a Saturday night, and it's sort of surprising they're empty. Maybe since the gala is taking up several ballrooms on the other end, they couldn't rent these out tonight.

I spot the ladies' room, and I walk in. He's right. There's nobody down here. In fact, the lights seem to sense my presence as they flick on, and I glance around the room as my heart pounds so loudly I think Madden might be able to hear it.

These aren't usual bathrooms with just sinks and stalls. There's a small lounge in the front with a fancy, ornate couch on one end. Maybe it's for nursing mothers, or maybe for an elderly grandmother waiting for someone. Or maybe it's for something else entirely.

On the other end is a long counter with a mirror above it. This might be where a bride comes to fix her hair or where an entire bridal party gathers to do their makeup. Little stools are pushed in beneath the counter as if the room has been recently cleaned and is just waiting for the next party to come along.

It's there where I stand when I see the door open in the reflection of the mirror. I draw in a shuddering breath as Madden Bradley walks into the lounge. He flips the lock I hadn't even noticed, securing us into privacy. For what, I'm not sure yet. But I'm trembling as I wait to find out.

CHAPTER 20
KENNEDY VAN BUREN

Tell Me How Bad You Want It

I don't turn around, mostly because I can't seem to make myself move at all. I'm frozen in place as his eyes meet mine in the mirror. He stands by the door for a beat, and I wish I had a window into his thoughts as he stares at me.

He slowly saunters across the room toward me, and he stops within a few feet of me, his eyes never leaving mine. He's close enough to smell but not close enough to feel.

Yet.

He closes the distance as he reaches out, and his fingertips glide from my neck halfway down my spine to where the zipper of my dress begins.

I tremble under his touch, and then he moves in closer to me until I feel his heated front against my back. God, how badly I want to lean back into him, to close my eyes and let him snake his hand around to the front, to slide his hand into the slit of my dress and explore what's beneath it.

I can't seem to make myself move, though.

We still haven't spoken a word, but as he moves in closer to me, his eyes seem to take on a desperation I've not yet seen in them. He drops one of his hands to the counter, boxing me in here much like he did against a wall a week ago, and his other hand moves first to my hip before sliding down to the obscenely high slit of my dress. His fingers dip inside the fabric, the heat of his fingertips electric against my upper thigh.

"I haven't taken my eyes off this slit all night," he murmurs. "I've been watching it like a goddamn hawk, hoping for a glimpse of something forbidden."

Oh my God. His words set me on *fire*. Heat and fire move everywhere through me, starting from the place where his hand makes contact with my skin and detonating explosively from there.

He breaks our eye contact only to move into place to press a kiss behind my ear. I shiver at the feel of his lips on my skin. I'm torn between letting him do what he's doing and spinning around in his arms to press my mouth to his to finish what we started last week.

As he kisses my neck and I shiver, he slides his hand down by my slit up until he feels my hip. "I need to touch you," he murmurs, and I nod, desperate for his touch.

His fingertips trail along my hip bone down to the line of my panties, and he pulls at the fabric to slide his finger underneath.

I close my eyes and lean back into him, feeling myself melting at his touch. He moves his finger along the path where my panties fall into place, teasing me, and I can't help when my body seems to take over all by itself, pushing down to try to urge his fingers over to where I need them to be.

The ache between my legs is unreal. It's been unreal since the moment I met him, but it intensified last week with that kiss, and no amount of touching myself has come close to what he's about to do to me.

I want him to make me fall apart. Right here. Right now.

His fingers toy with the elastic against my skin before he slips one under the fabric. A soft moan falls from me, and he inches his finger over achingly slowly.

"Jesus," he rasps, drawing out the *e* sound as he feels the moisture dampening my panties. "Is this for me?"

"God, yes," I moan as he slides his finger along the outside of my slit.

"Eyes open," he demands, and my eyes fly open at his words. So he's hot, smart, athletic...and dominating during the sexy times?

What am I getting myself into here? I'm not quite sure, but suddenly I want to please him. I want to obey him. I want him to command me.

His eyes are on mine as he slides his finger along the lips of my pussy, and I gasp when he plunges that finger through my slit and directly inside me. He's not gentle as he shoves his finger into me, and holy hell, it unleashes a fucking fountain of need—and more lubrication straight from my own pussy as I drench his finger with my need.

He pushes in as far as he can, and I feel his finger curling inside me as he starts to reach places that have never been touched before. He pulls out and adds in a second finger, and his voice is sexy as all hell by my ear when he asks, "Has this cunt been waiting for me?"

"Mm yes," I moan, and I'm so tempted to close my eyes, so tempted to give in to the pleasure he's giving me. He pulls his fingers out and slides some of the moisture up over my clit before slipping back inside me, driving into me over and over, slow, long drives that make me wish it was his cock there instead.

I don't dare ask, though. I can't. I can barely breathe at this point. I'm heaving as I climb closer and closer to an orgasm, small gasps and needy moans the only sound in the room aside from the rhythmic sound of his fingers as they plunge into me with all of my body's extremely wet natural reaction to him.

It's like he knows what I want anyway. He slams his hips against my ass at the same time he drives his finger in. I feel his erection with each of his thrusts, and maybe I'm going crazy for him, but that tells me he's going crazy for me, too.

We do this to each other.

It's a frenzy of need and lust and anger and heat and the forbidden all coming to a head at once right here, right now.

"I'm going to bury my cock so deep in this cunt that you won't be able to sit tomorrow without remembering I was there," he says.

Oh, great. So he's all the things—athletic, smart, hot, whatever else was on that list—and he's a dirty talker, too?

How is this man still single?

It's probably a question better left for later, not that I'd be able to coherently form words to ask him that in this moment anyway. Some strange grunt comes out of me instead.

"Do it," I manage to moan.

"Tell me how bad you want it."

"God, I want it. I want your cock. I want you to fuck me right here, Madden. Right now." It's a whiny plea.

He's still fingering me when he asks, "Are you on birth control?"

I haven't had a reason to be, and I shake my head.

"Fuck," he mutters, and my heart drops since we won't be able to have sex. But then he pulls a condom out of his back pocket. "Was hoping I wouldn't have to use this with you so I could wreck that sweet pussy with my hot cum."

He tears it open with his teeth, and it's a move that's so sexy I feel like I'm about to come.

"Oh God!" I scream, and my eyes start to flutter as the climax amps up to crash into me. "I'm about to come!"

He pulls his fingers out of me immediately, and he unbuckles his belt and reaches into his slacks to pull his cock out. He's behind me in the mirror, and I shift over to get a glimpse of his cock as he starts to roll on the condom, and…

Holy shit.

"Oh my God, Madden," I moan. He's huge. Thick, long, full of these sexy veins that I actually want to taste when I've never had that urge with a man before…and admittedly a little intimidating.

His eyes meet mine again in the mirror. "You're wet as fuck, babe. Don't worry. It'll fit."

It'll fit. It'll fit? Will it, though?

"Bend over," he commands, and I do it as he reaches under my dress. He slips my panties down my legs, and I step out of them. He gathers the bottom of my dress and lifts it up, and he runs his hand along my ass before he gives it a little slap. It's a loud crack in this silent room, and I startle a little at the feel. But then he smooths his hand over my skin, and it's like he's soothing what he just did.

Why the hell is that so hot?

It's demeaning, right?

It doesn't feel like it is right now, though. It feels like he knows how to deliver pleasure and line it with just the hottest edge of pain.

I never craved pain before, but right now, I want that cock to fucking spear me and drive into me until I can't see straight.

He's right that I won't be able to move tomorrow without remembering this moment, but I'm pretty sure I'm going to remember this moment for the rest of my life anyway.

And then he bends down so he's eye level with my pussy and my ass, and he leans forward and licks my clit.

He fucking *licks* my clit.

I'm about to fall apart. I'm barely holding on here, my fingernails clawing at the countertop like that's going to give me any sort of relief.

"Fuck," he hums against my hot, wet, needy skin. He leans forward and sucks on my clit, and my legs tremble as he does it. He lets go only to dip his tongue into my pussy, and I'm seconds from coming when he straightens to a stand. He bends down over me so his body heats mine, and he says, "Your pussy is fucking perfect."

He pulls back to grip his cock, and he fists it, running his hand along it a few times before he aligns with my body. He slides his cock through my folds before he pushes into me with just the tip, and my eyes practically roll to the back of my head at the feel of him.

"God, yes, Madden!" I yell, and I shift my hips back to take in more of him.

He inches his way in slowly, pulling back to tease me or to give me a little space before he pushes in just a little more. It's some mix of pure heaven and absolute torture. I need him all the way in, so I push my hips back again at the same time he thrusts forward.

"Yes, baby, take it all like a good girl," he murmurs.

He's slow at first, giving my body time to adjust to his size, but then he starts to pick up the pace.

He collars the back of my neck, driving my head down as he grips my hip in his other hand. "Eyes open," he demands again, and they fly open to watch him.

He's clenching his jaw as his half-lidded eyes meet mine. His are full of this demanding intensity, raw and real as he moves deliberately into me over and over again, driving my body to heights I certainly wasn't expecting it to be taken to when I agreed to attend this gala tonight.

Mine are full of need. The need to come. The need for him. The need for more.

His body slaps against mine, the only sound in the room aside from our breathless panting mixed with the grunts and moans of what can only be described as the hottest sex of my life. He lets go of his grip on my neck, and he reaches around me and right into the top of my dress. He finds one of my breasts, and he massages it and grips onto my nipple. His touch sends a shockwave through my core.

His jaw is locked as his lip curls up a little, and those heavy eyes are hot on me when he says, "Tell me how much you love it when I'm fucking you."

He's so goddamn hot in this moment that I can't even handle it. From his messy hair to the sexy stubble on his jaw to the way he looks in a tux…holy hell. And somehow *I* am the object of his interest. I'm not sure how I got so lucky, but now that we're here, I know there's no going back. Not when we're this good together.

I moan before I manage to say, "I never want you to stop."

"That's right. This cunt is mine now."

"Yes. Yes!" I cry. "It's yours." I don't even know what the hell I'm agreeing to in the moment before something snaps inside of me. I tumble headfirst into the most intense orgasm of my life made all the more powerful by the way our eyes are locked as I come. I reach back to claw at something, anything, and I grip onto his thigh, which only pulls him more tightly against me as my nails dig into his pants. Pulse after pulse of sweet relief crashes over me, my body throbbing everywhere for this man and what he's doing to me.

"Fuck, that's so tight," he mutters, or at least I think that's what he says, but I'm not entirely sure since I'm lost to my own orgasm at the moment. A roar of a growl escapes him, and I feel him swell inside of me as he pushes in as deeply as he can. He pants out a series of grunts as he reaches his climax, too.

I watch his face as it happens. His eyes are still on me, his lids almost closed, and his jaw is clenched tight as he grips my breast harder and his fingers dig into my hips. He rides it out, and I watch in awe as the fog of bliss envelops me.

He folds down on top of me for a few beats once he's finished, and it feels like a warm, sweet hug after what we just did.

Eventually he slips out of me and lifts up off me, and he drops my dress, smoothing it down over my ass before he excuses himself to one of the bathroom stalls.

I take a minute to step back into my panties, and I stare at myself in the mirror for a beat.

My hair is a little mussed, but not bad. My makeup is still perfect. I look about the same as I did when I walked into this bathroom.

But I'm leaving it a totally different person.

Not only have I added plus one to my body count—which was embarrassingly low at just two other guys—but it was with the very forbidden, very sexy, very untouchable Madden Bradley.

I blow out a breath.

Holy shit. Holy shit!

I can't believe I just got railed by Madden Bradley in the bathroom.

God, that was hot.

I want it to happen again. Anywhere. Bathroom, bedroom, out in the gardens at this banquet hall.

Tonight, tomorrow, the next day.

Over and over again.

But as he steps out of his stall and washes his hands, neatly tucked back into his pants once again, I can't help but worry that this is a one-time event. We gave into the pull that was between us, and that might be that on that.

I hope not, though. Because one taste of Madden Bradley simply isn't enough. I'm already addicted.

CHAPTER 21
MADDEN BRADLEY

The Most Delicious Thing I Ate Tonight

Fuck. I couldn't help myself, and I shouldn't be surprised that it was that good.

The chemistry between us has been on point since day one, and tonight was inevitable. Part of me thought I could fuck her out of my system, but as it turns out, quite the opposite happened.

I need more. Tonight.

"Come back to my place with me after the gala," I say once I'm done washing my hands, and I join her in the lounge again. It's not a question.

"I don't—" She begins her protest, but I hold up a hand.

I don't have an overnight bag. I don't have clothes for morning. I don't even like you. Whatever she was about to say is simply an excuse, and as we all know, excuses are like assholes. We've all got one.

"Don't make excuses," I say.

She presses her lips together, and she lets out a deep breath before her eyes meet mine again. "Okay. Just…" She trails off, and it's as if she thinks twice about what she was going to say.

"Just?" I prompt.

She clears her throat. "Don't hurt me."

I take a step toward her, and another, and then I reach out and close the gap between us so I'm holding her in my arms, and nothing has ever felt quite so right. "I can't make that promise. Physically, I won't. Unless you ask me to." I flash her a smirk, to which she rolls her eyes.

I lean forward and press my lips to hers, and the kiss quickly intensifies as she opens her mouth to mine and shoves her fingers into my hair.

Strange how this is only the second time we've kissed. We just had sex with no kissing, and it might've been the most intense sex of my life. I've also never fucked someone who hated me until I was inside her, so there's that.

I don't think she hates me anymore. I'm not sure she ever really did, but certainly not after the last few minutes.

But we still have that little issue of working together coupled with the fact that our fathers are actual enemies for reasons we really still don't understand.

Maybe we never will. But maybe we can be the examples here. There's no reason we can't explore this very tangible thing between us in secret and deal with the rest when we need to.

She pulls back first this time—mostly because there's no way in hell I was going to stop the kiss first this time. Not when she ran last time.

"We should get back out there," she says. "I need a minute or two in here if you want to go first."

It's her gentle hint to get rid of me so she can use the bathroom, and I take it. "Are you okay?"

She nods, and her eyes twinkle at me. "I mean, aside from the shaky knees from what you did to me, yeah."

I chuckle. God, she's pretty. I flash her one more smirk before I turn to head out of the bathroom, but her words stop me.

"Oh, one more thing," she says. I turn back around, and she's the one smirking at me this time. "Your breath smells like my pussy, so you may want to hunt down a stick of gum."

I can't help but bark out a laugh at that. I shake my head as I raise a brow. "Oh, hell no. I'm not getting rid of the aftertaste of the most delicious thing I ate tonight."

Her cheeks flush, and I flip the lock on the door.

I turn back toward her. "See you out there."

I head out, and the hallway is clear. I've been to this place lots of times for various events, and I knew these restrooms would be vacant since usually they're used during weddings for the bridal party. It wasn't the sexiest place to hook up with a girl, but when you're desperate, well, you take what you can get.

I spot Ford just outside the ballroom as I approach, and I stop to talk to him. His brow raises at me as I approach. "Where have you been?" he asks.

Ford is the traditionalist of the Bradley boys, and I don't think he'd understand me betraying the family name with a competitor.

That's how they'll see it. Everyone in my family will see Kennedy Van Buren as the competition. I just see her as a beautiful, intelligent woman who both challenges and captivates me, and those are two traits I haven't found in a woman in a long time. Maybe ever.

There's a connection I can't deny, and I need some time to explore it before I say a single goddamn word to anybody about it—Ford included. I don't really talk to my brothers about my conquests, anyway. Maybe Dex, since he's the closest to me in age and we've discussed this sort of thing in the past, but he's busy living his life in Vegas right now.

"Around," I say, dodging the question. "You?"

"I'm ready to call it. You want to share a car?" he asks.

I shake my head. "Can't. Dad expects me to stay until the bitter end. Or at least until I can close another deal or two."

"What's it like having all that pressure to carry on the legacy?" he asks.

"Exhausting," I admit.

He chuckles. "I can imagine. Dad's never been easy on any of us, least of all you."

"I'm pretty sure he's doing whatever he can to make sure I have the life he wanted for himself," I say dryly, but I also think it's true. After finding out he played football and couldn't continue because of an injury, he did whatever he could to give us opportunities, and now handing over the family business without regard to whether or not I actually want it—it sort of feels like what I just said to Ford is actually true.

"What do *you* want, bro?" he asks.

I twist my lips and bite the inside of my cheek as Kennedy's face flashes through my mind. Then her ass. Then that sweet pussy.

Fuck.

I'm in a boatload of trouble.

I blow out a breath. "Another beer," I finally say.

He nods. "Enjoy. I'm out."

"Did you tell Mom and Dad you're leaving?"

He shakes his head. "Nope. Bye."

"Traitor," I mutter toward his retreating figure, and he just laughs as he walks out the front door.

I spot Kennedy walking into the ballroom, and she's poised and even more beautiful than before with a glow in her cheeks, her head held high with confidence and conviction.

"You ought to stop looking at her like that," a voice behind me says, and I spin around to face my father. "If I didn't know better, I'd think you had a thing for the Van Buren girl."

"Don't be ridiculous," I say.

"I hope that's all it is. Because trust me when I tell you that she's the wrong person to get mixed up with." He raises his brows pointedly, and I'm not sure exactly what he means. I want to believe it's because we have to work side-by-side with them on the SCS project, but it feels like maybe it goes deeper than that. Maybe it goes deeper than either of us realized.

I lean in closer to him and lower my voice. "You're the one who wanted me to win her over, remember?" I say it to throw him off, not because I'm intending to actually betray her.

I would never.

I meant it when I told her she could trust me, and I won't go back on that promise. Not for business, and sure as fuck not for my father.

I turn and head back into the ballroom, and now it's more fighting against looking for her in every corner of the room paired with long, lingering gazes once I do.

The night feels interminable, but she's still here when I'm ready to call it a night. I send a covert text to her with my address.

Me: *Heading home. Will be waiting with more white wine.*

Her reply doesn't come right away, but I don't expect it to since she's busy networking.

I've only been home about ten minutes and haven't even changed out of my tux yet when my phone rings with a call from my building's concierge. "Kennedy Van Buren here to see you," the doorman, Joseph, says.

It's only then I realize that if we're sneaking around with the intent to keep this a secret, having her show up at my place isn't exactly doing that. Joseph is bound with nondisclosure agreements, but anyone could see her coming or going.

"You can send her up." I glance around to make sure my place isn't messy, a rather ridiculous thought. I'm nothing if not a neat freak, and I have the place cleaned once a week. I'm hardly here anyway, and when I am, I'm careful to keep things clean.

I start my day by making my bed even when I'm in a hotel, if that says anything about me.

Still, this is her first time seeing my home. I wonder what she'll think about it. What she'll think about *me*. What secrets my home will unveil about me.

What secrets I'll unveil about her tonight.

The urge to know everything about her is strong, and maybe tonight's the night where we can explore those kinds of things, where we can get to know one another.

But I have this feeling like maybe I won't know her personally any better, but I'll know her body a hell of a lot better. What makes her moan. What makes her smile. What makes her come.

I shrug out of my tux jacket and hang it in my front closet, and I loosen my tie. I grab a bottle of white wine from the wine cooler along with a glass, and I fill it up for her. I grab myself a beer, too, and I hear a tentative knock on my door a minute later.

I pad over to the door and open it, and she looks nervous and gorgeous standing there. I hand her the glass of wine, and she leans in and presses a quick kiss to my lips as if she's greeting her boyfriend. It's both sweet and sexy at the same time.

"Welcome to my place," I say, and I hold out my arm as she walks in. I close the door behind her, and she walks in with a bit of awe in her eyes.

It *is* a pretty killer place. It's mostly monochromatic with white walls and countertops, light hardwood floors, and a few black and gray accents and pieces of furniture. It's the view that's so amazing here, and she wanders straight for the wraparound windows to check it out.

Her eyes settle down on Navy Pier, and she sighs. "I don't know why, but I've always found the pier really romantic." She takes a sip of her wine and offers a quiet *mmm*.

I open the glass door so she can walk out onto the balcony, and her breath seems to catch. She looks a little fearfully between the open door and me.

"What's wrong?" I ask.

"Oh, nothing. I just don't *love* heights. And dogs. Dogs and heights."

"Well, good news, tiger. I don't have a dog." I give her a light chuckle, and she looks like a deer in headlights.

"We don't have to go out on the balcony, but if you want to check it out, I promise it's safe," I say.

"Yeah, and everyone promises their dogs are friendly when their unleashed beasts come running up toward me." She lifts a shoulder, and it's strange seeing her vulnerable. I thought I was the only one who was going to show another side tonight. Guess I was wrong.

I step out first and hold out a hand to assist her if she wants it. "You can stay inside, or you can come stand right up against the building. But I swear, the view out here is worth it."

"I want to try," she says. "I'm not *terrified* of them or anything. I just don't love them." She slips her hand into mine, and it's ice cold and trembling a little. She steps out onto the balcony.

"Good girl," I say absently, and her eyes fly to mine with a little heat in them.

She stands just on the balcony side of the door, her back against the glass of my windows.

We each sip our drinks, a little lost in thought for a minute or two as we stare at the pier.

"Is this okay?" I ask.

She nods. "Yeah. It's not so scary up here, and you're right. The view is worth it. But can I ask you a question?"

I brace myself for it because I just never know what to expect from her, and I tilt my head to tell her to go ahead.

"Why'd you invite me over here?"

I glance over at her, and she's looking at the pier, not me. The lights of the Ferris wheel sparkle in the distance, lighting her eyes as I think through how to respond to that question.

"I wasn't ready to say goodbye," I admit quietly.

I hear the vulnerability in my own voice. I'm not used to this shit. I don't invite women back to my place after fucking them in the bathroom. It's not my style. I got what I wanted, so I should be done. Hands washed. Game over.

I don't know what makes her different. She wasn't just some girl I fucked in a bathroom. She's a business associate, a competitor, and she's captivated me in a way no other woman ever has.

Do I want to get inside her pussy again? Of course I do. I'm only human.

But if that doesn't happen, if we stand out here where she's close enough that I can smell her coconut as she sips her wine, that's fine by me.

And *that* is the crux of what makes her different. I just haven't put my finger on why that is.

CHAPTER 22
KENNEDY VAN BUREN

This Place is Sexy

It's strange being here, standing beside this person I'm not supposed to like, feeling like there's something more than a healthy work rivalry between us as he's sweet enough to hold my hand to help me out onto his balcony.

I quiet the fear with my usual grounding technique—the 5-4-3-2-1. It's second nature to find each thing and takes under five seconds in my mind now. Five things I can *see* are the pier, the table on the balcony, my wineglass in my hand, the balcony wall built to keep us safe even though it's more glass, and, of course, Madden. Four things I can *touch* are my wineglass, the fabric of my dress, the doorway, and, of course, Madden. It's quiet, but I can *hear* the sound of an airplane in the distance, my own heart racing, and Madden's voice. I can *smell* my wine and Madden, and one thing I can *taste*? Madden, naturally. Which is why I have the sudden urge to kiss him.

Like kissing him will be the elixir I need to be safe out here.

He's been a little quiet since I arrived, and I'm surprised. I thought being at home would put him more in his element, something I was interested to see. But to tell me he wasn't ready to say goodbye…I'm not sure what he means by that, and I'm positive I'm too scared to ask.

I chug down my glass of wine, which is likely not my brightest move since I showed up riding on the wrong side of sober as it was.

I set my glass on the little table he has between two chairs perched out here, and I walk over toward him, surprising us both, I think. Shocking myself, to be honest.

I set my hands on his chest, and I move my body up against his. If I hadn't had that wine, I'm certain I never would've gotten up the nerve to do this—both because we're out on a balcony seventy-five stories up in the air and because I'm seducing Madden Bradley. "Well, I'm here now. What are you going to do about it?"

He stares down at me, his nostrils flaring as he starts to breathe a little heavier at my proximity. What *is* he going to do?

I'm dying to know. I move my face so my lips are mere inches from his. He only needs to bend down to close the gap, and I'm suddenly blind with lust for him.

He's still holding his beer, which he moves to set on the table beside us, and then he moves back into place, resting each of his hands over mine where they lay on his chest. He slides one of his hands around my neck, and he leans down at the same time. His nose brushes beside mine the way he did that first night we kissed outside the bar.

It's sexy. It's nearly a tentative move from this disciplined, confident man. It's unexpected, and it gives me a second to breathe. I suppose it gives me a second to run, too, but running isn't on tonight's agenda.

Unless he gives me a reason to.

"I didn't take my time with you at the gala. It was rushed. I had to get it out of my system. Get *you* out of my system," he murmurs, pulling back just slightly, though still too close for these confessions. He brushes my lips with his, and I close my eyes and lean into him. "It didn't work. One time just made me want more." He brushes my lips again, and his hand that's still covering mine on his chest moves down toward my waist. He wraps that arm around me and hauls me into him, and then he kisses me.

He *really* kisses me.

His mouth opens to mine, and our tongues dance as his hold on me tightens. He flattens the hand he has on my back and starts to move it, exploring my curves as his mouth holds me captive. He reaches down to squeeze my ass, which only has the effect of pulling my body closer to his.

I move my hands from his chest and around to his back. His body is firm and solid everywhere, and I hope this time I'm lucky enough to see his naked form as he hovers over me.

The thought sends a searing pulse of need straight through me, and as much as I want him to take me right out here on this balcony, I'm too scared for that to happen tonight. I'm not closing the door on the possibility of it forever, though.

I reach down and squeeze his ass, too, and holy *hell* is it firm. This man is just firm *everywhere*, and I've never been with someone so fit. He's a professional athlete, so I get it, but hot damn. I'm not sure I can keep up with this.

He stops the kiss first, and he pulls back, not moving his arm from around me. His eyes focus on mine for a beat before he moves away, and it's almost as if he's double-checking that he's not offending me. "I don't want you to be uncomfortable out here, so let's go inside," he suggests.

I melt. It's hot and heavy out here, and yet he *stopped* it because he was worried I might be nervous out on this balcony.

I am. But in his arms, I feel safe.

And that's a wholly unexpected feeling.

I nod, and I bolt inside first. He chuckles as he grabs my wineglass and his beer bottle, and he follows me inside. He fills my wineglass without me asking, and he tosses his beer bottle into a bin in his pantry and grabs himself another.

I take this moment to explore a bit. His layout is interesting, with a huge family room on one side, the balcony doors in the middle, and a living room space on the other side that appears to have been converted into an office-slash-game room. It has a poker table in the middle and a desk along one of the windows looking out over the view. The entire place is encased in glass, an acrophobic's worst nightmare, but somehow being here with Madden makes it seem not as terrifying.

And really, the view is lovely. I bet it's even prettier in the daytime when he can actually see out over Lake Michigan. He can sit on his balcony and watch the boats in the summer, or keep an eye on the Ferris wheel, or watch the traffic with all its mesmerizing red taillights.

It's neat, I notice only now. The family room side has a couch with several comfortable-looking chairs around a coffee table, all pointed at a television mounted on the wall with a fireplace beneath it. The couch is white, and the accent pillows and throw blankets are gray and black. The coffee table is black with some small silver decorations sitting on top of it.

There isn't a cup out of place or a magazine to make it look lived in. Instead, it looks like some sort of model home.

He returns and presses the wineglass back into my hand, now filled, and I hold it up and tap it to his beer bottle before I take a sip.

"Do you actually live here? Or is this some staged model you bring all the girls to?" I ask.

He chuckles. "Come here," he says, and I follow him through the kitchen and into one of the bedrooms. "This is where I work out." I glance at the equipment, and it looks standard enough, but it's the stuff hanging on the wall that tells me this does, in fact, belong to Madden.

Framed photos of John Madden are on one wall, mostly of his college playing years, along with what must be a very rare signed jersey. There's also a huge framed blow-up of a video game cover with what looks like a screenshot from the game and a guy that looks like a video game version of Madden in his Bears jersey with Bradley 80 on the back.

"Okay, this is more what I was expecting. But, like...do you use this room? Because it smells good in here, and there's not even a towel out of place."

"Yes, I use it," he protests. "Daily. Usually multiple times a day. And I confess, I'm a self-diagnosed neat freak."

I laugh. "I wouldn't have expected that from you."

"I'm full of surprises," he says with a wink.

"Show me the rest of your place."

He glances at my wine.

I hold up a hand as I giggle. "I promise I won't spill."

He seems to really think it over before he nods, and I probably shouldn't make promises I'm not totally sure I can keep since I'm not exactly the most graceful person to ever exist, but I take a long, healthy sip so there's less to spill should that happen.

He takes me through the two guest bedrooms that look mostly unused, and then he shows me the primary bedroom.

It's simply breathtaking. It's in the corner of the penthouse with wraparound windows. One side looks out over the lake, and the other shows some of the city. A gray couch sits along the windows across from the bed, and the bed itself looks plush and inviting with about a thousand pillows and the softest-looking gray blanket I've ever seen draped across the foot of the white comforter.

My brain immediately goes to sex. Sex on that couch. Sex on the little ottoman that's used as a decoration beside the couch. Sex on the bed. Sex up against the windows because if he's inside me, I don't think I'll be worried about the heights thing.

He shows me his bathroom, and yep. Sex in that tub for sure. And in the glass-encased shower with multiple shower heads and a bench.

Yeah...this place is sexy.

Madden Bradley is sexy.

"Wow, Madden. This place is amazing."

"Thank you," he says, and he ducks his head a little as if he's nearly embarrassed at my compliment. He must know how great this is since he lives here.

And I live with my parents.

Suddenly it feels *mortifying* to admit that.

Clem and I were saving for something better, but it just didn't work out. I'm sure he would understand, and I'm sure he wouldn't care. But I do. It's another reminder that I failed.

We head back to the kitchen, where he pulls out a chair at the round table and offers it to me to sit.

"You're quiet," he muses.

"So are you," I counter.

He lifts a shoulder. "I'm not used to giving gorgeous women a tour of my place."

"You don't invite women back here all the time?" I tease, though I suppose my tone is a mix of surprised and skeptical.

He shrugs. "Once in a while."

My synapses seem to fire with anger as I put the pieces together. "And you invited me here because you're trying to prove I can trust you. But why, Madden? What do you want from me?"

I'm expecting his answer to be business. He wants the trade secrets from his father's biggest rival—as if I have any to offer.

His next words, however, completely blow that thought out of my mind.

"What do I want from you?" he asks quietly. He finally glances up from his beer bottle at me. "That's a complicated question, Kennedy." He glances out the window, and when his eyes return to mine, they're full of fire. "But the more time I spend with you, the more I want everything."

CHAPTER 23
MADDEN BRADLEY

Show Me the Goods

She looks shocked by my words, and frankly, I'm shocked I said them.

This is horrible timing.

I'm leaving for San Diego for what very well could be my last season playing. We're business rivals. Her father hates my family, and I think the feeling might be mutual.

It's the worst-case scenario.

And yet…

I find myself diving in headfirst anyway.

Why did I invite her here tonight? Exactly why I said. I wasn't done with her.

And the more time I spend with her, the more I fear I will *never* be done with her.

But how the fuck am I supposed to run Bradley Group after this season, or next, or the one after that…when she's in line to run one of our biggest competitors?

"When you say *everything*, can I ask what that means?" she finally asks, her voice hoarse and soft.

I press my lips together, and then I drain my beer. I stand and carry the bottle to the sink, where I rinse it out. I toss it in my recycle bin, and then I move over toward the window. The whole time, I'm trying to figure out how to answer that.

"I don't know." That's where I land, and I rake my fingers through my hair at the confusion, tugging on the ends a little. It's strange feeling so fucking out of control, but that's what she seems to do to me. "I don't know what I want. I don't know what my future holds. It feels like everything is spinning away from me. My career, my choices, my future. But then I see you, and it's like this fucking lighthouse in the goddamn storm, Kennedy. I don't know how, and I don't know why, but I know I need more of it."

I choke out the last few words over the emotion suddenly clogging my throat, and it feels both terrifying and liberating to make this confession. She's seeing two very different sides of me this evening, sides that don't emerge very often. The vulnerable, emotional side making these confessions and the dominating side of me earlier who gave her demands that she bended to. Jesus, that was hot.

I have no idea how she'll react. Maybe she'll take those words and throw them back at me later. Maybe she'll use me to her advantage when it comes to business.

But if she does, the few moments of bliss, even if she's pretending, would be worth it.

I can't figure out *why* I feel this way. I never have before. I still hardly know the woman, yet the way she fits here makes it seem like she's always been a part of it. I'm not sure if I'm talking about my heart or my home. Maybe both.

All I know is that this is different. I feel something where I've always felt a void. And to me…that's worth exploring.

She stands slowly from her chair. She pushes the chair in, and she turns to face me. She's moving tentatively. Slowly. As if she moves too quickly, she might spook me.

Too goddamn late. I'm fucking spooked.

I don't know what the hell I'm doing as I stand stock-still and wait to see how she's going to react to my words.

She steps toward me, and she rests one of her hands on my cheek. I lean into her comforting touch, closing my eyes as I feel her warmth all around me.

She moves her hand and wraps her arms around my waist, and she rests her head on my chest as she hugs me.

I can't remember the last time someone hugged me like this. Maybe never. Sure, I hug teammates in celebration after a great play or family when we greet each other, but those are different.

This one is full of comfort and care, gentle warmth, and strong coconuts.

I slip my arms around her and hold tightly to her. I don't let my vulnerable side out. Ever. I'm strong and solid. I'm the oldest Bradley brother, a natural-born leader because of my birth order. I'm untouchable.

But Kennedy Van Buren has managed to touch me in unprecedented and totally unexpected ways. She can take me down with just one lift of her brow, one steely look, one tip of her lips into a smile, one soft swipe through her drenched cunt.

And it's only just the beginning.

I blow out a shuddering breath as it feels like my world centers again with her in my arms, and that's when I know I'm fucked. I'm in a boatload of trouble when it comes to her.

She pulls back out of my arms to tilt her chin up, and she lifts to her tiptoes to press a soft kiss to my lips. I grab onto the back of her head, holding her there in place as I let go of the fears of falling. I give in to it. I can't fight something this strong, and I won't. We'll figure out the rest later.

I open my mouth to hers, and this kiss is intense. It's fast and messy, teeth clashing and tongues battling. She softens a little, her body melting into me, and a quiet moan that's my total undoing escapes her.

I'm still kissing her as I start guiding her backward toward my bedroom. I want her in my bed. I want her tangled in my sheets. I want to go to sleep tomorrow night smelling coconuts and sex and thinking of her.

It's slow progress this way, so I rip my mouth from hers and sweep her up into my arms. She doesn't protest, doesn't yell or scream to put her down. Instead, she links her arms around my neck and leans forward to kiss me there, and Jesus Christ, why is her mouth on my neck so goddamn hot? My dick hardens painfully as if it's not already semi-hard every second I spend around her.

We get to my room, and I carry her to the bed, where I toss her and immediately climb over her. I settle in between her legs, and thank God for that gorgeous slit in her dress because she widens her legs and wraps them around my body, feet still shoved in the heels that've managed to drive me insane with lust all night.

Fuck, she's something else.

I pump my pelvis against hers so she can feel how fucking hard she makes me, and my mouth moves back to hers. She wraps her arms around me, too, so I'm cocooned in her warmth, and I never want to leave. I could kiss this woman forever, and that's certainly another new experience for me. Usually kissing is nothing more than some vehicle to drive us to the good part, but with her, all the parts are the good parts.

Still, I need more. I need all of her, and I want to take my time in a way we didn't get to a few hours ago at the gala.

I pull back from the kiss, and she unlocks her legs from around me as I move down the bed. I reach under that dangerous slit and slide her panties down her legs, and I flip her over and unzip her dress. She slips the straps down each of her delicate shoulders, and I slowly ease the dress down her body until she's lying on my bed naked but for those heels.

I climb off the bed and gaze at the picture of perfection on my bed for a beat. Jesus. She's gorgeous.

I grab a condom from the nightstand drawer where I keep them, and I pull off my tie first. I toss it next to the condom on the bed, and then I unbutton my shirt, starting with the cufflinks. She watches with rapt attention as I slip the shirt off and set it on the ottoman next to the couch. I pull off my undershirt and set it on top, and I glance over at her. Her eyes are on my abs, and the way she's looking at me like she wants to lick my entire body makes me grateful for the hours of hard work and discipline I put in to shape this body. Her appreciation feels like a validation I didn't know I craved.

Well, there's more to appreciate.

I slip out of my shoes then unbuckle my belt and drop my pants. I step out of them and peel off my socks, and she's watching my every move like a hawk. Or a tiger. *My* tiger.

My cock swells as I study the look of need in her eyes, and my eyes travel hotly down her body from her perfect tits to her stomach to the curve of her hips and finally down to her pussy. I lick my lips as my mouth starts to water. I only had a taste before. I need a meal now.

I kneel between her legs as I get ready to dive in mouth first to her pussy, and she lets out a huff of protest.

"You're going to stop there?" she demands.

"Huh?" I grunt, not sure what she's talking about.

She runs the pointed front of her shoe along the waistband of my boxer briefs.

"Show me the goods." She licks her lips, too, and I get the hint.

I stand again and finger the waistband of my underwear, and then my eyes connect with hers. "Crawl over here and take them off if you want them off."

My voice is back to being disciplined and firm, and I feel like I get a little of my sensibilities back with the demand.

She raises a brow, but then she does it.

And fuck, is it hotter than hell to see a woman crawling across my bed on her hands and knees wearing those devilish heels. She moves slowly, deliberately, and I don't think she has any idea how sexy she is.

I lick my lips as my heart rate skyrockets, and when she gets close enough, she folds her knees under her and sits back on them as she sets her hands on my hips. She slips a finger between the elastic band there and my skin, and my breathing quickens as I watch her. Her eyes are focused on the bulge beneath my boxers, and all I can do is appreciate the angle I have. Her tits are sweet, perky handfuls that look heavy with need, and since she's sitting on her knees and they're slightly parted, I'd have a direct view of that sweet cunt if I bent down.

I draw in a harsh breath as she plays with the band, and then she starts to lower it. My cock springs free, long and hard and *needy*, and she grips me in her hand. She makes a fist and slides it along my length a few times, and I'm so desperate for her that precum starts to leak out of me. Before I can stop her so I can eat her pussy first, she leans forward and takes me into her mouth.

I grunt out some loud noise at the feel of her perfect mouth as it wraps around me. She takes me as far back as she can before she pulls back, and she drops me from her mouth to run her tongue along my length before she takes me deep into her mouth again.

I set my hands on the back of her head as she starts to move in a rhythm, and she adds her hands into the mix, fisting me at the base of my cock and following the path of her mouth while she takes my balls into her other palm, gently fondling them as she sucks me off.

I don't want her to stop what she's doing, but I need to taste her, too. What I really want is for her to sit on my face, but we have time.

I think.

Maybe not.

Maybe this is it. Maybe she'll realize she shouldn't be doing this with me when she wakes up in the morning.

I'm not sure where the thought comes from, but I'm suddenly worried she'll leave.

It's a deep-rooted fear that pulses into my mind unbidden, and maybe it's something I need to explore later.

Wherever it came from, it's telling me that I need to take what I can while I have her here.

"Fuck, baby. Your mouth feels so good," I say, and my words seem to encourage her to keep doing what she's doing.

She moans over me, the hum sending vibrations through my cock that are out of this world.

"Lay on your back," I finally grit out, and she slowly moves my cock out of her mouth, sucking hard and giving me a loud pop when she finally lets go.

I climb over her and set my knees on either side of her shoulders, and then I slowly trail down her body, stopping to suck a nipple into my mouth on the way. I align my cock over her mouth again, and she grabs onto it and gives me a few long strokes before taking me into her mouth.

I push her knees apart and lean down. I swipe my tongue from her clit nearly down to her ass, and her hips jerk wildly as she moans loudly. I do it again, and fuck, she tastes good. She's as wet as she was back at the gala, as if I didn't just give her an orgasm a couple hours ago, and that only tells me that she's already as addicted as I am.

I push my tongue inside her, and she pushes her hips toward my mouth. I do the same to her, grinding my hips down so she can take me even further back than before.

It's a lot to coordinate, but I'm nothing if not skilled when it comes to moving my body. I fuck her mouth while I tongue her cunt, and it's fucking glorious.

Between the way she tastes and the way she's handling my cock, I'm not going to last long. It's too many pleasurable sensations plowing into me all at once.

I shift my hips out of the way and out of her mouth because hell if I'm going to come in her mouth and miss out on getting inside her pussy again.

She lets out a grunt of protest, and I hum against her pussy. "If you keep doing that, I'm not going to get to fuck this cunt for a while. And I really, really want to fuck this cunt right now."

"God, you have a dirty mouth," she moans as I use said mouth to continue pleasuring her. I suck her clit into my mouth, and her hips jerk again. She reaches up and slaps my ass, and I can honestly say I've never had a woman slap my ass. Something about it is…fuck. I don't even know. Hot as hell. She really is a fucking tiger.

"You love my dirty mouth," I say after I let go of her clit, my breath hot against her hot pussy.

"I love it when you're sucking on my clit," she clarifies, sassy as ever even when I'm eating her out.

I laugh against her pussy, but I take her clit in between my lips again anyway. Maybe I was demanding and dominating back in that bathroom, but I want her to see that she can be in charge, too.

"Do you want me to make you come with my mouth or my cock?" I ask.

"Pretty confident you're going to be able to do it at all," she remarks, and I laugh.

"I can assure you, it's going to happen. You tell me how."

"Fuck me, Madden," she demands.

Her wish is my command. I climb back down, grab the condom, and roll it on all in the space of about five seconds, and then I slide back into position over the top of her. I fucked her from behind the first time, and this time I want to sink into her as she writhes beneath me.

Her eyes are hot on mine as I slide my cock through her slit. I pump myself against her clit a few times, and her eyes close as she gives in to the pleasure. I stop what I'm doing, and her eyes open with a bit of curiosity in them as she waits patiently. Once they're open and on mine, I push into her.

I don't make my way in as slowly this time. We've already done this once, so I know she can take it.

"Oh, God," she cries as I push all the way in. Her pussy grips greedily onto me, as if she's giving the truth about how much she wants me even if Kennedy hasn't voiced that yet.

"Your pussy was made for this cock," I grunt, and she cries out in agreement as she wraps her legs around me, locking them at her feet. Her fingers trace tenderly up my back.

I start to drive into her, but I keep the pace slow as I lean up on my arm over her to study her as I thrust leisurely but forcefully. She meets my thrusts as she tilts her hips for me, her eyes on mine but her brows moving with my thrusts as if she can hardly take it each time I give it to her as deeply as our bodies will allow me to go.

This connection with her is un-fucking-real. I'm pushing her body to heights I'm not sure she's ever been, and in doing so, she's taking me places I've never been before, either.

Each time I stroke in deeply, she claws at my back. She's leaving sexy scratch marks, little souvenirs of this night together, and I fucking love it.

"It's so sexy when you claw at me," I say, and she stops for a second as if she hadn't realized she was doing it. She seems to get self-conscious for a second, and I lean down and press a kiss to her lips. I trail down to her neck as I continue to drive into her, and I move my lips toward her ear. "Keep doing it. I fucking love it."

She scratches the fuck out of me at that, and the pain is somehow a heady contrast to the pleasure I'm currently feeling. It drives everything up a notch, pushing me into what feels like it's going to be a long and intense orgasm.

And then it edges up on me out of nowhere. I don't want this to end. I want to keep fucking her all night like this, slow and steady and deep. It's creating a new connection between us, forming a stronger, more intimate bond as we create a new memory of each other that I know I'll dig up often in the days and weeks to come.

I only wish I could blow my load inside her to mark her with my cum, to watch it as it drips out of her pussy after I wrecked her. Maybe another time. Maybe when we know each other a little better. Maybe when we've fallen even deeper and agree there's room for a future together.

"Fuck, Kennedy," I rasp. "I can't hold on anymore."

"Give it to me!" she screams at me, and I don't know where that feral cat just came from, but it's extraordinarily erotic and sensual. Her body coils tightly as she says it, and then she starts to unleash her wild side as the orgasm seems to race through her. She's clawing at me and moaning my name as she says, "Fuck, Madden, yes! Oh God, yes!"

I lose it at that. Heat races through my entire body as the explosion detonates, and the sweet relief of a climax pumps out of me and into the condom, jet after hot jet. I grunt my way through it as I slow my thrusts to longer, still deeper strokes. She hangs on, fighting her way through her own climax as my mouth drops to hers for an intense, deep kiss as we ride it out together to the end.

I'm depleted as I come down from the high of an orgasm, but I kiss her gently, tenderly, slowly after the rising heat we just raced through together. I shift out of her, immediately missing the grip her pussy had as it clenched onto me.

I move to the side of her, breaking our kiss, and lay on the bed, pulling her over so she's resting on my chest.

"Your heart is racing," she says after a few quiet beats.

I lean down and press a kiss to the top of her head. "That's what you do to me."

I don't think I realized how much my heart was already tangled up with her until the words slipped out of my mouth.

I can't be doing this. I can't be falling for some girl in Chicago when I'm set to move to San Diego.

I can't create a life here with someone I'm going to have to leave for the next seven months, whom I might get to see once or twice a month if I'm lucky.

But as I hold her in my arms, the thought slips into my mind unbidden. What if I can?

What if I finally found something worth taking a risk on?

CHAPTER 24
KENNEDY VAN BUREN

I Didn't Peg Him as a Romantic

Well.
Wow.
I can't think coherently enough to come up with more than that.
Wow.
That was…
That was something else.
That isn't even in the same league as the two losers I was with before. Madden Bradley isn't just a professional athlete set to take over his father's real estate development business when he retires from playing football. He's also apparently a sex god.
I've never been banged like that. I've never had someone with such a dirty mouth say such naughty things to me in the heat of the moment. And if they did, it came off as weird or cheesy.
Not with Madden. Not when he knows what he's doing and has the most perfect equipment that he definitely knows how to use. Skillfully. With expertise.
He knew exactly what to do…and he did it. It's like he knew all the secrets to my body. Secrets maybe I hadn't even uncovered.
He understood the assignment. He knew. He seems to know me down to my soul, and even though we still have a long way to go to really know anything about each other aside from

surface stuff, it feels like we'll be able to get there quickly and easily since we have this intimate knowledge of each other already.

I'm half asleep when I feel the bed dip, and I'm suddenly lying on pillows rather than on Madden's chest. I suppose I should get up and use the bathroom. Ideally a shower would be nice to rinse off after not one but two romps with this man.

But I'm just so deliciously, achingly exhausted. I don't want to move.

And I don't have to.

I hear water running, and a few moments later, I'm woken with feather-light kisses along my arm. My eyes flutter open, and I see Madden there. I swear, I have heart eyes as I look at him, and I was sure, *so* sure, that he was all wrong for me.

I'm starting to change my mind.

He hauls me into his arms, and a moment later, he's setting me in his luxurious bathtub.

It's filled with bubbles that smell like him, and he has the jets of the whirlpool tub already running as he sets me into the warm, soapy water. The jets are heaven on my exhausted body, massaging me in all the right places.

He lit a few candles, and my glass of wine is filled again and sitting on the side of the tub. He also dropped off a glass of water in case I needed any, and honestly, that sounds more necessary than more wine at this point.

I didn't peg Madden Bradley as a romantic, but here we are. He squirts some of the body wash on a washcloth, and he runs it over the parts of my body not submerged in the water. I lean my head back on the towel he propped there, and I swear I could fall asleep in here.

He pulls one of my legs out of the water and washes it, taking time to wash and massage the aching feet that were jammed into those heels all night. He does the other leg, too, and then each of my arms. He helps me lean forward to wash my back, and then he washes my front. He reaches into the water to run the washcloth between my legs.

It's sweet and passionate at the same time. He's taking care of me after he put my body through the wringer, and all I can do is lie my head back and freaking enjoy it.

"I'm going to take a quick shower," he says. "Do you want to get in bed or watch from the tub?"

"Watch," I say immediately, and he turns on the water, and I swear to God, it's like watching one of those erotic car or cologne or men's underwear commercials where the camera stops just short of the goods…except I get the full view of this very entertaining show.

He's not even trying to be sexual as he simply washes himself, and yet as he closes his eyes and leans back so his neck is corded as he rinses suds from his body…

Yeah. It's sexual. I'm tempted to reach into the water and rub myself to another orgasm. Or let one of those tub jets work its magic on my clit.

I don't.

I gawk as I drink my water, and he chuckles when he shuts off the water and catches me staring.

I start clapping. "Best show I've watched in a while."

He laughs as he towels off, and then he holds up a hand to help me up. He wraps another towel around me, and he lifts me out of the tub and onto a rug to finish drying.

He pulls me into his arms once I've tucked the towel around myself, and he buries his face in my neck. "You smell like me."

I laugh. "And you always smell like heaven, so I'll take it."

He raises a brow. "Heaven? Really?"

I lift a shoulder.

"Well, whatever that coconut stuff is smells like pure joy, just so you know," he says—or growls. I'm not sure. How does he make even words like that sound sexy as hell?

He's got a real talent.

"Do you, uh, want to stay the night?" he asks. I can tell he feels awkward asking, but the truth is that I hadn't considered *not* staying the night. I'm a grown-ass adult, and I don't need to explain myself to anybody—my parents included, not that they'll even notice if I don't come home tonight.

"Is it okay if I say yes?"

"I'd like it if you said yes," he admits.

"Then yes. I'd love to."

"Do you want something to sleep in?" he asks.

I can't exactly sleep in the emerald gown I wore to the gala. "What do you wear to bed?"

"Nothing, usually," he admits.

I snag my bottom lip between my teeth. He's going to be naked next to me for the entire night?

I don't know if I'll be able to keep my hands off him. Yeah, I'm tired, but my pussy is perking up at the thought of a naked Madden in bed beside me.

I drop the towel to the floor. "Then let's wear matching outfits."

He laughs, though he does bend to pick up my towel and hang it on the towel bar. He hangs his own, too, and then he smacks my ass as I scamper into the bedroom and dive under the covers.

He takes my wineglass to the sink, sets the water on the nightstand beside me, and slips into bed. He gives me the kind of kiss that I'll be able to dream about all night, and then he settles in beside me. I turn away from him so I can snuggle my back into his front, and I feel his cock as it's semi-hard again. Already.

He pushes it near my ass, and I shift back toward him.

He moans. "I know you're exhausted. You better not start that now."

I laugh, and I push back again. "I'll stop. Goodnight."

His lips find my neck. "'Night."

I fall asleep for a bit, and I wake to the feel of his fingertips brushing along my nipples. It's dark in here, and I have no idea what time it is, but even a few hours of sleep have me feeling refreshed and ready. I moan at the feel of his fingers, and when he hears my consent, he applies a little more pressure, massaging each of my breasts and tweaking my nipples between his fingers and thumbs.

I shift my hips back, and I can feel how hard he is. The man is always horny, and it's a good match since I'm feeling greedy.

"God, I want to fuck you bare," he moans.

"Do it," I murmur. If I weren't half asleep, I might think twice about telling him that.

He's awake enough not to. He reaches over me and grabs a condom, rolls it on, and then he settles back into place. His fingertips trail down, and he slips a finger into me as he thrusts his cock against my ass again. I cry out at the feel. I want his cock inside me, and it's like he knows exactly what I need the second I need it. He pushes my leg out of the way and then pushes his cock into me from behind. He reaches around me and rubs his fingers on my clit as he starts to pump into me.

It's slow and sleepy and perfect all at once, and it feels like this one's different. I feel a pulse of emotions for him as he does this to me in the dark, as if he couldn't wait until morning to be with me. As if whatever we have is so strong that he was awakened in the middle of the night needing me. And I need him, too. He's filling me with his cock, yes, but he's also filling some need in me I didn't even know existed until he was there to fill it.

I'm lost to him as he makes love to me in the dark. I want to lean into him, to kiss him and hold him and feel him, but this is good too.

And it's as I start to come that I realize I'm not sure I'll ever have enough of this man.

I'm falling already. It's too fast, and I'm still not quite sure what his intentions are, but I'm in this. Deep.

CHAPTER 25

KENNEDY VAN BUREN

Scrambled

When I wake in the morning, I glance at the clock to see it's after nine. I don't typically sleep in quite this late, but we were up late and then up again in the middle of the night. The other side of the bed is empty, and my first thought is that I hope I'm not being a rude guest overstaying my welcome. I wonder how long he's been awake.

I force myself up, and my entire body feels deliciously achy after he put me through the wringer last night.

I pad over to the bathroom and do my thing, and I spot a T-shirt on the counter. I wonder if he left it out for me, and as I pick it up to bring it to my nose to smell it, I spot a pair of boxer shorts under it.

I slip the shirt over my head since I feel weird walking out into his condo buck naked. What if he has guests? I pull the shorts on, too. He thought of everything, and I can't help but think how romantic even this small act is.

I walk into the kitchen to find him standing at the counter stirring something in a bowl. I stand on the other side of the counter and stare at him.

"Good morning," he says, and he's more chipper than I am after the amount of wine I drank last night. "Do you prefer your eggs scrambled or fried?"

"My eggs?" I repeat stupidly, and he chuckles.

"Yeah. I'm making you breakfast. Scrambled?"

Scrambled? He means, like, my *brain* right now. Right?

"Sure," I murmur. He's making me breakfast?

"I have sausage links ready to go in the pan. I was just waiting for you to get up. And I'm whipping up a batch of my special protein-packed chocolate peanut butter pancakes. Unless you have food allergies. Do you?"

I shake my head, still a little stunned he's doing all this.

"Do you want anything else?" he asks.

"Sounds downright gourmet compared to my usual breakfast."

He laughs. "What do you usually have?"

"A cup of yogurt. Sometimes just a protein shake," I admit.

"Well, that won't do at Casa de Bradley," he says. "The coffee pot is full, and there's cream in the fridge and brown sugar syrup in the cabinet above the pot. If you want orange juice, there's some in the fridge."

"You didn't have to go to all this trouble." I've never had a man cook me breakfast after a night like last night.

Okay, fine. Full disclosure, I've never had a night like last night.

"It's no trouble at all. I actually enjoy cooking, and I try to make a batch of pancakes every Sunday so I have breakfast ready to go all week. In the offseason, anyway." He shrugs, and he pours the batter onto a prepared sheet pan sitting beside him on the counter.

"You use a sheet pan for pancakes?"

He nods. "And get this, I cut them into *squares* instead of *circles*. Weird, right?"

"I can honestly say I've never had a square pancake. Bring it on, Bradley."

"Bradley? No more mule?" he asks.

"After last night, I don't think I can call you a mule anymore."

"I can still call you a tiger," he says, and he raises a brow as my cheeks turn bright pink.

"Can I do anything to help?" I ask, changing the subject as I think about what I could call him after last night. Sex god?

He shakes his head. "You can help yourself to coffee, but I've got this under control."

I go ahead and do that, and I perch on one of the stools at the counter so I can watch him do his thing. Once he gets the pancakes into the oven and sets a timer, he walks around the counter and drops his lips to mine for just a quick kiss. He rounds the counter to wash out the batter bowl, and he dries it and puts it away before he gets started on the sausage.

He's meticulous in everything he does, and I could literally sit here sipping coffee and just watching him all day.

"When do you have to go to San Diego?" I ask.

"Midway through next month is when OTAs start, but I've got a trip booked for a long weekend this week, and I should get there a little more often to start bonding with my new teammates," he says. He doesn't turn to face me as he answers, instead keeping his focus on the food.

"OTAs?" I ask.

"Organized team activities," he clarifies. "The ones in May are voluntary, but they're sort of the unofficial kickoff of the season. My first chance to work out and start drills in the actual facility instead of at off-site gyms."

It's too soon to ask how that'll affect whatever it is we're starting. It's too awkward to ask if we're actually starting anything at all or if last night was an anomaly. It doesn't feel like it was.

It feels like something passed between us last night that bonded us in a new way, and to be honest…I don't *want* him to go to San Diego. I want to have the time to explore whatever this is, even if we have to explore in secret because of our fathers and business and all the other crap in our way.

He sighs as he turns to face me. "My father said he's opening a branch of Bradley Group in San Diego so I can work on my days off."

My brows shoot up. "In San Diego? When?"

He shrugs. "I didn't ask. I don't know, but it's just another way for him to keep tabs on me."

I tilt my head thoughtfully. "VBC has a branch in LA, you know."

"Really?"

I nod. "It's not in LA itself. I forget the town. Aliso Viejo, maybe? It's in the southern part of the greater Los Angeles area, so we all just call it the LA office."

He tilts his head, too, as we both think that one over.

Neither of us says it, but the distance between LA and San Diego isn't really all that far. Especially if he's in the northern part of the San Diego area and I'm in the southern part of Los Angeles.

We could try to make it work. But it might be hard to sell my father on why I want to move to the LA branch considering I don't have any work there when I do have a big project here.

"Do you get many days off when you're in season?" I ask, changing the subject before we go down a road neither of us might be ready to tackle.

He shakes his head. "Tuesdays. Sometimes Mondays. That's it apart from our bye week."

"Is real estate development what you want to do with those days?" I ask.

"Fuck no. It's my one chance to reset and recharge, to bond with teammates off the field, to participate in community events or charity or do whatever the fuck I want. Going into the office is not part of that plan," he says.

My brows dip. "What about the SCS project?"

"I figure by the time the season starts, we'll be on the permit phase, and that always takes forever." He shrugs. "I'm hopeful I can get through the season without having to do much because all the plans will be in place, and we'll just be working on the backend stuff that isn't really part of my job description anyway."

"So you'll pawn it off on someone else?" I demand. "Who am I going to be working with?"

He chuckles. "Me. But, yes, I'll pawn a certain extent of it off on someone else because I physically won't be able to make certain quick decisions. I've already pegged Margot and filled her in on the basics."

I note that Margot is most definitely a female name. So either she's the best choice, which is logically a possibility, or he doesn't want me working with another man.

Sort of like I didn't want to hand the project off to Sara.

Is Margot pretty? I want to ask. I don't. I'm not ready to show my insecurities to him, and it's a petty thought to have anyway. It doesn't matter. He's not making *her* breakfast this morning.

"My trip to San Diego this weekend is to pick out a place to live while I'm playing there," he says.

"Are you renting?" I ask.

He nods, and his brows dip together. "Would you want to come with me and help me decide where to live?"

I physically reel back a little in my seat at his surprising question.

"No, forget it. Sorry. It's too soon to be asking questions like that." He shakes his head and turns back toward the food, and we're both quiet for a few beats as he cracks some eggs into a bowl. "You hated me until last night. I shouldn't have asked."

"I didn't hate you," I say softly. Silence moves between us, and it turns nearly awkward when I finally break it. "What if I was about to say I'd love to?"

His head whips up, and his eyes meet mine. "Were you? I mean...*can* you?"

I shrug. "Why not? I can check out the LA office while I'm there." And we can have loads of that addictive sex, though I refrain from actually mentioning that.

He stares at me as we both consider it, and eventually the sausage starts to scream and sizzle in the pan, so he turns his attention back to it. And then, to my total shock, as he stares at the sausage, he says, "I'd love that."

And I melt just a little more as I find myself attaching to someone I'm not supposed to, scrambling me just a little more.

His phone starts to ring, and he answers it. He listens for a second, and then he says, "Yeah, you can send it up."

I don't ask because it isn't my business, but a few minutes later, there's a knock at his door, and he comes back carrying a fairly large box.

"What's that?" I ask.

"A welcome package from the Storm."

"That was nice of them."

"It's pretty standard." He sets it on his counter, and he gets back to cooking.

"Don't you want to open it?"

He shrugs. "Not really."

"You didn't want this trade," I muse.

"I didn't. Not really. But it's my reality. I like the guys in San Diego, and eventually it'll be home." He clears his throat. "You can open it while I finish up breakfast if you want." He pulls a box cutter out of a drawer and sets it on the counter for me, and I grab it and slice the box open.

I open it and find a note on top. I pull it out and hand that to Madden since it might be personal, and then I pull out a Storm baseball cap, joggers, a sweatshirt, a bunch of T-shirts, some other gear, and finally, at the very bottom of the box, a jersey.

I pull it out and hold it up. "Bradley eighty," I read off the back. He glances over at me, and he lets out a small breath. "Try it on," I say quietly.

He sighs, but then he turns off the burners and relents. He pulls his shirt over his head, and I allow my eyes to fall on those sweet abs of his. I hand him the jersey, and he pulls it over his shoulders.

It falls into place, and I stare.

I gawk.

I swoon.

I get even more scrambled.

I get hot and need some water.

Holy hell, this guy's hot. Business attire, naked, in a jersey…they're all great looks, and I can't decide which I like best. I'll take them all.

Did I really just think that?

"That looks good on you, Madden," I say, my voice a little shy.

"It's not Bears, but I do feel a sort of new energy having all this shit. It's becoming real, and I guess I'm starting to get excited."

"Have you made friends out there?" I ask.

"I'm starting to. The other wide receivers are all pretty good guys."

"I bet none of them look like *that* in the jersey, though," I muse.

He laughs, and then he takes it off and trades it for his shirt.

But I will definitely allow my dreams to be filled with Madden Bradley and all his different looks going forward.

CHAPTER 26
MADDEN BRADLEY

The Future CEO

When I get into the office on Monday morning, I'm still in a haze over my weekend. She left shortly after breakfast yesterday, but she did love my pancakes—even in their strange, square shape.

And something happened.

Something big.

Something deep.

When she left…I didn't want her to go.

That's not me, and it never has been. I've never allowed myself to get attached. So what the fuck makes her different? I have no idea.

I stop at Starbucks for some caffeine and the chance to run into her, but she's not there. We've both eased into more projects at work that keep us separated, though I'm wondering if she's come up with a way to get to the LA office.

I don't hear from her during working hours, but I'm busy with projects anyway. I do, however, stop into my father's office after lunch.

"You mentioned a San Diego office. Tell me more about it," I say, sitting in the chair across from him.

"Coming around, I see," he says. He pulls open something on his tablet, and he passes it over to me. I glance at the information on the office building he chose, and it's in Carlsbad. As I recall, that's north of San Diego, and perfect given what Kennedy and I talked about yesterday.

I shouldn't be having those thoughts, yet they are certainly ever-present. *She* is certainly ever-present.

I haven't stopped thinking about her since the moment I met her, and now we're going to spend a weekend together in California? It seems dangerous somehow, yet I can't seem to stop myself from moving in that direction anyway.

"What do you think?" he asks.

"Carlsbad isn't very close to the practice facility, but I can make it work," I say rather than the other rushing thoughts in my head regarding our competitor.

"Pick a place to live halfway between the two," he suggests, always full of answers. I don't *want* to pick a place further from our practice facility, but the thought of Kennedy having to drive further to her office isn't exactly appealing, either.

Wait a second.

What the fuck did I just think to myself?

I'm considering *a woman's* commute in my thought process of where to live?

But…why?

We've been together exactly one night. I have no idea why it feels like more, but suddenly it's like I can see a future with a person I just met.

Maybe it's because we bonded on more than one level. She isn't sure she wants her family business, and neither am I, yet we're both destined to fulfill a role someone else chose for us. And then there was her hate for me melting into something else.

There was Saturday night and breakfast yesterday.

There's always California.

I never really pictured my life after the game since it was always mapped out for me, but I'm starting to picture it now. And I like seeing *her* in that picture.

It's a hard reality I never wanted to face, but with this being the last year of my contract on top of a trade, I'm not sure I can see myself playing beyond this year. It's better to quit while I'm ahead. I've got my health, though who knows what's in store for me this season. More years would equal more money, but there's plenty of cash to be had in the real estate development market, too.

Just ask the billionaire sitting across the desk from me.

"Is there anything else?" he asks.

"Send me the details on the office," I finally say, relenting. I like what I've seen so far of San Diego, and maybe after a year there I'll decide I'm ready to call it a day on icy winters, lake effect snow, and unpredictable weather. "I can swing by to check it out in person this weekend."

"We've already rented the space, and I've already tagged who will be running that office," he says.

"I thought you wanted me to do it," I protest.

"And I thought you didn't want that."

"If I'm the future CEO, I'd at least like to have some say in these decisions."

"If?" he repeats, and I forcibly restrain myself from rolling my eyes. "I'll remind you that yes, you are the future CEO, but I am the current one."

Thanks, Pops. Really needed that reminder.

Normally on a Monday night in the offseason after the Bradley family dinner, I'd be getting paid to make an appearance at a bar or club nearby. But tonight, I had no offers. And so I'm sitting at home on my balcony thinking about the kiss I shared with Kennedy a few nights ago when I decide to send her a text.

Me: *The view isn't as good tonight.*

I take a photo of the pier and attach it, and her reply comes quickly.

Kennedy: *Turn the camera around and try again.*

I laugh at her text, and then I do it and send her a cheesy selfie.

Kennedy: *Much better.*

Me: *Send me one, too, but with your tits in it.*

Kennedy: *Definitely no.*

Me: *You're no fun.*

Kennedy: *You weren't saying that on Saturday night in a bathroom at the gala. Or those times afterward at your place.*

Me: *You were definitely fun then, tiger.*

Kennedy: *[tiger emoji]*

Me: *[laugh emoji]*

I can't quite figure out why getting a tiger emoji has me laughing at my phone, but I feel light and excited as I think about what to text her next. It's as I'm thinking that a new message comes through from my brother, Dex.

Dex: *You home?*

Me: *Yep.*

A minute later, my phone rings, and it's the front desk of my building.

"Send him up," I answer, since that will be Dex.

I open my front door, and the elevators open on my floor a moment later. Dex steps off, and I greet him with our usual hug where we pound each other on the back.

"Couldn't make it in time for family dinner?" I tease.

He rolls his eyes and shakes his head as if the thought of attending it is more than he can deal with.

"What the fuck do you want?" I tease some more.

My phone dings with a new text, and it's probably from Kennedy. I want to look at it with everything in me, but I know if I do, I'll get that stupid grin on my face again, and then I'll be subjected to Dex's questions that I'm certainly not ready to answer.

"I got into a little trouble in Vegas. Can I lay low here for a few days?" he asks. He looks…well, a little more haggard than usual.

"When you say *trouble*…" I hint, trailing off, and he sighs.

"I'd prefer not to get into it." He walks past me and into my place, and I slam the door behind him.

"And I'd prefer not to harbor a fugitive. Out with it."

He sets his hands on his hips. The family resemblance is strong with him—with all my siblings, really, except for Archer. "Fine. Wild night out, wrong crowd. There were some drugs, a fight broke out, and a few photos were taken that could show me out of context, so my publicist suggested getting out of town. I got here intending to stay with Mom and Dad, but then I realized there is absolutely no part of me that wants to do that, so I'm here begging for a place to stay. I just need a few days. A week tops."

"When you say there were some drugs…were you doing them?" I ask carefully.

He presses his lips together. "No."

"Not in the photos, or not at all?"

"Not at all, man," he says defensively. "Who do you take me for? I've got a career I'm not ready to fuck around with. I was in a bedroom with a woman when it all went down. It was honestly wrong place, wrong time. My publicist is trying to cover it with a deepfake, but it's anyone's guess whether it'll work."

"What's a deepfake?" I ask.

"You know, those artificial intelligence images that are generated to look like someone or something else is going on."

"Isn't that illegal?"

He shrugs, and I probably don't want to get caught up in this, but he's my brother.

I sigh. "Okay. You can stay here. I'm going to San Diego Wednesday evening, so you'll have the place to yourself if you're staying longer than that." I'm giving the hint so he'll reply with when he plans to leave, but he doesn't say.

"Thanks, man."

"Did you bring luggage?" I ask.

He shakes his head. He's sort of the Bradley rebel, if there was one, and he tends to make impulsive decisions that can potentially put the rest of us into situations we don't want to be in.

"You're an idiot. You know that?" I press.

"Fuck this," he mutters. "I'll just go stay with Mom and Dad."

"Knock it off. But pull yourself together, yeah? You can borrow whatever you need short of my toothbrush. I have some spares in the guest bathroom. And clean the fuck up after yourself."

"Yes, Father," he says.

Jesus. Do I sound like Dad? I sure fucking hope not.

I send him in the direction of the guest rooms and tell him he can take his pick, and then I head out to the balcony to check that last text from Kennedy.

Kennedy: *What are you doing now? We could have some more fun…*

That's the text I missed because of Dex?

And now my cockblock of a brother is here, so I can't even invite her over. I'm not ready to reveal the fact that I'm seeing someone, especially not if Dex happens to find out who she is.

Me: *My brother just showed up from Vegas. I'm so sorry. If he wasn't here, I'd be all over having more fun. Actually, I'd be all over YOU…*

Kennedy: *Bummer. How long is he staying?*

Me: *No idea. He's here laying low. Lucky me.*

Kennedy: *I'm sorry.*

Me: *I'll text you my hotel details in San Diego. I just changed to a place in Carlsbad, so it's not as far for you.*

I'm not sure why I give her that little detail. It's definitely showing my vulnerability, something I wasn't quite ready to do.

Kennedy: *You didn't have to do that.*

Me: *If it were up to me, I'd just keep you there all weekend.*

Kennedy: *What would you do with me?*

She's bold, and I like it. My cock likes it, too. He perks up at the mere thought of having her in my hotel room all weekend.

I decide to take a page from her book and be bold right back.

Me: *Tie you to my bed and make you beg me for my cock.*

Kennedy: *Whoa. I'm listening. What else?*

Me: *Fuck you slow. Fuck you hard. Fuck you deep.*

Kennedy: *So lots of sex.*

Me: *So much sex. And lots of orgasms.*

Kennedy: *How many?*

Me: *What's your single-night record?*

Kennedy: *Three.*

Three? I gave her three on Saturday night.

Holy shit. The realization washes over me.

How many men has she been with? Wait…no. I don't want to know the answer to that.

But now my wheels are turning. She wasn't a virgin, but maybe she's not very experienced. There was something innocent about her, and the way she bent to my will was hotter than fuck. I want it again. I *need* it again.

I'm not prepared for this. And certainly not now that my fucking brother is here.

I blow out a breath and sidestep that question for now, though curiosity will eventually get the best of me. Still, even if I ask her, am I prepared to share my number? Likely not. Maybe we won't need to.

Me: *What about you? If you could do whatever you wanted to me, what would it be?*

Kennedy: *You'll laugh if I say it.*

Me: *I promise I won't.*

Kennedy: *I'd kiss you.*

All the things in the world she could do, and she chooses…kissing?

Me: *Kiss me?*

Kennedy: *You're a really good kisser. My stomach flips every time you kiss me. And then I'd let you kiss me wherever you want because you're also very good with your mouth.*

My chest tightens at her words. Her stomach flips when I kiss her?

It just makes me want to kiss her more. I want her to feel that exciting flip of her stomach every time she's in the same room as me.

What the hell is happening to me?

Me: *I can't wait to show you how good.*

The door to my balcony opens. "Mind if I join you out here?" Dex asks, interrupting my intense texting conversation with Kennedy.

"Do I have a choice?" I joke.

He chuckles, and he sits *beside* me, not across from me, so I can't even text her without him looking over my shoulder.

My phone dings with another text, but I don't look to answer it. Instead, I make small talk with my brother while I wait for the moment when I can pick up my conversation with the woman I seem to be falling for hard and fast.

CHAPTER 27

MADDEN BRADLEY

Clay Mack and Mad Brad

Kennedy is flying out Thursday after work, so I have an entire twenty-four hours in San Diego by myself. I text Clay, and he invites me to his gym so we can work out together on Thursday morning as we continue getting to know each other. He tells me he likes to swim as part of his workout, so I throw swim trunks into my gym bag at the last minute.

He's waiting for me by the entrance when I walk in, and he slaps me on the back before we hit the weight room first. He spots me, and I spot him. We shoot the shit about life in San Diego, but it's all surface shit.

He seems like someone I can talk to about Kennedy, but I'm not sure how to bring her up. While my immediate family is the worst choice to make my confessions, he might be someone who can help me put things in perspective.

We run on the treadmills and work up a sweat, and I peel off my shirt and hang it over one arm of the machine as I scale back my speed to start cooling down.

He glances over at me after he slows, too, and he says, "You seeing anybody?"

"Who's asking?"

"Me. Wondering who left those scratch marks all over your back."

"Unfortunate run-in with a tree branch," I lie.

"They look more like fingernail scratches, but if you say so."

"My cat," I lie again.

He laughs and holds up both hands. "Like I'd believe you have a cat. You don't have to make shit up."

"It's this woman back in Chicago. It's just the worst possible timing, you know?"

"Because you're moving here?" he guesses.

I nod. I don't want to give too much away since I don't know him, yet this sort of feels like a bonding moment.

"Can she move with you?"

"We *just* started seeing each other," I say. "It's complicated."

"Yeah. Anyone who leaves marks like that is definitely complicated."

I chuckle. He's not wrong. "I've never been in a serious relationship. Have you?"

He nods. "Once. But I was young and fucked it up, so I swore them off. What's your excuse?"

"My career." I shrug. "It's just easier this way. Less to manage."

"Women certainly do complicate things, don't they?"

I press my lips together and nod. My life feels like it's been one complication after another since I bumped into her at that Starbucks one fateful morning, and here I am, mooning over the fact that I've started falling for her when I should be focused on workouts and the upcoming season with a new team.

"So the question is, can you live without her in your life?" he says. "If you can, then you can leave her behind in Chicago and explore the vast and wonderful opportunities here in San Diego as my sidekick. But if you can't, well, you figure that shit out. I'm not your man for advice on that."

I bark out a laugh. "One thing, Mack," I say, and he glances at me with raised brows. "I'm nobody's sidekick."

He laughs with me, and we call it a day on the treadmills and head for the pool.

I don't feel all that much better about my situation, but I do feel a new bond with a teammate. That's the thing about working out. Sometimes you're working out more than just your body, and your mind gets some benefits as well.

I guess it feels like a bit of a load off my shoulders. It doesn't solve world issues, but it helps that I already have someone here I can confide in, and I can see us becoming good friends. He's been here in San Diego a few years now, and he's a lot like me. He's a wide receiver, he's single, and he doesn't bother with relationships. The other receivers—Spencer Nash, DJ Evans, Trey Clark, and Zach Moore—are all either married or have significant others.

So it's Clay Mack and Mad Brad for the win, a phrase I hope to hear a lot this season.

After workouts, I touch base with a realtor recommended by Spencer. He put together a schedule of places to view this weekend, and I'm more excited than I should be that I'll have Kennedy with me to give me another perspective as I click through the photos he sent over.

I shower, and it's as I'm getting out that I hear a knock at my door. I glance at the clock and realize I lost track of time, and I run over to the door as I wrap a towel around my waist, my hair still dripping with beads of water as I open the door.

I find Kennedy standing there looking as gorgeous as ever. Her hair is down and a little wavy, and she's wearing a pair of jeans and a plain white T-shirt.

Her surprised eyes immediately and greedily dart down to my abdomen. I glance down at my body with the small hotel towel wrapped around it. "Sorry. I lost track of time."

"Uh," she says, dragging her bottom lip between her teeth. "No, uh. Actually, this is perfect." She sets her hands on my abs and pushes me into my own hotel room, and I laugh as she yanks her suitcase in and kicks the door shut behind her. She stalks toward me.

Saturday night was our night together. We haven't seen each other since she left on Sunday. It's been only four days.

And somehow with her here in front of me again, I realize one important fact.

"I missed you," I say as she moves in closer.

She runs her fingertips along my forehead, and she curls her finger around my ear as her eyes find mine. "I missed you too."

I lean down and press my lips to hers, and she melts right into me. It's the way she does that, how her body just seems to mold to mine, that makes this so fucking addictive.

I have nowhere to go tonight. I wasn't planning on leaving this hotel room. I was going to order food in and spend the evening naked.

And it appears her plans are in line with mine as she tugs at the spot where my towel is tucked into itself. We both let it drop to the floor.

She's been here less than a minute, and I'm already naked, my mouth opening to intensify our kiss as she kisses me back with urgency and need. She reaches between us and tugs on my cock, and all the blood in my body rushes right there at the feel of her hands on me. I grunt into her mouth as she starts to stroke me off, and I'm desperate to feel her, too, but she's got me by the balls.

Literally.

She breaks our kiss and bends down. Her hands never leave my cock, and she holds me around the base of my cock, wrapping her thumb and forefinger around me as best she can with my size, taking my balls in her palm as she starts to stroke me. She stops at the tip of my cock, and she licks the bead of precum that's already formed there. Her tongue flattens as she licks me from tip to base, and she follows the movement with her fist around me.

"Jesus," I mutter, drawing out the *e* sound at the feel of her mouth on me.

She sucks my tip between her lips, and I feel like I'm about to shoot four days' worth of buildup to the back of her throat. She feels so fucking amazing, and it's just the tip. Then she deep throats me, taking me all the way back until the tip she just had between her lips bumps the back of her throat, and I grip onto the back of her head to hold myself there for a few seconds. I let go, and she sucks in a breath before we do it again.

"Do you like it when my cock fills your mouth?" I ask, and she looks up at me, and I'm fucking done.

Is there a more beautiful sight than my cock in this woman's mouth while she looks up at me with that begging look in her eyes like she wants me to give her everything I have?

I shift my hips back to let her answer.

"I love it. But I love it more when it's filling my pussy." She's panting, and she pulls me right back into her mouth as soon as the words are out.

Holy fuck.

"We have all weekend for that," I grit out, my jaw clenched as I force myself to hold off. "And right now, I want to fuck your mouth."

I start to move, shifting my hips back into her, and she simply opens her mouth and accepts it. She keeps her fingers around the base of my cock with my balls nestled in her hand, and the other hand follows the path I make as I move in and out of her mouth each time.

Her mouth is hot and wet and perfect, and when our eyes meet again, I'm fucking done. She's looking up at me with all this innocence and need, as if she can't quite get enough of me even though I'm stuffing her mouth with my cock, and she's just so fucking pretty like that on her knees for me.

"Fuck," I mutter as I feel my balls draw up. She seems to get more enthusiastic in her sucking, as if she can tell I'm about to lose it. "I'm gonna come," I say, a little warning in case she doesn't want my seed going down her throat, and she doesn't shift a fucking centimeter as my body erupts.

White-hot jets of cum spill out of me, and I feel her swallow around me as my climax goes on and on for what feels like forever. Her mouth is pure magic, and she swallows down every last drop I have to give. She licks me clean like she can't get enough, and it's just one more thing to pull me even closer to her.

I'm fucking spent, and she hasn't removed a stitch of clothing yet.

She gently lets me go, and she pushes to her feet. "I just love my first time in San Diego so far," she says, her voice hoarse and low as her eyes meet mine. She winks at me, and then she takes off for the restroom.

I grab the towel from the floor and wipe myself off as I can't help but think I'm growing to like this town more and more with every visit.

CHAPTER 28

Lock and Key

Well, I've never done that before. I've never just shown up at a guy's hotel room and sucked his dick the second I walked into the room.

I guess I'm experiencing a lot of firsts with Madden Bradley.

He's making me want to experience so much more with him, and maybe we can do whatever we want here in San Diego. We can be whoever we want since we don't have the threat of our fathers hanging over us out here.

Maybe we could even go on a date. We don't have to be secretive here the way we do back home.

And if we're caught and exposed? We're working on the SCS project together. We have that excuse, at least…not that my father would necessarily buy that. And Madden is a celebrity. He could be recognized. Maybe a date is a bad idea.

Still, we have the entire weekend ahead of us, and we've never had the promise of this amount of time together. Between his brother crashing at his place and both of our busy schedules this week, I've relied on our text conversations for the last few nights. But it's nothing compared to being in the same room as him.

It's a little terrifying, but I think it might be time to make the admission that I'm more than just a little interested in him. I'm pretty sure this is falling.

I can't recognize it for sure since it's never happened to me before, but it sure as hell feels like that's what it is.

I'm standing by the balcony doors looking out over a gorgeous view of palm trees with water in the distance when Madden walks into place beside me. He's dressed now, and he slips his arm around my shoulders. I lean into him. It's easy, and it feels right. It feels *good*.

"Are you hungry?" he asks softly, and he leans over and presses his lips to my temple.

I rest my head on his shoulder as I nod. "Yeah, I could eat."

"Want me to order something in?"

"That sounds great. Let's get seafood since we're by the ocean," I say.

"Fish tacos?"

I nod. "Perfect."

He chuckles. "God, you're so…I don't know. It's easy with you. I always avoided this kind of thing because women were always so complicated. You're not like that."

"Avoided what kind of thing?" I ask, clinging onto that statement because I need the reassurance that whatever it is that I'm feeling isn't just me.

He clears his throat and keeps his eyes trained on the view. "Relationships." He stiffens at the word. "Whatever the hell this is."

I lean in and slip my arm around his waist, and I squeeze him in a side hug because it's my instinct to make him feel more comfortable. "It's okay if we don't define it right now."

He pulls out of my arms and turns to look at me. "What if I want to?"

"What would you call it? Two business rivals messing around?" I lift a shoulder.

His jaw clenches, and I see those muscles working back and forth the way they sometimes do. "Is that what you'd call it?"

I shake my head and avert my gaze to the ground, suddenly vulnerable. His fingertips come under my chin to tilt it up so I'm forced to look him in the eye.

"Listen to me, Kennedy. Whatever it is…it's different for me, okay? I'm thirty-five, and I've never done this. Some might call that baggage and run scared, and if that's what you want, it'll be easier to walk away now."

My voice is a whisper when I say, "I'm not going anywhere."

His forehead drops to mine. "Good. Because I'm not, either."

I tip my chin to catch his lips with mine, and it's an important moment for us where it feels like something shifts.

We're no longer just two business rivals messing around. Maybe we didn't exactly define it, and maybe he darted around the topic by saying he's never done *this*. I don't know what *this* is, but I also know I've never done it before, either.

He orders our fish tacos from room service and adds margaritas for each of us, and he lets me know our food will be here in a half hour.

"Mm, a half hour? Sounds like just the right amount of time," I hint, and I wrap my arms around him.

He chuckles. "For what?"

I pull back out of his arms, and I'm not here to play games. I lift my shirt over my head and drop it to the floor, and I unhook my bra and drop it on top. "For this."

His mouth curls into a sly smile as his eyes zero in on my tits. "Fuck, I love these," he murmurs.

I freeze a little at his use of the word. He didn't say he loves *me*, but my tits are a part of me, and he loves those.

I've never heard those words from a man before. In fact, I've rarely heard them at all in my life.

He moves in. His eyes are still on mine, and he wraps one arm around me until my tits are crushed against his chest. His eyes move to my lips, and his palm moves toward my neck. He drops his mouth to mine, and as he kisses me, I feel it.

We're not there. We're not ready to say the words. Not by a long shot.

But I think I can get there…and fast when it comes to him.

He kisses me with all the pent-up emotion we've both been scared to unleash on the other, and I hope he feels it back.

He pulls back only to peel my jeans and panties off, and he lifts me into his arms. He carries me to the bed, and he kneels between my legs.

He dips his tongue inside me, humming into me as he tastes me again, sucking my clit between his lips and pelting me with pleasure. He's quiet, his usual dirty talk and commanding directions tamed in this moment as I let go and let him do whatever he wants to me.

I'm nearly tipping over the edge. He doesn't let me crest over it just yet, though. He's already learned my body in this short time we've been together, and he stops short of giving me a climax.

He rolls on a condom and climbs over me. He hovers on top of me, his eyes on mine as he pushes inside me.

And then he makes love to me. I can feel his emotions through his actions, and I cling to him as he drives into me, pushing both of us to heights our bodies have never seen since they've never had this emotional connection before in a moment like this.

My stomach clenches as the need to come pulls over me. I squeeze my eyes shut as I feel the start of it climbing over me, and a series of moans escape me as it plows into me out of nowhere. I cry out his name as I hit my peak, and my body squeezes him inside as I hear him grunt, "I'm coming."

We ride out the wave together, two sated bodies pulling pleasure from the other, and he drops his mouth to mine as we each start to relax at the same time. He kisses me slowly and tenderly for a few glorious seconds, and then he pulls back and trails his lips toward my ear. "Your body was made for mine."

His words send a shudder through me.

It's supposed to be forbidden. Wrong. But nothing about being with him feels wrong.

Instead, it feels an awful lot like his words are exactly right.

Maybe I was put on this earth to find him. Maybe I'm the lock, he's the key, and together, we'll fit together to unlock the mysteries of our family legacies.

CHAPTER 29

MADDEN BRADLEY

A Jock Being Handed the Company

After fish tacos and margaritas, we head outside to take a walk. We end up on the beach, and we each take off our shoes. We hold hands and hold our shoes in our other hands, and the moon reflects on the water as we walk slowly in the sand.

The beaches back home aren't like this, and usually it's too windy or too cold to enjoy them anyway. But this? Walking here with Kennedy's hand slipped into mine after sex and fish tacos…this is pure fucking heaven.

I know it won't last because everything in this life is fleeting, but somehow it feels like San Diego is already *our* place. Chicago can't be. It's too wrapped up in our histories and our families to feel like *ours*. But this feels like a fresh beginning here away from those histories and families, and it's something that's just for us.

I have to admit…I already love how that feels.

What kind of woman pushes me into my hotel room to suck me off and then rips her shirt off to tell me she wants to fuck before dinner arrives?

Only the kind of perfect woman I don't ever want to let go.

I think back to Clay's question just earlier today when he asked me if I could live without her, and I thought I knew the answer to that.

Turns out I was wrong.

The truth is, now that she's here, I just can't see myself here without her.

But that's definitely a complication. For one thing, I don't know if she feels the same. And for another thing, I don't know if she even has the ability to move here. It's way too soon to be thinking these things, but here I am, thinking them anyway.

It's late, and we head back to the hotel to get some sleep. She's going into her office tomorrow, and I suppose I have to do the same since I told my father I would.

When morning dawns, it feels right to wake with her beside me. For a moment, I wish we were getting ready together and going into the office together.

I realize what a ridiculous thought that is immediately.

But then, like the Kombucha girl GIF, I rethink that. Maybe it's not so ridiculous.

It's not like it's something I can bring up now when we're at the early stages of whatever this thing between us is. She's supposed to be staying away from me, and it would likely be smart for me to stay away from her as well.

I can't. I won't.

Today isn't the day to discuss potentially merging companies, but if this works, and someday down the road we're CEOs of competing companies and we're planning our future…why not?

It's not what my father would want for his company, and it's not what her father would want for his. But if they're leaving us in charge whether we want it or not…we're free to do whatever the fuck we want.

I head into the shower with those thoughts swirling around. I don't want to bring it up because I don't want to scare her off. I also don't want her to think I'm trying to gain access to her clientele or her company. That's not at all what this is.

It's simply a thought about the future and how it could be so much better for us to work together rather than apart.

She's up when I emerge from the shower, and she's sipping coffee that she made in the hotel room coffee maker as she stands by the windows and stares out over the view.

"I could get used to this place," she says as I stroll over and move in behind her, wrapping my arms around her waist in a backward hug.

"The view got better once you arrived." I drop my head and press my lips to her neck.

"Mm," she moans, and she leans back into me as she reaches up to wrap her hand around the back of my neck. "You better stop that or you're going to make me late."

I laugh. "Then be late."

She twists in my arms so she's facing me. "I can't. I said I'd sit in on a meeting that starts at nine, and I have no idea what traffic will be like during the morning commute to get up there."

"Too bad," I murmur.

"I know. We have tonight, though. And tomorrow. I need to go shower." She tips her chin up and kisses me, and then she heads toward the bathroom.

I get ready to head into my own office, and that idea of merging companies is still swirling. We say our goodbyes once she's ready, and I head over to the office space I didn't even know my father had already rented.

I text John, the man my father chose to run the San Diego branch, when I arrive, and he meets me in the lobby. I'd guess he's in his fifties, and he introduces himself and shakes my hand before he accompanies me up via the building elevator to show me around.

We're renting half of the top floor of this building, and the space looks like it's just about ready for us. His office is, anyway, and we sit in there and discuss the opportunities available here in the greater San Diego and Los Angeles areas. There is plenty of development to be had despite the already crowded nature of both areas, and they're both highly competitive markets.

I think Bradley Group can do some really great things here…but I also know one of my competitors is meeting with her staff right now probably thinking the exact same thing.

"Your father said you'll be around more once you move here," John says.

"He told me that as well," I say dryly, and John laughs. "And I will stop in on occasion, but I'm not taking over Bradley Group until I retire, and I'm very much still playing."

"Good luck to you this season, Madden. We'll all be watching. In terms of business, your father trusted me to take on the managing responsibilities here at this location, and I plan to do just that." There's a bit of warning in his voice, as if he's telling me not to step on his toes because he's the one running this place.

I realize he's older than me, but he's not in line to be the CEO. Part of me wants to put him in his place, and the other part of me doesn't have enough fucks to give him one of them.

So I let it slide.

We talk until lunchtime, and then we go out for a working lunch as we discuss the goals of this office.

He never says it, but I get the feeling John sees me as nothing more than a jock who's being handed this company. And honestly, yeah. That's partly true, and I get it. I *am* a professional athlete. I *am* being handed this company thanks to that little old thing called nepotism. I didn't earn it. I was born into it.

I may have focused on football for the better part of my life, but every summer since I can remember, I worked at Bradley Group. I have a vast knowledge of this business even though I spend the better part of six months out of the year away from it.

I'm smart, and I'm capable. And I'm tired of trying to prove that. I don't *need* to prove that. But maybe I do need to put this guy in his place.

I don't. Not today. I don't have time since I promised I'd meet Clay at the gym for a few hours.

I don't want to, though. I just want to get back to my hotel where I can get back to *her*.

And that's a really goddamn terrifying thought that's brand-new to me.

CHAPTER 30

KENNEDY VAN BUREN

The Math Isn't Mathing

The office visit goes surprisingly well. The entire time, I can't help but feel like this is where I'm supposed to be.

I'm a Chicago girl at heart. It's why Clem and I moved on our own to the city. We wanted to experience independence, to be city girls living our best lives.

It didn't exactly pan out that way, but even so, Chicago has my heart.

But I think California might have my soul.

The proximity to the beach and the mild weather are lovely traits. But I think it's the fact that Madden Bradley is going to be living here for the next year that really has me looking at things through a different lens.

We're *just* getting things started, and the thought of being away from him, of trying things long distance…it's overwhelming. It'll be far too hard on a burgeoning relationship like ours.

We meet back at the hotel for dinner, and we decide to take the risk and eat at one of the restaurants in our hotel. We have a private corner booth, so neither of us is worried about being caught.

After we place our orders and our drinks arrive, he asks, "How was the commute?"

"Not bad. I listened to an audiobook, and it made the time pass faster. How was your day?"

He lifts a shoulder. "It was fine. I met with John, the man my father chose to run this office, and I just got the feeling like he doesn't really respect me."

"Why would he? He doesn't know you."

"You're right," he concedes. "And I know respect has to be earned. But he was a little on the condescending side, and I was trying to piece together if it's because he thinks I'm nothing more than a jock or if it's because my father is handing the company over to me."

"Do you think those might be your insecurities speaking out?" I ask, though truthfully, I often think of the second thing he just said only about myself.

"Absolutely. But I still felt it coming from him."

"I get that. I feel that way too. Not the jock thing, but the being handed the company thing. I didn't earn it, and I guess being born into a role isn't what little kids dream of when they're imagining the future, you know?"

He nods. "But you took the job to escape a bad situation. We've talked about how that was a smart move on your part."

"Right." I take a sip of my wine. "But it doesn't change the fact that I was able to leave another job and step right into the place my dad was reserving for me when that time eventually came. And maybe the people I met with today didn't outwardly make me feel that way, but it doesn't mean they aren't thinking it anyway."

"Do you like what you're doing there at VBC?" he asks.

I nod. "I do. I'm growing to like it more and more, actually. It's not graphic design, but I do think there are a lot of opportunities for me to put those skills to use, and the more I'm there, the more I'm starting to sort of *want* to be there. It's nice knowing I have a stable career in front of me, and I'm nothing if not a hard worker bent on achieving the best for my company. What about you?"

He presses his lips together and stares into his beer. He glances up at me when he finally answers. "It's not football." He looks torn by that.

"No, it's not. But you can't play football forever."

"No, you're right. I can't. But between my trust fund and my paychecks from the league, I can't say I really *need* a job to fall back on. Especially not one as intense and exhausting as being the CEO of a multi-billion-dollar company when its billionaire CEO retires." He twists his lips.

Wait a minute.

Billionaire CEO?

I haven't looked at the financials for VBC, but a billion dollars is a hell of a lot of money. Our companies are probably worth that, but our fathers?

That seems somehow wrong. Maybe it's just a turn of phrase, but the math isn't mathing for me. I don't think my dad is worth *billions*. Millions, yes. Eight figures, likely. Possibly into the low nine figures.

But ten figures?

It's a reach that seems unlikely.

I push it away. I'm sure it's nothing. Maybe just a turn of phrase on his part.

"So are you saying you don't want to take over Bradley Group?" I ask quietly.

He chugs down a few sips of beer. "No. I'm not saying that. I like the industry. I like what we do. I like a blank canvas, and I like to build. But sometimes I wish things were different and that I could do it because I wanted to do it rather than because I'm expected to do it."

"So do I," I admit, and it's fascinating to me that I have so much in common with this hot guy who bumped into me at a Starbucks one morning not so long ago.

We take another walk on the beach, we make love, and we sleep. I feel this pull to him as we bond over these unexpected similarities between our families and our futures.

And as I feel that pull toward him, I start to see the future more clearly. It's mapping itself out before our very eyes.

We look at houses on Saturday, and we find one that's perfect for him. He signs the lease that will start next month. We have no idea if he'll be here a year or more, but it's close to his practice facility, and it's on the north side of town, so it's only about a fifty-minute drive to the Aliso Viejo office for me.

And then we celebrate. Naked.

I'm sad when Sunday rolls around and I have to head to the airport. He's staying through the day tomorrow to get in more workouts with his local friends, and I'm glad he's finding people to bond with on his new team. He drives me to the airport to drop me off, and he kisses me goodbye from the driver's seat.

I don't know when I'll see him again. I don't know if his brother is still staying at his place, and I can't exactly invite him to my place since I'm living with my parents.

But after this weekend, I have this lovely, strong feeling that we'll find some way to make this work. It feels like San Diego is our safe haven, and I can't wait to get back there with him to make more magic. Sooner rather than later, preferably.

That feeling is shot to hell the minute I get home.

My dad sent a ride from the company for me, and as I walk through the front door with my suitcase, my father is standing in the foyer as if he was waiting for me.

"Why were you photographed with Madden Bradley leaving a hotel in Carlsbad?" he demands.

My heart palpitates. "Excuse me?" I ask, setting my hand on my chest.

"You were supposed to be in Los Angeles. You checked into a hotel there. So why were you at Madden Bradley's hotel in Carlsbad, a full forty miles from the Aliso Viejo office?"

"Dad, calm down," I say as I feel anything but calm. I scramble to come up with some excuse. "We were working out some details for SCS while we were both in town, and we met for dinner halfway between San Diego and Aliso Viejo."

"I will not calm down. Are they opening an office there? They can't win that town, too. I won't allow it," he hisses.

"They're opening a branch in San Diego, yes. With Madden moving there because he's playing there, his father wanted him to have a local office so he can continue working on his projects while he's in season," I say.

"Why do you know so much about this, Kennedy?" he thunders at me.

Jesus, Dad. I haven't even set my suitcase down yet. I take the opportunity to do that.

"Because we're working together on SCS, and sometimes conversation drifts, okay?" I say. It's clear that he would never, ever be okay with me being in a relationship with Madden.

To be perfectly honest, I've never been all that close with my father. And the way I already feel about Madden in such a short period of time…well, the choice is pretty clear. If it comes down to some ultimatum, I'll do what I have to do to put my own happiness first.

And maybe spending less time with my father would lead me to a little more happiness. The kind of happiness I experienced in San Diego.

But I'm just starting to warm up to the idea of running VBC. If I choose Madden, or, rather, if I *don't* choose my father…then what the hell will my future even look like?

CHAPTER 31
MADDEN BRADLEY

My Girl

Over the next month, we see each other as much as we can—which is actually quite minimal since Dex thinks he lives with me now. On more than one occasion, I've rented a hotel room for the night so we could meet somewhere for a quick dinner and a long fuck before we each had to head home.

San Diego felt so much easier. We were away from all these stupid pressures and expectations and could focus on the two of us.

But it feels like she's not going anywhere, and neither am I.

Well, except for San Diego. My house is ready, and I need to get there, move in, and get ready for OTAs, which start next week already.

It's two weeks of team activities, and since I'm new to the team, I need to be there. Clay's going, too, along with Spencer, DJ, Trey, and Zach. It'll be a chance for the six of us to bond. Together we'll start learning plays, and I'll focus on getting to know my new playbook, working out, and figuring out my place with my new team.

I'm hopeful I'll be a starter. I have been my entire career, and I don't see that slowing down now. But Chicago didn't exactly have a winning record, and they made changes from the top down. One of those changes included trading me.

It's the night before I'm leaving. The place I rented comes furnished, and I ordered anything else I thought I'd need to arrive the day after tomorrow. I'll get set up over the weekend, and that'll be it. Home sweet home.

And rather than spend tonight at my place with my brother, I got a hotel for my girl and me.

Yeah, *my girl*.

Over the last month, that's how I've started referring to her in my mind.

She *is* my girl. I'm not seeing anyone else, and neither is she. We're in this, and tonight, I plan to tell her that I want to make it work even when we're apart.

I want her to see if she can work out of her LA office more often so we're in closer proximity. I want to reclaim the magic we had for that one perfect weekend in San Diego.

I want to give this a real try with her away from the spotlight of my family here in Chicago.

I'm going to ask her to move in with me...sort of. To stay with me when she comes to town. To see if there's a future here.

I'm nervous. We've seen each other as much as we can over the last few weeks, but we've really only known each other a couple of months at this point. Still, I don't see another option than this since we're running short on time.

I realize how lucky I am to play professional sports, but that doesn't mean life's perfect. Sometimes I wish I had the capability to work a normal job where I'm not committed day and night for half a year.

Sometimes I wonder where I'd be now if I'd just started working for Bradley Group fresh out of college. Would I be married? Would I have kids? Are these even things I *want* for my future?

I'm not sure. I guess I've never been sure since my post-playing career was already mapped out for me. I figured someone would make those choices for me, too.

Only now I'm thirty-five and still don't have any of the answers. It's all a little fucked.

Not one of the seven of us Bradley siblings went to work for the company. We've all worked in different capacities over the years, but none of us were chomping at the bit to make this a career. It was a nice way to earn some extra cash in the summers or even in the offseason before big contracts came along. But my brothers all committed to sports, and my two sisters never really wanted anything to do with the company.

I've only been at the hotel a few minutes when I hear a knock at the door. I open it and find Kennedy standing in front of me. She's worrying her bottom lip between her teeth, and I immediately haul her into my arms. I hate that she feels any sort of anxiety, no matter the case. But I feel like it has something to do with me.

I feel like it has something to do with the fact that I won't be here in Chicago by this time tomorrow.

Things are about to change no matter how we look at it, and whatever this is will either thrive or not survive.

The door clicks shut behind her once she's in my arms, and I press my lips to the top of her head while I hold her.

"You okay?" I ask.

"Not really," she mumbles into my chest.

"Talk to me."

"Total honesty, I'm scared I'm here tonight so you can end this when it feels like it's just getting good," she says.

I squeeze her more tightly against me for a beat before I pull back and meet her eyes with mine. "Let me assure you that's not my intention tonight."

"Then what is?"

I guess it's time to ask, but I'm not ready. I draw in a deep breath and do it anyway. "I love you, Kennedy. I want a future with you, and I know it's early for us, but I want you to stay with me when you're in San Diego. I want you to spend more time there. I want to be able to see you, to continue getting to know you, to fall harder for you."

"I love you, too," she whispers, and my mouth crashes to hers before she can say more words.

I want to show her with my body how deeply I've fallen for her, but I also don't want tonight to just be about sex. I don't want it to feel like a goodbye since she came here with the anxiety that a goodbye was exactly what this was going to be.

But then her hand comes down to cup my cock over my jeans, and whatever coherent thoughts I just had about tonight not being about sex fly right out of my head.

My hand wanders up toward her chest, where I massage one of her tits over her shirt. She moans, and my cock stiffens at the hot sound.

I shove my hips toward her palm as I continue to kiss her, and she groans as she feels me getting harder and harder for her.

I pull back and study her for a second before I say, "Tell me what you want."

"You, Madden. I want you."

"Tell me what you want me to do," I urge.

She seems shy for a second, but then her words are fucking fire. "I want you to fuck me so hard that I'm sore for a week and think of you every time I sit."

Jesus.

She adds more. "And I want you to suck on my tits so hard that you leave bruises behind."

Fuck.

"Take off your clothes and lie on the bed," I demand.

I watch as she takes a step back. She starts by kicking off her shoes. She pulls her shirt over her head and lets it flutter to the floor. She drops her jeans and then her underwear, and she strides confidently over to the bed, where she lies on her back and waits for me.

She takes direction well, and it's hot as hell.

I pull my wallet out of my back pocket and grab the condom I slipped in there earlier. I stare at her naked form on my bed for a few seconds as I debate where to start. She wants me to fuck her so hard she can feel it, and I briefly think about taking her ass. I haven't had the pleasure just yet.

But I need to prep her body for that. So instead of fucking her there, I think I'll start the prep tonight. First, though, I need to taste that cunt.

"Bend your knees and part your legs," I say.

She follows the direction, and I stare at her sweet, glistening pussy. She's already wet for me. I can see it from here.

And fuck, that's hot.

I take a few steps over toward her.

"Wait a minute," she says. "I want you naked, too."

As much as I want her to come over here and unwrap me if she's the one who wants me naked, I don't want her to move a muscle. I want to stare at her pink flesh a little longer.

So I slowly undress, dropping my clothes on the floor even though my instinct is telling me to pick up my clothes and set them over a chair. It's fine. I'll get them later.

I move slowly toward her, and I settle onto the bed between her legs. I bend down, and I realize this is my favorite place in the world. Right here between her legs.

I suck her clit between my lips, and her hips jerk. I'm a quick study who already learned what she likes, and I do everything I can to give it to her.

I slip my tongue inside her, and she moans as she gyrates her hips to the rhythm of my tongue.

I drag some of the moisture down and push a finger into her ass.

Her entire body bucks up, and she lets out a feral moan that I'll hear in my dreams tonight.

I pump my finger in and out and lick my way through her pussy until she falls apart. I feel her body start to clench beneath me, and I know her orgasm is coming, so I push a finger into her pussy at the same time. I'm filling both holes and sucking on her clit when the intense pleasure takes her body into another realm.

She comes harder than she ever has with me, and as her legs clamp around my ears and her fingers tug on my hair and her body explodes into a contorting, spiraling mass of pleasure, I like to think she's coming harder than she ever has with anybody.

And I can't wait to be the man who makes that happen again and again.

CHAPTER 32

KENNEDY VAN BUREN

Falling Directly Onto My Lap

I didn't come here tonight with high expectations. I thought for sure he was going to let me down gently, that he was going to tell me that while it's been fun, he's got a football season he needs to start thinking about. I was bracing myself for him to say something along the lines of how it's better to cut our losses while it's early days before we fall in too hard.

But I guess we're there. We've both fallen in pretty damn hard.

And speaking of pretty damn hard, he let me bask in the afterglow of my first orgasm for a few glorious minutes before he pushed into me and granted my wish for him to rail me so hard I'd be thinking of him for the next week.

The truth is that I would've been doing that either way, but this way I'll have that deliciously sore ache.

My father's confrontation when I got back from California apparently had little effect on me. I'm not ready to give up what the two of us have started, least of all for someone who makes demands of my life, my time, and my future when I'm not even close to him.

My mother's oblivious to everything, worrying instead about ridiculous things like gold facials and laser skin resurfacing, while my father continues to run VBC as he hands more and more responsibilities over to me. I continue to prove myself, and the more involved I become, the more I wish I would've started here out of college instead of asserting the independence I wound up giving up anyway. I might not have the same pressures on top of me if I would've just taken this position years ago.

Or I might have even more pressure. Who knows? I can't change the past, so all I can really do is figure out how to navigate my current reality instead.

After the best sex of my life, we have dinner together at the small table by the window in our hotel room, and then he has to go.

"What time is your flight tomorrow morning?" I ask after I set my napkin on top of my plate.

"Seven." He twists his lips, and I wish I could take that sadness away, but it's hard since I feel it, too.

"Safe travels," I say.

He presses his lips together. "When will I see you again?"

"I'm not sure. I've been looking into some projects in California that'll allow me to travel there more often as an excuse, but after my dad confronted me about that photograph of us leaving your hotel together, I have a feeling he'll start to get suspicious. I keep thinking maybe we should just come clean."

He shakes his head. "Would it be easier to come clean? Absolutely. But with SCS splitting the work between us, it becomes a conflict of interest if we're together. We can't have stakeholders wondering whether we're making decisions based on what's best for the project or what's best for ourselves. And on top of that, if other developers figure out we're together, they may assume we're collaborating, and we could be seen as a threat to fair competition. Not to mention the threat of internal gossip with all the nepotism shit."

I twist my lips. They're all very good, very valid points. But it also tosses another concern into the conversation. "So does that mean we just... *never* get to go public with this?"

He lifts a shoulder. "I don't know, Ken," he says, and it's the first time he's ever abbreviated my name. It's a whisper, and it's sort of sexy coming out of his mouth when I've never really cared much for the nickname that's a male name. "It feels like things will fall into place at the right time just like they're supposed to."

I wish I shared that same sentiment, but as we say our goodbyes and I head toward the door, a feeling of dread pervades. It feels like this is the beginning of the end, but at the same time, it's almost like we never really got a chance to get started.

He kisses me goodbye, and it's deep and intimate as he holds me close and pushes his feelings into this simple connection.

It should give me a sense of relief. He's in this. He told me so. He wants me to basically live with him when I'm in California.

But he's going to San Diego, and I'm staying here. We have no real plans for what comes next.

And that's scary as hell given how deep my feelings already run for him.

I head home, have a good cry with Clem for a bit, and then I pull myself together. I open my laptop and start researching development opportunities in California. I reach out to Oliver, the head of the LA office, with some different ideas I generate in my simple search, and I hope I found something he hasn't already been working on—something I can show my father from Oliver that says how he'd love for me to come help with a new opportunity.

And then I wait for a reply.

I don't get a reply from Oliver, but I do wake up to a text from my father.

Walter Van Buren: *Come to my office when you get in.*

MAD RIVALS

Yes, I have my dad in my phone by his name. Not by *Dad*. Not by *Father* or *Pops* or *Daddy*. By *Walter*.

It feels an awful lot like I'm getting called into the principal's office, and I don't like that sense of dread that accompanies it. I already had dread inside at the fact that Madden is currently on an airplane flying far away from me, but this just couples on top of all that.

Clem and I haven't been carpooling since we leave the office at different times, but we do meet in the kitchen for breakfast each morning.

"What's on today's agenda?" she asks when she walks in. She grabs the box of Cheerios from the pantry and helps herself to a bowl while I pick at my yogurt and berries.

"My dad wants to see me in his office when I get in," I mutter.

"And you're feeling a certain way about that?"

"No," I say, and I glance around the kitchen and lower my voice just in case my mom's somewhere around, but it's Friday morning, which is facial time, so I think I'm safe. "I'm feeling a certain way about Madden leaving."

"That explains the crankiness," she says lightly. She's teasing, but I'm too cranky to give it a pass. Instead, she gets a glare.

"And you're awfully chipper."

"It's Friday, but…" She glances around, too, and lowers her voice as well. "I finally broke Lance in. He asked me out via text last night, and we're grabbing drinks after work tonight."

She's blushing and giddy, and I do my best to meet her with the enthusiasm she deserves.

"Oh my God, Clem! That's amazing!"

"Thank you."

I narrow my eyes at her. "So *that* is why you're looking extra cute today."

She wrinkles her nose. "Cute? All this effort and I just get a *cute*?"

"You look fab, babe. Sexy, hot, fuck-a-licious. All the best things. He's a lucky guy."

"It felt forced, but I'll take it." She shoves a spoonful of her cereal into her mouth. "Are you doing okay with all of this?"

"I don't have a choice. Time marches on, and he'll be back in nine months or so. Maybe we can resume then." I shrug half-heartedly.

"Or maybe you're writing the end when it's really just the start of a new chapter."

"A hard chapter," I mutter.

"Maybe. Probably. But the best things in life don't come easy, so stop sulking and start fighting."

I sit with those words and wonder whether she's right. I'm not giving up. It's just the first morning he's gone, and truthfully, it hasn't affected us yet. I wouldn't have seen him this morning anyway. It just feels different, and I need a minute to get over that.

I'll get there.

I'm allowed to be cranky. I'm allowed to miss him. I'm allowed to want to fly to San Diego tonight to see him.

I blow out a breath, finish my yogurt, give Clem a hug, and head into the office.

I walk straight toward my dad's office when I arrive, and he glances up when he hears my light knock on the doorframe.

He raises his brows. "Shut the door."

Fuck. I feel like I'm in trouble. Like I'm twelve all over again and he's yelling at me for stealing eyeshadow from Target when it was Lynne Morris who did it. Like I'm fifteen all over again and he's yelling at me for sneaking vodka from the liquor cabinet.

Okay, fine. That one was me.

I'm not sure what I'm being scolded for this time, though—unless he knows about Madden and me.

I slip into the chair across from him, and he fixes a glare on me. Or he's studying me. It's hard to tell the difference.

"I got an interesting email from Oliver out of the Aliso Viejo office."

I raise my brows and play dumb. "Oh?"

He nods. "He said he has several ideas for new projects in the area, but he's already overbooked. He said he'd like to hire a new developer. He has several bid walks lined up in the coming months, and I thought it over and came up with you. Not as a new employee, but as someone already versed in bids and bid walks. You won half the work from SCS as we worked together, and since that's the main project you're heading up here, I can afford to have you commuting between here and LA if that's something you'd be interested in."

Is he kidding me right now?

Is this seriously falling directly onto my lap as if my prayers are being answered?

I just went from not being sure when the hell I'd see Madden again to being offered the chance to work out of the office a mere hour away from him.

The light that fills me from the inside is surely shining brightly in my expression, but I'm careful to school it so my father doesn't catch it and figure out why I'm so eager to get to the LA office.

"I have several other projects here, too," I say, trying my best to sound defensive but already knowing what he'll say. "I'm not sure I could afford the travel commitments."

"I've considered that, and I think Sara could likely take on your additional projects here. I don't want you to give up SCS, but we're on permitting now anyway, so it'll be a bit before you have more to do there. You could probably get away with spending the next week or so in LA if it's something you'd be interested in."

I twist my lips as I pretend to think it over. "What about accommodations?"

"I don't love the idea of you living out of a hotel, but Oliver has some resources for home rentals if it comes to that. My initial thought was getting you a hotel at first, allowing you to get your feet under you, and then you can decide how much time you think you'll need. We could rent a place for a month or for the year, and then you'll have a home base for when you're going back and forth. VBC would pick up the cost, obviously."

I refrain from mentioning that I in fact already have accommodations in town. Instead, I say, "That's fine. Let's start with a hotel and go from there."

"So you'll do it?" he asks.

Fuck yeah I'll do it. I think about adding Clem to my list of demands, but she's happy here.

I don't know how happy she'll be staying with my parents while I'm not there, but she's going on a date with Lance tonight, and I'll be commuting back and forth anyway.

We'll still see each other plenty.

Instead of saying any of that, I say, "If it's what you need me to do, then that's what I'll do."

He tilts his head as he studies me, and then he nods. "Fine. I'll need you to work out details today for what your schedule will look like based on your SCS timelines, and I'll need you in California by Tuesday."

Hell, I can be there tonight if that's what he wants. I nod. "I'll get started on it now." I move to stand, but his voice stills me.

"One more thing, Kennedy."

I glance up at my father.

"The Bradley boy," he says, and my heart stutters in my chest. "Stay away from him. He's nothing but trouble."

I press my lips together and nod. I can't find it in me to reply with words because I don't want to tell a lie.

But the very last thing I plan to do is stay away from the Bradley boy.

CHAPTER 33

KENNEDY VAN BUREN

The Best Luck

I work my ass off all morning to come up with some sort of travel schedule that might work around SCS, but the fact that the person I'll need to touch base with the most on the project will essentially be my roommate makes things a bit easier.

I text Clem before lunchtime.

Me: *I've got big news. Can you do lunch?*

Clem: *If I couldn't, I'd cancel just to hear your big news.*

My heart warms. She really is the best friend.

We make a plan to meet at twelve, and we head down to our favorite sandwich shop. After we order and we find a table, she finally asks, "When are you planning to spill this news, VB?"

I laugh. "My dad wants me spending more time in the LA office."

Her jaw drops. "So you'll be an hour away from the pro football star who just moved there?"

"Forty minutes with light traffic," I correct, and she grins. "But since he basically told me I'm staying with him when I'm in town, it'll be inches."

"You really have the best luck out of anyone I know, you know that? First the hot football star bumps into you at Starbucks, and now you'll be taking his inches in as his roommate."

My cheeks flush, but I laugh. "All nine of them."

"Nine? Jeez Louise, Kenny. That's…"

"Big," I say dreamily.

She giggles, and I hear my name at the counter, so I head over to grab our food.

"Will you be okay staying at Casa de Van Buren without me there full time?" I ask.

"It'll be weird, I think. I've been banking up my paychecks for the last couple months, and with a steady paycheck not dependent on commission, I think I can finally afford a place to stay that isn't in the bad part of town." She reaches over and squeezes my arm. "And I have you to thank for that, by the way."

"I'm glad we made the change when we did. Honestly it feels like that's when our luck started turning around. Things just feel like they're falling into place, don't they?"

She nods. "To be perfectly honest, I already felt like I was overstaying my welcome with your folks. I've been putting out feelers, and Lainie in the marketing department is actually looking for a roommate. Her current one is getting married and moving out soon, so it's perfect timing."

"You've been putting out feelers?" I ask. "What about our pact?"

She purses her lips. "You're breaking it first."

"I'm sorry," I say, and a little bit of sadness pulses in my chest at the end of this era.

She shakes her head. "Don't be. It's not going to change our friendship. We just won't be living together anymore."

I hope she's right. It'll be strange not being together after all the years we have been, but truthfully our work schedules, Madden, and the fact that she's dating Lance now tell me that things were starting to change anyway.

"Love you," I say.

"Right back at you." She smiles, and then we both attack our sandwiches.

When I get back to the office, I email my dad a draft of my travel schedule, and then I dig into work on SCS. I chat with Sara about some of the projects I'm handing off to her, and when I get back to my desk, I see a reply from my father.

This looks good. Send it to Darla for booking.

I can book my own travel, but he never really thinks about that since Darla does everything for him. He assumes Darla does everything for everybody, I guess.

And so I let her book my flight to LAX, which heads out Sunday evening, and my hotel near Aliso Viejo. I'll stay for the week and return next Thursday night.

I hate to waste the company's money, and furthermore, I hate to fly into LAX when the San Diego airport is much closer to Madden's place.

But for now, these are the prices I have to pay in order to keep my relationship with Madden a secret. I just hope it'll all turn out to be worth the effort in the end.

I wait until I'm in my car on the way home to call Madden.

"Hey, babe," he answers, and I'm smiling just at the sound of his voice.

"Hey," I say. "How's California?"

"Lonely without you here."

My chest warms. "I have some good news, then."

"Oh?"

"My dad wants me to take on a bigger role in the LA office. Oliver runs that location, and I reached out with some ideas. He told my dad he needs help, so my dad asked me if I could give up all my projects except SCS here and commute back and forth."

"Are you serious?" he asks. It was the same reaction I had in my own head when my father first presented the idea to me.

"I am. He said the LA office had some new ideas and wanted to hire a new employee, but he basically offered me up instead so they don't have to worry about the training curve."

"Holy shit. That's incredible, Ken." His voice is warm, and I can hear the excitement in it—a relief to the insecurities that made their way into my brain. "When do you get here?"

I don't know why I was worried. Whatever this is, it's genuine. It's more than just sex, though the sex is incredible. He might've fallen first, but I'm right there with him. "Sunday night."

"I wish it was tonight instead," he says.

"So do I," I admit. I was trying not to make anyone suspicious, which is why I waited until Sunday. I don't see why my father would have any knowledge of Madden's schedule when it comes to football and moving to San Diego, but we can't be too careful.

Especially since we really won't *need* to be careful when we're two thousand miles away from home. Or at least not *as* careful.

We're taking risks, for sure. Both here at home and in California. We've already listed all the reasons why it's not smart for us to be together publicly.

But that doesn't seem to be stopping us privately.

CHAPTER 34
MADDEN BRADLEY

Guilting Me

I roll onto my side, bliss freely floating through every part of me. I'm exhausted after an intense workout with Clay this morning followed by two rounds of the best sex of my life with the lady by my side.

She's here. I'm here. We're together. And I'm trying to live in that knowledge rather than focusing ahead. It's not like me, and I don't think it's much like her, either. We're a couple of Type-A people who usually know our plans for the next month down to the minute.

But from what I've heard, love throws all of that out of proportion. And from what I've experienced so far...she's fully worth it. Whatever *this* is between us, it's fully worth it.

I just don't know how we take things to the next level. I don't know how we move beyond this part. I'm not sure either of us are ready for that anyhow, but the thought is there, pressing into me as I think about how this is going to get harder before it gets easier. The thrill of secrecy is wearing thin, and part of me is ready to shout to the world that she's mine. The other part of me knows we can't.

In the morning, I make us breakfast, and she heads out for the morning commute up to Aliso Viejo with her romance audiobook set to entertain her while she drives. I send her with a key to my place just in case she gets home before me.

I hate saying goodbye, but I'm also heading into the office this morning. My father told me John had some opportunities he wanted to discuss, or rather, my father demanded that because I'm already out here and not yet playing football, I had the time to head in to be his representative.

As if I have nothing else going on.

And he told me not to disappoint him.

Despite my reservations, like a good boy, I head in. It's not like I *hate* the development game, and honestly, working with Kennedy, who has a similar feeling about taking over her own family business, has been a bit of a game-changer for me. I'm starting to see the benefits of having this business to fill my hours when I'm done playing, and as we turn toward the start of another season, it's feeling more and more like it'll be my last.

I haven't admitted that out loud yet. Not to anyone—not to Dex, my pseudo-offseason roommate while he continues to lay low in Chicago, and not to Kennedy, who might benefit the most from knowing that. It feels like bad luck to talk about it now, and I don't want anything getting out before I'm ready for it to get out. So it'll stay in the recesses of my mind. For now. Like a lot of things lately, really.

I head into the office, and John is ready with a presentation for me.

"I heard from some inside sources that Newman Winery in Temecula is looking to expand with tourism amenities and a possible luxury rebrand," he begins, and he takes me through more details before he finishes. "The winery is owned by Grace Nash, wife of Spencer Nash. I think we have a good chance of landing this project if you can get your new teammate on board."

I've gotten friendly with Spencer over the last few months since the trade deal went through. We play the same position, and we've worked out a few times together when I've been in town.

Maybe it's time to get even friendlier so I can seal this deal. It'll make my dad proud, and who the hell wouldn't want to work on a project like this? We could propose anything from a luxury hotel to a boutique resort, event spaces, or even venues for festivals or concerts. The winery itself is situated on seventy-five acres of land, and the Newman family just put in a bid to buy more fields nearby to expand. There are endless possibilities for that land, and my mind is already in overdrive dreaming it all up.

"What's their timeline?" I ask.

"This isn't public yet, just a tip I heard from an insider, so I'm not sure yet. But I was thinking that you could talk with Spencer and find out more, if that's something you're comfortable with."

Aha. So that's why my dad sent me here this morning. It had nothing to do with me having the time to stand in for him or not disappointing him and everything to do with guilting me into getting my teammate to choose Bradley Group for this project.

"I have OTAs starting Wednesday of this week," I say. "I'll see what I can do."

"Let's discuss what we want the bid to look like first," he suggests, and we spend the rest of the morning brainstorming what types of things we'd be able to include in the expansion. He has additional projects to tackle, so after lunch I spend some time drafting up a bid with our best ideas on it. It's not done by dinnertime, but I want to get home to Kennedy.

After all, we only have tonight and tomorrow, and then OTAs start. It's the first time this season the practice facility will be open to players, and I'm ready to get on the field and start learning the dynamics of this team.

It's only four hours of practice on Wednesday and Thursday, but I'll meet with the other wide receivers for film analysis and additional workouts before I head home. And then Kennedy has to head out Thursday, which feels far too fast.

I want her here all the time, not just Sunday through Thursday.

I have plenty to keep my hours occupied, especially now that offers are starting to come in for different types of engagements. I'm getting paid offers for corporate events, youth camps, charity events, media interviews, meet-and-greets, influencer partnerships, community events, sponsorships, and, of course, the bar and nightclub scene. If I so desired, I could have something booked every night of the week—and I do, in fact, have several nights booked out with Clay.

Maybe I should book a few with Spencer, too—see if I can get to know him a little more off the field.

As it turns out, Kennedy is already home when I get there, and I've never really done this thing before where the woman is home waiting for me to arrive.

She greets me with a kiss, and it's both strange and wonderful. It feels like something I could get used to. It feels like *home* even here in this city that's new and strange to me.

"I thought about making dinner, but I wasn't sure when you'd be home," she says, and I hold her close a few extra beats.

"Let's just order in," I murmur.

"Before or after?" she asks.

I pull back a little and tilt my head, my brows drawn together. "Before or after what?"

"The sex."

I laugh. "After. Definitely after."

We make good on that pact, and when we're finally eating an hour later, I ask her how her day was.

"It went really well, actually. Oliver had several projects he needed to hand off, and I'm really excited about one of them."

"Want to talk about it?"

She twists her lips. "It's sort of on the down low for now, so I really shouldn't."

Oh. "Right."

San Diego was supposed to be our safe space.

We're competitors in different markets that still share overlap, so I guess I get it.

Still, though. It feels like one more thing that has the ability to divide us when we're just coming together.

Our time together feels fleeting as I make my way to OTAs on Wednesday morning.

The team meets first in a lecture room, where the room buzzes with excitement as teammates new and old greet each other. I'm sitting between Clay and Spencer when our coaching staff walks out onto the stage to greet us.

The head coach introduces players new to the team, including myself, and then we break up into smaller groups by position. Coach Clark, the wide receiver's coach, goes over a few different plays with us, and then we head out to the field to practice.

The second I step foot onto the grass again, it feels like home. It's not Chicago. It's not where I've played and practiced and lived for my entire career.

But it's a field, and field means home.

I feel like I'm living two lives, like my personality is split in two. There's the businessman my father wants me to be, the one I guess I'm even sort of training to be once my football career is over. And then there's this…the athlete who always feels at peace on the field.

I don't know which side of me is going to win in the end, but as I make a catch, pull the ball in tight, and race toward the end zone, today it feels like this is where I'm meant to be.

CHAPTER 35
KENNEDY VAN BUREN

Felt Like Forever

The last two weeks have been a total whirlwind as I commute between Chicago and California. The schedule is already pressing on me, and I'm not sure I really *need* to be working in the Chicago office as much as LA needs me.

And that's what I tell my dad on a Friday morning when I'm back from another blissful few days with Madden.

"I could fly home when I'm needed for SCS and otherwise work out of the Aliso Viejo office," I say. "But after only two weeks, I already know I can't do this long-term. Four hours on a plane plus a time change is killing me."

My father clears his throat as he stares at me. "You look exhausted."

"Thanks," I mutter, but it's true. My flight got in late, and by the time I waited for my luggage and drove home, it was well after midnight. Now I'm back at the office bright and early at eight, but the jet lag is real and definitely pulling me down.

And, you know, the extracurricular activities, I suppose. Madden and I shared a few late nights, and I plan to use the weekend to catch up on sleep. But my dad doesn't need to know that.

In fact, he can't know that.

"Is this what you want? Or would you rather stay here?" he asks. "Answer that honestly."

"Yes, it's what I want." I wish I could be even more honest than I am when I give him my answer, like *why* it's what I want. "Oliver has several projects that feel really exciting to me, projects I want to work on and be a part of."

"That's the kind of enthusiasm I've always wanted from you, Kennedy. I'll have Darla put together some housing options so you don't have to live out of a hotel, and we'll go from there. We'll get you a hotel until you have a chance to look at them. I don't want you to go, and I'll still need you coming back here when SCS calls for it, but you don't need to be going back and forth weekly."

"Thanks, Dad," I say.

I head to my office, and instead of working on anything I have going on here, I continue working on one of the California projects—the one I'm most excited about.

I actually end up spending the entire weekend working on it so I can present it to Oliver on Monday morning, and I return to Los Angeles on Sunday night with excitement for the project but even more excitement to see Madden.

I have a couple of places to look at this week thanks to Darla setting up appointments for me, but it doesn't really matter where I live. I picked out a few I liked in San Clemente since it's only twenty minutes from the office and under a half hour to Madden's place. Maybe we can even stay at my place sometimes this way.

I invited Madden to my hotel room tonight so I can actually get some use out of the room my dad's paying for, and with any luck, I'll find a place to live while I'm here this week, and I won't have to worry about actually showing up at the hotels and having to check in just in case my dad's keeping tabs on me.

My dad told me he arranged a car for me, so I look for someone holding a sign with my name on it. I find it, and rather than telling me he'll help me claim my luggage, he presses a set of car keys into my palm.

My brows crash together as I look up at the man in confusion. "Your father bought you a car to use when you're in town. I'm happy to take you to it once we get your luggage."

Well he's certainly full of surprises.

The man leads me out to a silver Volvo SUV, and he puts my luggage in the trunk. "Anything else I can help with?" he asks, and I shake my head.

"Thank you for everything," I murmur as I get into the driver's seat of my new car.

I navigate to my hotel in the lighter Sunday evening traffic, and I use the digital room key on my phone to get into my room.

It's the same key I shared with Madden earlier, and he's already in the room waiting for me when I walk in.

He drops his phone on the desk where he's sitting and darts out of the chair. He strides over toward me and pulls me into his arms. His lips drop to mine. "How has it only been three days since I last saw you?" he asks, resting his forehead against mine before kissing me again.

I pull back. "I missed you."

"Felt like forever," he says, and he kisses me some more. The urgency is there, and I'm desperate for him. I've never been like this with anybody before in my life. I've enjoyed sex, I guess, but with him, it's like I'll never get enough. But it's more than just that. We've got this deeper connection between us, these similarities that help us relate on multiple levels.

I'm addicted to him. Clem will always be my best friend, but he's quickly becoming someone I can trust and rely on…he's becoming the person I want to talk to first when the day begins and last before I go to bed.

"Take off all your clothes and lay on your stomach," he demands, and he doesn't have to tell me twice. I leave my suitcase where it is, and I strip naked in about three seconds flat.

He chuckles but seems to take his time getting to me. Eventually I feel the bed dip, and his legs move on either side of me as he straddles my ass. He's stripped down to his boxers, I think—at least as far as I can tell.

And then I feel a warm liquid as he pours something onto my back. A minute later, he's giving me the greatest massage of my life. His hands work the muscles in my back, muscles that haven't been getting the workout they need lately as exercise has fallen off the priority list given my current travel and work situation.

I moan at the feel of his hands as he digs into the muscles near my shoulder blades, and I nearly cry out as he works my lower back. Airplane seats aren't great for much more than stiff backs, to be honest.

I'm nearly asleep when I feel his hands on my ass. He kneads the muscles there, too, and down my legs. He massages my thighs and my calves, and then he works my feet. I'm more relaxed than I've been in weeks as he seems to know exactly what to do to fix my tired body.

The sensations stop, and I find myself in a strange state that lands me somewhere between totally horny due to the feel of his hands all over my body and totally sleepy.

But when his voice sounds low and deep next to my ear, I'm suddenly wide awake again as the horniness takes over. "Spread your legs so I can fuck that sweet pussy."

My God, this man has a way with words. And his hands. And his dick.

I don't flip over but spread my legs as directed, and he gently lifts my thighs to set a pillow under them to give him the right angle to fuck me this way.

I feel his fingers first, and he slides them down right into my waiting, greedy pussy.

He hisses when he feels how wet I am, and I cry out at the feel of his fingers inside me.

He pulls his fingers out of me and slides them down to my clit, and my hips buck before he moves back inside me.

And then he moves his wet fingers out of my pussy and slides them up toward my ass. He slips a finger in there at the same time that he takes his other hand and slips a finger into my pussy. The full feeling is absolute bliss as he starts to work both zones simultaneously. I push back to meet each of his fingers thrust for thrust, and the sudden desire for him to fuck me in the ass washes over me.

I've never wanted that before. In fact, I've been terrified of it. But Madden knows what he's doing, and I trust that he'll do everything he can to take care of me.

"I want you to fuck my ass," I murmur into the pillow.

"Are you sure?" he asks softly, and he slips a second finger into my ass.

"Oh, God, yes," I moan.

Everything stops as I feel him move off the bed, and I feel the bed dip again when he returns a moment later.

"Condom or no?" he asks.

"No," I cry.

"Fuck," he hisses. I hear the sound of a bottle squirting, and he pushes a cool liquid into my ass with his fingers a second later. He squirts some more, and I open my eyes and turn to look at what he's doing.

He's stroking his own cock with the lube, and the look of absolute pleasure on his face as his neck is corded and he faces the ceiling will forever be burned into my memory.

He leans forward when he catches me looking, and he presses his lips to mine. He opens his mouth, and his tongue tangles with mine even from this strange angle. And then he pulls up, moves over me, and says, "Relax. I'll go slow. If you need me to stop, just say 'stop.'"

I'm already relaxed thanks to the massage, so I nod into the pillow as I face down. I force my body to relax as much as I can, and then I feel the tip of his dick poking at a virgin territory.

He pushes in, and it's a little uncomfortable. It's bigger than his finger—even than two of his fingers—and I'm not used to his size yet.

Still, I don't want him to stop.

"Jesus, that's tight," he murmurs, and he inches his way in a little more. "Fuck, Kennedy, your ass feels so goddamn good." He inches in a little more, and it's some mix of a burning, painful sensation with this flicker of pleasure. "You okay?" he asks gently.

"Yes!" I cry-moan. "It hurts and feels good. Keep going."

"Up on your knees," he says, and he pulls at my hips to help me into position. And then he reaches around me to brush my clit with his fingertips.

I moan as he starts to rub my clit in earnest, and I'm biting my bottom lip between my teeth as I reach to grab my nipple. I need some friction somewhere else, some other place to focus some pain, and I pinch myself hard between my finger and my thumb. It sends a shot of pleasure straight through me, and as I moan, he slips a finger into my pussy at the same time he slowly pulls his cock back a bit and then slowly rears it forward again.

Holy shit.

It's full, and it's wet, and it's fucking beautiful as I think I start to see stars. It's him bare inside me, fucking me in a place that's never been touched by another man before, and this is a new, shared, intimate and erotic experience for us. It's as if what we're doing is forbidden, and yet…it isn't. It's normal and natural and oh-so-fucking hot.

It draws my soul somehow closer to him as he works hard to pleasure me, picking up speed as he fingers my pussy and fucks my ass. He slips his fingers out to give some attention to my clit, and that's when I fall completely apart.

I scream out incoherently about the fact that I'm coming. I can't writhe the way I want to with his dick in my ass, but my knees give out. He follows me down as my body moves back into the position we started in, his arm basically crushed under my hip as he continues to stroke my clit even from an odd angle, and his cock continues to fill my ass.

"Oh, fuck, Ken. I'm coming, fuck! I'm coming so goddamn hard in your ass, baby. Oh, fuck," he groans.

It feels still more slippery as he finishes then pulls out of me, and I wince when he's fully out. He leans down and peppers kisses all over my back as his warm liquid starts to leak out of my ass, and he gently reaches down to massage his cum around the ring he was just inside. It's gentle and soft, tender in comparison to what we just did.

"Fuck, that's hot," he says. "I want to push my cum into your pussy. I want to fuck your pussy bare next," he practically snarls, his voice raspy and growly all at the same time. "I want to mark you as mine."

"I'm yours," I murmur from beneath him.

He leans down, his body warming me as he presses his lips to my cheek. "And I'm yours."

He moves off me, and I hear the bathtub running a moment later. He returns and gently turns me to pick me up into his arms as if I weigh nothing, and then he carries me over to the tub. He gently scrubs my shoulders, and the entire room smells like him and his gorgeous shower gel.

I'm spent. Totally wasted. I can't even lift an arm to help him, and he's taking care of me in a way that tells me I don't need to worry about it.

And that's what this is. That's what tonight showed me. It was more than just giving him a part of me I've never given anyone.

It's building our trust further, falling deeper, connecting on a new level.

And now that I've leveled up to here, there's no turning back.

CHAPTER 36

MADDEN BRADLEY

A Little Research

We're at my place on Monday night after work the first week of June, both of us skirting around what we did at work today. I don't want to tell her about the project I've been spending all my time on, and I'm guessing she feels the same way since we're still competitors when it comes to business.

I don't have OTAs this week, but mandatory minicamp is next week. It's quite a bit more intense than the team activities, so I've been spending a lot of time at the gym with the other receivers in a bid to get myself ready for practice next week.

As for Kennedy, she came home late today from the office, and so as we finish up dinner, I ask, "What have you been working on?"

"No work talk at the dinner table," she chides, and I chuckle.

"Fine," I say, holding up both hands. "I get it. I've been working on a project that's not very well publicized, but it's one I'm excited about."

"Good. I am, too, actually, and I'm glad you're starting to enjoy what you're doing."

"I guess I spent so long pushing back against my father that I didn't take the time to see that I actually sort of enjoy all this. And with the tens of billions invested in Bradley Group, I guess I can think of a lot worse things to do after I retire from playing, you know?" I ask, and her brows furrow.

She tilts her head as she studies me. "You know, you've mentioned that before. Billions. That's a lot of money, Madden. I haven't taken a close look at our books, but I'm fairly certain we're not in the billions, let alone the tens of billions."

I've never really given it much thought. I haven't studied our books, either. But my father started this business from the ground up, and from what I know, he didn't come from a ton of money. His dad was a construction worker, so he grew up around buildings, and his mother stayed home to care for him.

The business he built focuses on luxury and large-scale projects. Billions are feasible, aren't they?

I think through our last few projects that I know of.

They were all million-dollar ventures. The SCS project is one of the biggest we'd ever bid on, and we were only awarded half the work. While my father's company has beat out VBC and others like them on several occasions, he doesn't *own* Chicago. There's still a market of competition there.

It's not something I've ever questioned, but suddenly I'm curious.

Curious enough that I want to do a little research. I have no idea what I'm looking for, so I wait.

She's tired after a long day at work, and she heads to bed early. I take the opportunity to slip into my office.

My father gave me access to all of our client portfolios, and as I open the first few alphabetically, I don't really know what I'm looking for. It all looks standard.

I sort in a different way instead, and I open one of the most recently updated files. It's SCS, and everything in there looks fine.

I look through a few more files that were updated today, and I'm still not finding anything out of the ordinary. But even so…none of these companies would contribute to the billions Kennedy was questioning.

Is she right?

I'm not sure, and I don't know where else to look.

I flip through a few more files, and then I decide to call it a night.

I guess I could just ask my father about it, but I don't even know what I'd say. *The girl I'm supposed to be getting info from for you but instead fell for is questioning how much we're worth.*

Yeah, probably not the best plan.

The next day after workouts, I spend a little time doing some more research. I have projects to attend to, but now that I've started, I can't let this go.

When I look at what I consider some of our top clients, there simply isn't enough cash flow to call this a billion-dollar company. And yet when I look at the bank statements…we are.

I decide to skirt around it with John just to see if he knows anything. I pop into his office a little before the end of the day.

"You ready for the bid on Newman?" he asks before I get the chance to move in with my question.

I nod. "Two more weeks. From what I've heard, they're keeping it very quiet, and they're only accepting three bids. I haven't heard who the other companies are just yet. Have you?"

He shakes his head. "No, not a word. They're keeping it all very hush-hush, which is probably to their advantage since if other developers knew about it, they'd have a million and one bids to sort through. They want to get moving quickly, and I hope that's reflected in your plan."

"I can send it to you if you'd like to look it over," I say since he's clearly indicating that he doesn't think I have my shit together.

"I trust you."

Yeah, right. On that note, I ask, "Who would you consider to be Bradley Group's biggest clients?"

His brows dip. "In California?"

I shrug. "Sure. Or overall."

He names off a few that I already checked, and I nod.

"Why do you ask?"

"Just thinking out loud. If we snag Newman, maybe they'll be our biggest."

His brows dip. "Maybe, but I'd think the project out in Oak Park is bigger."

"Yeah, you're probably right," I say. I glance at my watch. "I'm going to call it a day, but I'll see you tomorrow."

I head home and find that Kennedy isn't here quite yet, so I pull open the files and continue my search.

I keep hitting dead ends.

And that's why, when Kennedy does get home and she walks into my office, I don't immediately close down the file I'm looking at.

In fact, maybe she can even help me.

"Tell me I can trust you," I demand without so much as a *how was your day, dear?*

Her brows dip. "Of course. Always. With anything."

I narrow my eyes at her. "With Bradley Group's books?"

Her eyes widen a little, but she nods. "Yes, Madden. I swear, if there's something you need me to look at, it's between us. Always."

I have never put my trust into someone else like this, but even though it's only been twenty-four hours, I'm frustrated as fuck. I'm on a tight timeline to figure out what the hell my father is hiding, and I need help.

Preferably from someone who's familiar with this business the way Kennedy is.

I draw in a breath and plow forward before I lose my nerve. "I've been searching for two days now to try to figure out where the money is coming from, and you're right. Our top clients aren't generating billions for us. But our bottom line shows billions." I shrug. "I'm at a loss, and I don't know where else to look."

"Do you have access to the ledgers?" she asks.

I nod. "My father gave me full access this summer. I don't think he assumed I'd be looking into it, but I needed access for some other projects I was working on."

"See if you can search your income statements," she suggests. "You should be able to get a snapshot of large sums of money coming or going."

I open the file and click around, but spreadsheets and financials…they're not really my forte. Yes, I have a business degree, but I really only took two accounting classes, and I may or may not have been getting naked with the class's TA on the side to help me pass. "How?"

"How is your ledger organized? Can you search by transaction type?" she asks. She starts to move around my desk to take a look, but she freezes. "May I?"

I nod, and I slide my chair back so she can sit on my lap. She takes control of my mouse, and that's not a euphemism, as she starts to search the books. "This is the same software we use, so I'm sort of familiar with it. I'm not sure where to start, but I do know that typically these big companies don't pay actual cash, so if there are any fishy cash transactions, that might be a good place to start digging." She clicks around a bit, and then she finds a search bar and types in *cash*. She clicks a link to cash transactions, and then she sorts from largest to smallest.

And we both immediately see it.

Cash transactions labeled *warehouse expenses* and *consulting* in amounts well into the tens of millions of dollars populate the screen.

Every single one of them is attributed to one of the same three companies: Vivicorp Commercial Ventures, Peoria Property Group, and Geneva Holdings.

"That seems weird, doesn't it?" I ask.

She nods, and she pulls out her phone and opens her calendar. "These last few were all deposited on Monday mornings. Isn't that also a little strange?"

I reach around her to open a search on Vivicorp Commercial Ventures, the one that seems to come up the most. Nothing comes up on a simple search, so I head to a website where I can search businesses.

I drop the name in there, and I find the name of the director of the company.

Vivienne Bradley.

My mother.

My surprised eyes meet Kennedy's.

What the fuck?

CHAPTER 37
KENNEDY VAN BUREN

Warehouses

My brows dip together as I try to piece out what might be going on. Something illegal, that's for sure. And my brain chooses that moment for my father's words to come back and haunt me.

Back when we were in the running for the SCS project and found out that Bradley Group was one of our competitors, my father said that Thomas Bradley has the kind of connections you just don't fight against.

What kind of connections?

Did he mean *illegal* connections? *Dangerous* ones? What am I getting into by digging into this with Madden?

It's all very fishy, but I also need to handle this with extreme care. He trusted me by asking me to look at this with him, and I need to prove I'm a partner he can trust.

"What about the warehouse transactions?" I ask. "If all these cash transactions are related to warehouses or consulting, maybe we can figure out what's going on in that warehouse." It's the only lead we have to go on right now, but if his dad was doing something illegal in a warehouse—say, storing drugs or weapons or something—then he wouldn't run it through his real estate development business, right?

If he's trying to clean dirty money, he might.

"I don't want him to know that I'm onto him," Madden says quietly as I stand and walk around the desk to sit across from him. "But I want to find that warehouse and figure out what the hell he's doing."

"So let's go find it," I say. I'm not quite sure *why* I say it. I guess I assume he'll say that's a bad idea, or that he needs to do this alone, or any one of a plethora of other ideas that might keep me safe from whatever this could be. He doesn't say any of that, though.

Instead, he nods. "I have minicamp this week, but I can get out there as soon as Friday. Actually, I can be out there for the next month, really, after minicamp."

I press my lips together. "I need a reason to get out there. My father just approved me to be *here*."

"SCS. I'll call a meeting for a progress update early next week," he says.

"God, it's hot when you go into smart businessman mode. And athlete mode. All the time, really."

He laughs. "Allow me to show you just how smart I can be." He pats his lap, and I stand up from the chair I just occupied, walk back around the desk, and straddle his lap as he pulls me down for one of those intense, soul-shaking kisses of his.

Neither of us brings up our mission for the next week, but he's busy with minicamp, and he appreciates the full-body massages I give him when he gets home sore and aching as he complains about how he's getting "too goddamn old" for this.

It's starting to feel like a real, actual relationship. I'm taking care of him when he gets home from work, just like he took care of me when I was exhausted from flying back and forth to Chicago.

And speaking of flying, we head back to Chicago together on Friday night ahead of our meeting at SCS on Monday morning, and we land a little after nine.

Before we deplane, he glances over at me. "I know we're not supposed to be seen together or whatever, but I want to get started on finding this place. I have a list of four warehouses I was able to find that are all under Vivicorp's name, and I want to go look at them tonight. Let's go to my place and grab my car. Dex should be gone since he had minicamp this week, too, so if you want to stay with me tonight, we should have the place to ourselves."

I nod. "I didn't tell my parents I was coming in since I wasn't sure what the plan was. And I haven't mentioned anything to Clem, either, but she moved out of my parents' house last Monday, anyway."

We take a rideshare to his place, and we run upstairs to grab his car keys. Sure enough, the place is deserted with a note from Dex on the counter.

Thanks for letting me lay low. Back to Vegas for now. Good luck this season except when you play us. -D

He tosses the note in the trash and picks up two cups that Dex must've left out. He places them in the dishwasher, and I can't help my giggle at his meticulousness.

"I mean, he could leave the place like he found it," he jokes.

"Yeah, two cups. What a dick," I agree with a heavy dose of sarcasm.

"Hey, that's my brother you're talking about," he warns, but the twinkle in his eye gives him away.

We both laugh as we head to the elevator, and then we start our mission to figure out what the hell Thomas Bradley is hiding. Our first stop is over at Logan Square, which is about a twenty-minute drive from Madden's place. He picked the one furthest away to check first, and we're making our way back toward his place with each of the subsequent stops.

Traffic is heavy, which makes the drive closer to thirty minutes, and when we get to the address, the lights are all off and the place is quiet and dark.

It's a total dead end.

He tries all the doors, but they're all locked. It's a warehouse, and the windows are way up high—too high to allow us to try to see in.

Maybe this was a bad idea.

We run into the same issue at our second stop in Bucktown and our third stop in Wicker Park. They're just quiet, empty warehouses.

He twists his lips. "Should we bother with the one in the West Loop?" he asks.

"It's on the way back to your place, so why not?" I shrug, though we're both pretty convinced that it's going to be the final dead end.

Only…it's not.

There isn't a parking spot to be had on the street, but that's not unusual for the West Loop on a Friday night. We end up parking a few blocks away from the warehouse and walking to it.

But this one appears to have someone standing out front. He glances around before he opens the door and lets someone inside, and Madden and I exchange glances. When we get closer, though, it gets even stranger.

"Mick?" Madden asks. "What are you doing here?"

Mick glances at me before he answers. "Expecting a warehouse delivery," he says smoothly.

Like…*too* smoothly.

Something is weird here.

"On a Friday night?" Madden glances at the street. "In this traffic?"

Mick nods. "I don't make the schedule. I just follow it."

"What sorts of items do you store in this warehouse?" Madden presses.

Mick clears his throat. "This warehouse is mainly construction materials. We have the extra flooring from the Cannings project coming in this evening."

A man in a suit walks by us, and Mick's shrewd eyes follow him as he walks by.

I get the distinct feeling that Mick wants to get rid of us so he can talk to the man in the suit, but I'm not sure why I feel that way. More suits walk past us, though this is a popular area. But still…it all feels very, very weird.

The door is shut behind him, and I can't help my next question. "Who did you let in there a minute ago when we were walking down the block?"

His eyes move to me, and he doesn't look very amused that I'm here asking questions. "Who are you?"

"Excuse me?" I set my hand on my chest.

"She's with me," Madden says. "What's going on here, Mick?"

"I told you, sir," Mick says, never losing his cool. "Expecting a delivery."

"Can I see inside the warehouse?" Madden asks.

"Be my guest." He opens the door, and the warehouse is dark inside, which only fuels my question about who he let in here a minute ago. Why would it be dark if someone was in here? And furthermore, if he was expecting a delivery, why wouldn't he have gone in and turned on the lights? Why would a delivery be coming in this door off the main drag when surely for a warehouse there's an easier way to get pallets of flooring inside?

What the hell is going on?

We walk in, and he keeps the door open. He reaches in and flicks on a light, and maybe I'm being ridiculous. It really is just a warehouse with rows and rows and rows of…flooring.

Madden and I exchange another glance.

It feels like another dead end.

But something is going on here, and I have a feeling Madden isn't going to stop investigating until he gets some answers.

CHAPTER 38
MADDEN BRADLEY

How Do I Get In

I can't let it go.
    Mick was up to something on Friday, but I don't know what.

It's a ten-minute drive from my place, and I decide to head back on Saturday morning with Kennedy since she's spending the weekend with me.

In the daylight, everything looks…well, pretty much the same. It looks like a warehouse, minus Mick standing out front.

I want to get back in there. I'm not sure what made me leave so easily last night other than the fact that Mick said there was flooring in here, and that's pretty much all I saw as we walked the aisles and aisles filled with various tiles, hardwood, carpeting, padding, foam, and stone.

I didn't look for another door. I didn't look for something that could indicate a separate area. But the more I thought about it as I didn't sleep at all last night, the stranger it became.

All those people dressed up in suits and dresses who kept walking by while we spoke with Mick outside. A dressy couple waiting around the corner when we walked back to the car. None of it added up. There are enough fancy places around here, I suppose, but I got the distinct impression they were waiting for me to leave.

The door is locked, and there's no getting in.

But I decide to play a little game.

I text my father.

Me: *I'm at the warehouse in the West Loop. I have a carload of extra tiles I've been storing at my place. How do I get in to drop them off?*

Rather than text me back like a normal person, my phone rings a moment later.

"Hey," I answer.

"How do you know about the warehouse?" he demands. No *hey, son,* or other similar salutation.

"I ran into Mick last night when I was out in the West Loop," I lie. If he can hide things, so can I.

"Hm," he grunts.

"So…how do I get in to unload all these tiles?"

"I thought you were in San Diego."

"I was. I have an SCS meeting on Monday, so I'm back for a few days." And, you know, I was checking out the warehouses.

It's a solid enough excuse that he buys it.

"Mick is driving me to a meeting of my own this morning. We won't be by to let you in until this afternoon at the earliest. Take your tiles and clear out."

Take your tiles and clear out?

Nah. I'll come up with some other way to get in.

"I can wait," I say smoothly.

I walk near the door and find a scanner that looks to be a facial recognition system of some kind.

I give it a try, though I highly doubt I'm in the system since my dad appears to be trying to keep me out.

But that's the question.

Why would he be keeping me out?

If it's just a warehouse storing flooring as he said it is…why would he care if I went into it?

My father sighs on the other end of the line.

"Why don't you want me in there?" I ask quietly. I glance up and lock eyes with Kennedy, who looks like she's waiting on the edge of her seat for the answer.

So am I.

"Because we can't just accept whatever load you have, Madden. That's not how it works. We need someone there to take stock of what you have, inventory it, and put it in the right aisle."

I grit my teeth together. I guess that makes good enough sense. Still, it feels like there's some reason he's keeping me out, and I wish I would've approached this differently. Maybe if I would've told him I needed some flooring for a project, I could've gotten in that way.

Somehow I doubt it.

So how do I get access to this place?

The two of us load back into my car, and we head back to my place. The answer doesn't hit me until I get back home and start unloading the dishwasher, where I see all of the dishes my brother used while he was staying here.

"That's it!" I say, snapping my fingers.

Kennedy is at the kitchen table, and she looks confused at my outburst. "What's it?"

"Deepfake!" I feel like this could actually work, and that sentiment is clear in my enthusiasm.

"Huh?"

"My brother—when he was here, he said he got into some trouble. Some pictures were taken of him that made it look a certain way, but he said his publicist was going to try to cover it with a deepfake."

"A deepfake? What's that?" she asks.

"It's like an AI-generated photo or video. I have access to the security footage at Bradley Group, so we could find someone who can do this, give them different angles of my father's face, and access the facial recognition software that way."

She tilts her head as she considers the idea, but then she has a question I hadn't really considered. "What if you get caught?"

I twist my lips, but I realize the answer to that pretty quickly. "So what? If my father is doing something shady, and he's handing this company over to me within the next few years, don't I deserve to know what's going on?"

She nods. "Yeah, you do. I just don't want you to have to do something illegal to figure out what's going on."

"Truth be told, I don't know if it's illegal."

"Do you even know someone who could do something like that?" she asks.

I shake my head. "No. But my brother does."

It's pitting one family member against another. I realize this. I already know what my father would say about the family legacy. But Dex doesn't have to know what I need this for, and it's the pressure of that legacy leading me to do this in the first place.

I was already teetering on the edge of not wanting this company after retirement. Kennedy started to change my mind.

But I flat-out refuse to get tangled up in illegal activities because my father is hiding whatever he's doing and using the business as a cover-up.

And I'm already convinced that it all starts with whatever is in that warehouse.

"Then make the call," she says.

I don't waste another second. I dial Dex, and he answers right away.

"What's up, OG?" he answers.

He's always called me that since I'm the *original* son, and it stuck.

"Hey, Dex. I need a favor."

"Anything for the bro who let me lay low in Chicago for a month."

"When you said it'd be a week," I say, rolling my eyes even though he can't see me.

"Yeah, yeah. What do you need?"

"First, a question. Did your publicist ever do that deepfake thing you told me about?"

"Yeah, man. He got fake photos up that painted me in a much better light. Nobody knew the difference," he says.

Okay, so there may be ethical issues with that, but I refrain from judging aloud since I have my own use for this. "Can you put me in touch with whoever did the deepfake for you?"

"Nah, man, no can do. My publicist didn't tell me who it was that did it."

"Well can't you find out?"

"What for?" he challenges.

I don't particularly want to let him in on what I'm up to. "I want to manipulate some videos, that's all."

He sighs as if he knows I'm keeping part of the story to myself. "I'll see what I can do."

"Thanks, man," I say, and I hang up before he can ask for more.

In the meantime, I start gathering some video footage of my father. Kennedy has her own work to do, and she's sitting at the kitchen table lost in thought when I walk behind her…and I see what she's working on.

I shouldn't look, but I do.

Now I have insider information about what project she's bidding on…and I'm not exactly sure what to do with it since I, too, am bidding on it, and I have a better chance of winning it since the client plays on the same team as me.

Fuck.

I don't get the chance to talk to her about it because Dex's text comes through with the deepfake guy's info. He prefers to be contacted via email, and Dex tells me exactly what he needs.

I get right to work. I set up a new email address to cover my tracks and send in my request complete with the video footage. And then I wait.

I hear back from the guy about an hour later letting me know he got my request and it'll take around twenty-four hours…and it'll cost me, of course.

I send in the payment, and then I wait.

CHAPTER 39
KENNEDY VAN BUREN

A Big Step for Us

I'm so focused on putting a bid together since the client will start accepting bids this Thursday that I don't even realize I've worked well into the evening. The final touches are coming together, and I'm ready to present this.

I'm ready to *win* this.

I don't know if there's ever been a project I'm so passionate about. Actually, scratch that. There never has been. I know there hasn't.

Rumor has it they're only accepting a few bids, and I'm prepared to go in swinging. If I can win this client for VBC in California, my dad will see that I'm a valuable asset out there. It's sort of my way of proving I deserve to stay there a while, even though I'm sure I don't need to do that. Maybe I need to prove it to myself.

I've spent so much of my time recently feeling like everything is out of my control. If I can win this, I'll be back in the driver's seat. I'll be doing this because I *want* to, not because I *have* to. Not because my dad dictated it to be so. Not for anyone else. Just for me.

I glance over at Madden, who's tapping away on his own laptop across the table. "Date nights used to be a lot more romantic," I say, and he chuckles.

"I can order us in some dinner if you're getting hungry," he offers.

I nod. "Or..." I say, drawing out the word. "We could go down to the West Loop for dinner and see what's going on over there."

He raises his brows. "Together?"

"You can wear a hat. I can, too. We'll disguise ourselves."

"Why didn't I think of that? You're so goddamn sexy when you're being all smart."

I laugh, and I close my laptop as I lean back in my chair and stretch. "Back at you, Bradley."

We head to Verde, where we eat way too much pasta, and we take a long walk afterward only to find the same man positioned out in front of the warehouse for a second night in a row.

Madden ducks out of view, and we watch from nearly a block away as he lets someone in a suit into the warehouse.

A few moments later, he lets in a couple. Another man in a suit.

"What the fuck?" Madden murmurs. "Flooring storage my ass." He pulls his phone out of his pocket, and he taps on the screen. "Aha!" he says a little triumphantly.

"What?"

"The deepfake came through. We can't use it now, obviously. My father might already be in there. But before sunrise, we're coming back."

"We?" I ask, a little nervous to be brought in on this plan.

He looks at me, and I'm surprised at the vulnerability in his eyes. "You've been with me this whole time. Don't abandon me now."

I nod. "Wouldn't dream of it."

We head back to his place, and we head to bed early since tomorrow will be an early morning.

And early it is. It's half-past four when the alarm goes off, and I'm snuggled into Madden's side and don't particularly care to get out of bed.

He jumps right up, though, eager to get to this warehouse and check things out.

I follow suit, throwing on a pair of leggings and a black shirt. We head out, park a few blocks away, and walk the rest of the way. The anticipation is killing me, and I'm one part terrified and one part thrilled he asked me to be here with him.

This is trust. This is a big step for us.

We stop a block away again to take a peek at what we're getting into only to find it's deserted at this hour. We check all around us as we make our way toward the warehouse, both for safety and to make sure we're alone.

We are. We get to that same facial recognition panel by the door, and Madden pulls up the video the hacker guy sent him. He flashes it at the screen, and we both wait with bated breath for a moment before we hear the click of a lock and neon words light up beneath the device.

Access Granted.

He pulls open the door, and we both look around as we step inside. Madden shines a flashlight. It's a quiet, deserted warehouse, just like it was the first night we walked in.

Rows and rows of shelves containing various flooring materials are before us, and Madden starts to slowly walk through the aisles.

I follow closely behind him, certain I don't want to get lost in here without him. This is actually sort of scary, to be completely honest, and my heart is racing and beating so loudly I can hear it echoing in my ears.

We continue walking the aisles looking for anything out of the ordinary, but there doesn't seem to be anything. "Do you think this really is just a warehouse?" I finally whisper.

He presses his lips together. "No, I don't." He glances back at me. "There's something here, and we're going to find it.

Maybe it's not in the aisles at all, but maybe it's…" He trails off as we round the corner and start down the next aisle.

There's a patch of carpet on the floor, almost as if it fell off a shelf. We walk toward it, and he kicks it out of the way.

And when he does, he reveals a manhole cover.

In the middle of a warehouse.

Our eyes lock as we both wonder what the hell that manhole cover is covering.

On closer inspection, we see a keypad on the cover. Madden taps six digits into it, and the cover pops open.

"How'd you know?" I whisper.

"My parents' anniversary. My dad uses that PIN number for everything. It was the same as our home security system growing up."

It's not the smartest move, but I think about my own parents and their penchant for living in the past. They use the same password on every account despite the warnings given to create unique passwords.

He pulls open the cover, but it doesn't lead anywhere. Instead, we hear a clicking sound near the far wall, the one opposite the entrance of the warehouse. We walk over in the direction of the sound, and we see that a hidden doorway has popped open right out of one of the concrete walls of this facility.

"What the fuck is this?" Madden murmurs, and he pulls open the door only to be greeted with another facial recognition device blocking our way through a heavy, wooden door. He flashes his phone with his dad's image at it, and the deadbolt on the door slides open. He tries the handle, and the door opens to reveal a staircase.

The contrast between this stunning, luxurious staircase and the concrete warehouse above it is striking. The stairs as well as the walls surrounding them are all made from black marble with white and gray veins, and I slowly follow Madden down the stairs. We move to turn the corner, but we're stopped by a rather large, burly fellow with his arms crossed.

"How'd you get in here?" he grunts at us. He must be the bouncer, here to guard whatever is on the other side of this wall.

"I'm Madden Bradley," Madden says confidently, as if that explains why he's here.

"Thomas said none of his kids know about this place. How'd you get in?"

"My father gave me the credentials." He tries to look around the man at what we're dealing with here, and I would love to try to look around Madden, but I'm behind him, and he's blocking my view completely.

"We're closed." The man's tone is firm and finite.

"I know. My father asked me to let you know that I was welcome to take a look around. He asked me to wait until off-hours, but since I'm the incoming Bradley CEO, this is all part of my legacy." He sounds convincing enough to me, and meanwhile I'm shaking like a leaf back here. We're caught! We're not supposed to be here! What the hell is this place? What is the Bradley family caught up in? Are we going to get in trouble?

"I'll just call him to confirm."

"At this hour? Don't be ridiculous. You know after last night, he'll be asleep. Look, I had the credentials to get this far. Are you really going to disappoint my father further?" Madden demands, and holy hell, he sounds all authoritative and freaking sexy.

"Who's she?" he asks, nodding at me.

"My assistant."

The man stares off at Madden a few extra beats, and then he seems to relent. He makes a good point about having the credentials, and the man steps aside. He doesn't exactly offer a tour, but as soon as I round the corner, I know exactly what I'm looking at.

It's one of those illegal, underground casinos you only see in movies or TV shows, but this is real life. The entire place is encased in that beautiful black marble from floor to walls to ceilings, and elegant chandeliers hang above different types of poker tables from blackjack to Texas Hold'em to baccarat. Leather chairs are pushed in at tables for craps and roulette, and a cashier lines one wall while a bar lines another. A third wall has counters for sports betting and lottery games, and there's a small area with a huge screen and gorgeous leather chairs.

It's certainly not like the casinos I've been to. This place is high-class, and I'm guessing it's also high-stakes.

And it would definitely explain where the large sums of cash on Monday mornings are coming from.

"My father mentioned that he wanted to expand the wine menu. I said I'd take a look through the selection," Madden says to me loudly enough that the burly bouncer dude can definitely hear him. We head over toward the bar, and he walks behind it to look at the wines. I, on the other hand, would like to just get the fuck out of here before we get caught down here with burly bouncer dude.

My dad's words about Thomas Bradley come back to haunt me once more.

He has the kind of connections we can't fight against. Was this what he meant? Does my dad know about this place? Does he know about the bouncers and the underground, illegal activities?

How did he get started in this? And furthermore, was he ever going to tell his kids about it?

Madden clearly didn't know. I wonder if the others do? According to the bouncer, no.

Are there more of these, or is this the only location? Does it change each week? Is that why there are four warehouses? Is the time and place a secret that only the members know about?

I have about a million questions and exactly zero answers.

And as I look over at Madden, who is secretly sneaking photos of this place from behind the bar...I realize that at least I'm not alone.

CHAPTER 40
MADDEN BRADLEY

Can You Ensure Her Silence

I'm not surprised when I get a voicemail from my father demanding to see me in his office immediately.

I broke into his top-secret warehouse, bypassed Goliath, and discovered his secret. Of course he wants to see me.

I didn't pick up when I saw him calling a little after eight, and that was probably my first mistake. I was at a restaurant eating breakfast with my girl, both of us in hats to try to stay under the media's radar while we decompressed after a rather intense morning, and I didn't particularly want to talk to my father.

Even so, it comes as no surprise that he's inside my penthouse when I arrive home with Kennedy in tow.

"You were supposed to be getting information from her, not sleeping with her," he hisses at me, pointing at Kennedy, and, okay, so that's how this is going to go.

He's just going to go ahead and blow up my entire life. Cool, cool.

She looks devastated by his words, and I try to reassure her.

"It's not like that, Ken," I say softly. "You know how I feel about you, and you know he's not going to take this lying down."

She snags her bottom lip between her teeth, and I feel like the scum of the earth right now. But my father just makes it worse.

"Excuse us," he spits at her. "I need to talk to my son. Alone."

She spins on her heel and walks right out the door we just came in through.

"Kennedy, wait," I call after her, but she just shakes her head, holds up a hand that clearly says I can go fuck myself, and lets the door slam shut behind her. I turn toward my father. "What the fuck?"

"I could ask you the same," he hisses. "You know we have cameras at the warehouse, right? Did you think I wouldn't find out you were there?"

"I knew you would. I just didn't care," I say.

His brows rise, as does his heart rate, I'm certain, since that vein in his forehead becomes a little more pronounced.

"If this is my *legacy*, I need to know what I'm getting into," I say, putting a little extra emphasis on the word *legacy*. He can be angry all he wants. He's not the only one.

"How did you get in?" he demands.

"Deepfake. It wasn't hard. Your state-of-the-art system isn't really all that secure, and you should probably be more creative with your passcodes."

"Deepfake?" he asks.

I blow out a breath. "I took some security footage of you from the office and had someone create a video of your face. I showed it to your facial recognition thing, and boom. Access granted."

He looks impressed, but whether or not he's impressed with my hacking skills is irrelevant to me. The only thing relevant just walked out my door, and I will figure out how to fix that next.

"Look, you weren't going to tell me what was going on, and now I know," I say as I eye my father warily. "I have about a million questions, but let me start with one. Were you going to tell me about this when you handed Bradley Group over to me, or were you going to continue laundering illegal casino money through your legitimate real estate business?"

He sighs and wanders over toward the windows. He looks out over Navy Pier for a long time before he answers me.

"Remember how I told you I was injured my senior year of college?" he asks.

"Your knee."

"Mm-hmm. I'd gotten involved in an underground poker ring, and I owed some people some money. When I couldn't come up with the money, they beat the shit out of me. Tore my ACL with enough nerve damage that they ensured I'd never play again. I guess it was then that I vowed I'd never be vulnerable to those types of people again. Instead, I'd be the one sending the henchmen to collect payment, so to speak. It's why I worked hard to create something out of nothing. It started as an underground ring, and when I found how lucrative it was, I saved money. I opened the development firm and ran the ring on the side. Eventually it became the members-only, high-class, luxury experience you broke into today."

"Evidently with poor security."

He gives me a wry look. "Evidently."

"So what happened with Van Buren? Is that related?"

"The client I won from under him years ago was a member. Of course he chose Bradley Group for his project. I opened a line of credit for him, and he awarded me the business. Van Buren has held a grudge ever since."

I blow out a breath. I wonder how many more examples there are of this exact sort of thing. How many clients are part of this ring? Where does it stop?

"I don't want any part of the illegal shit you're doing," I finally say. My voice sounds tired. I *am* tired. I feel like I've aged ten years in the last four hours.

"All the things I've done for you, done for this family," he says, and whirls around to glare at me.

"What, Dad? What have you done?" I demand. When he doesn't answer, I ask again, this time a whisper, as all the advantages in my life, everything that's always seemed to come so easily, flash before my eyes and the heavy truth falls into place. My stomach feels queasy as I ask, "What have you done?"

He purses his lips, but he doesn't answer. Instead, he starts to walk toward my door. "That's enough for one day. I trust you'll keep this to yourself?"

I guess he has henchmen to ensure I do.

"Yeah," I mutter.

"What about the girl? Can you ensure her silence?"

"She won't tell anybody." I try to be convincing because if I'm not, I'm terrified *he* will find a way to silence her. I don't know how far he's gone, and I don't want to know what he'll do if he's pressed further.

He walks out the door, and as it clicks shut behind him, I can't help but wonder exactly how much of my life has been manipulated by my father. How many decisions he's masterminded for me—and my siblings, too.

And for the first time, I can't help but wonder whether he somehow arranged this thing with Kennedy, too.

CHAPTER 41
KENNEDY VAN BUREN

Feels Fitting

I don't know where to go, and so I walk down the block as tears freefall down my face.

I should've known from the start that Madden Bradley would never have any interest in me. Of course he wouldn't. He's a pro football star. He could have any woman he wants. He only ever wanted to get a look inside Van Buren Construction, not actually get inside Kennedy Van Buren. That was just a hazard of the promise he made his father, I guess.

It feels like my heart is breaking. I wish I knew him well enough to read what the look he gave me was, but my heartbroken brain interpreted it as pity. Pity for the poor, stupid girl who believed he actually had feelings for me when he was secretly working for his dad all along.

I should trust in what we have. Something deep down tells me that. He brought me with him to make that discovery this morning, after all. Or maybe that was all part of the plan, too. Who knows? His dad kicked me out, and I wasn't about to stay as an unwelcome guest.

I should believe he was being honest and genuine with me and that he misled his father for whatever reasons he had. He's not close with Thomas Bradley, just like I'm not close with

Walter Van Buren. We had each other to rely on for a couple months there, and I thought we had formed something special.

But he has a legacy to protect, and so do I. It might do me good to remember that.

I feel a single raindrop as it splashes down on my head. It's not surprising that the sky is crying along with me. I heard on the radio on the way to the warehouse this morning that we weren't going to see the sun today. Feels fitting. There was only a thirty percent chance of showers. I guess this is it. I spot more drops on the sidewalk ahead of me, and I debate what to do. I don't have my car nearby. I could walk to the VBC office from here, or I could grab a cab and take it to…where?

My parents' house?

Clem's new place? I don't even know where she lives.

I pull out my phone to send her a text when the skies seem to freaking open up, and rain starts to hammer down on me.

Great. Just fucking great.

I slide my phone back into my pocket to try to keep it dry, and I find myself stuck in the middle of an empty sidewalk. I could run for cover, but I can't seem to make my legs move. It's like I don't care if I'm wet or dry. All I can feel is the slice in my chest at the fact that Madden was just using me that entire time.

Starbucks. There's a Starbucks a few blocks from here. I'm exhausted after getting up early to essentially spy on the Bradley patriarch and uncover his illegal secrets, and coffee will put all this into perspective. Coffee always puts everything into perspective.

I trudge in the rain toward Starbucks. A couple with an umbrella rushes past me, but I can't be moved to walk any faster.

I'm within a few yards of the door when I feel a hand grip onto my bicep.

I whip around and find myself face-to-face with Madden.

My traitorous stomach flips at the sight of him.

I'm squinting up at him through the rain that's pouring down on us. He might've betrayed me, but goddamn, he's gorgeous.

Those dark eyes look relieved as he pins his gaze to me, and the rain has flattened his hair as little droplets cling on, refusing to let go. I can relate.

"How'd I know you'd wind up at Starbucks?" he asks. There's a teasing quality to his voice, and honestly I'm not sure I'm quite there yet.

I blow out a breath as I try to yank my arm from his grasp, but I'm no match for a pro football player.

"What my father said…" he says, trailing off.

He pauses as if we're not standing out here in the pouring rain in the middle of the sidewalk. We could go inside and get a respite from the storm, but somehow this feels like it suits us just fine. It's been a bit of a stormy path anyhow.

"It's true. I told him I'd get close to you. But it was never my intention to steal sensitive information, Ken. You have to believe me."

"How can I trust you after what he said?" I ask.

"Because you know how we feel. You know this is real."

"And how do I know it's not just some act on your part?" The rain seems to pick up as a rumble of thunder shakes the sky.

"I'm not that good of an actor. You know I fell hard and fast for you. I've never felt like this, and I don't know what I need to do to prove that to you. Ask you to stay with me when you're in California? Done. Stand in the rain begging you to take me back?" He holds his hand up to indicate that's what he's doing right now. "Tell me what to do." There's an edge of desperation in his voice, and the intense sincerity in his eyes tells me everything I need to know.

That twinge in the back of my mind telling me to trust in what we have starts to speak a little louder.

Maybe I need to put my walls back up a bit, but with Madden, I don't *want* to.

I don't want to hide.

We have to—not from our fathers, necessarily, because honestly, fuck those family ties that don't really mean all that much to either one of us—but because of our clients and our positions as the future heads of our own companies.

It's complicated, but what relationship isn't?

We'll figure it out.

His eyes move back and forth between mine as he searches for the answer he's looking for, and that's when I crash into him, set my hand on the back of his wet hair, and pull him down for a kiss.

It's not even nine in the morning. What a fucking day this has been.

His mouth opens to mine, and as his tongue batters into my mouth and butterflies flap around my stomach, I can't help but give in. This feels good. It feels right. It feels like it's exactly where we are meant to be.

This is possibly the most romantic kiss of my life. The man just chased me down in the rain to make things right, and as he seems to intensify our kiss, making it more urgent as he tightens his hold on me, a crack of thunder roars through the sky.

It doesn't faze either one of us. I don't know how long we kiss there on the sidewalk, but I never want to stop.

Eventually he pulls back, resting his forehead to mine. "I fucking love you so much," he says, and the tears falling from my eyes mingle with the raindrops as I cling onto him.

"I love you, too," I say.

"We'll figure the rest out. Okay?"

I nod as this feeling of confidence fills me that he's right. We *will* figure this out.

We have to. It's the most important thing in my life, and I'm not going to give it up…least of all for a job I wasn't fully convinced I even wanted until a few weeks ago.

"Coffee?" he asks, and I chuckle as I nod.

We head inside, sheltered from the rain now but dripping on the carpet inside the store, and place our mobile order for our twin grande iced brown sugar oat milk shaken espressos, and then we walk slowly in the rain back to his place, hand-in-hand as we brave the storm we currently find ourselves in.

His front door has barely clicked shut behind us when his mouth is back on mine. We're wet, I'm wet, our mouths are wet, and I can't keep my hands off him anymore than he can keep his hands off me.

And just for the sake of logistics, we both finished our coffee on our slow stroll back here, tossing our empty cups into the trash can at the entrance of his building.

He starts tugging at my clothes, and we're dripping in his front hall, but neither of us cares. Or maybe he does, the cute little neat freak, but he'll clean it later.

I tug at his clothes, too, and before long, we're both naked in his entry as we kiss desperately, hastily, sensually. He thrusts his hips to mine, his hard cock settling between us. I part my legs and reach between us, pushing his cock down so it's resting between my parted thighs. He's not inside me, but his cock is close and warm, and I want nothing more than for him to slip inside me right the fuck now.

I claw at his back. "Fuck me, Madden."

"I don't have a condom here."

"I don't care."

He lifts me up as if I weigh nothing, and he pushes my back against his front door as I wrap my legs around his waist. His eyes are hot on mine as he reaches between us and slides his cock inside me. It's not the first time he's entered my body without a condom, but it's the first time his cock has been in my pussy this way.

And it's pure fucking heaven.

The way he slides into my body is a totally different sensation than with a condom. He buries his head in my neck as he starts to move, and I claw at his back as he pushes me closer and closer toward a quick climax. Even the way he's making love to me now feels desperate, as if the last five hours have been this frantic path to push us toward this moment.

His body is pressed to mine, but then he pulls back, and my tits bounce between us. His eyes move there, and then they move down to where our bodies are connected.

"Fuck, that's hot," he says as he pumps into me over and over. "I love watching my cock move into you over and over."

"It feels so good," I moan.

"It looks good, too," he grunts.

I grab onto him and pull him back into me, and he tips his head up to meet my mouth with his. He pulls his mouth from mine, and the look in his eyes is hungry as he pulls me away from the door, his cock still buried inside me, and he fucks me as he makes his way over to the couch.

He sits, pulling me down with him so his face is eye level with my chest, and he grabs one of my breasts now that he doesn't need his hands around my body holding me up.

"I fucking love these tits," he says. He sucks my nipple into his mouth as he squeezes the fleshy part, and I moan as I tip my head back, closing my eyes and balancing with my fingernails digging into his shoulders. I ride him, setting the pace between us for a bit since he's usually the one doing the work, and the way his huge cock hits inside me from this angle is nothing short of absolute perfection.

He continues working my nipple, and the feel of his mouth working one zone while his cock works the other pushes me into an orgasm far too quickly. It hits me out of nowhere.

"Oh, God, Madden, yes!" I cry out as I start to come, and he sucks my nipple harder as my body unravels around him as if he knows.

"Fuck yes, baby. Give me your orgasms."

I moan my way through the peak as I freefall into bliss, his words washing over me and filling me with warmth.

As the contractions of my body start to slow, he lets go of my tit and flips me over so quickly that I'm on my back before I know what's happening. He manages to move us without ever pulling out of me, and it's his athleticism on full display. He shoves into me a few times from this angle before he pulls out of me.

He grabs his cock in his fist, and he pumps it a few times before his hot cum shoots out the tip, splashing down onto my stomach. He aims a little higher, the next jet of cum landing on my tits, and as he comes down from his climax, he rolls the head of his cock around the cum. "Fuck, you're gorgeous with my cum marking you as mine."

I reach up and pull his head down for another kiss. I'm wet from the rain, and now sticky from his cum, and I've never been more satisfied.

He kisses me deeply for a few beats before he lifts me and carries me to his bathroom, where he starts the shower, and we proceed to wash each other tenderly.

Questions swirl in the air about our discovery this morning, about his father, about our future…but now doesn't feel like the time to talk about any of that.

Instead, we lie in bed and hold each other until we each fall asleep for a while, blissfully content for now as we both revel in the emotions we just shared.

CHAPTER 42
MADDEN BRADLEY

Bigger Issues

The check-in with SCS goes well, and we're on our way back to California by Monday evening. She's flying with me to San Diego to stay the night with me before she heads into work tomorrow morning, and I have plans to work out with the other wide receivers this week. On top of that, Newman is accepting bids on their expansion this Thursday, so I've got plenty to keep me busy.

She stopped in at her office but otherwise avoided her parents, and for now, that's likely for the best. I'm not sure my father will keep our secret under wraps, but if he wants me to keep his secrets, he'd be wise to keep his goddamn mouth shut until we're ready. Maybe he thinks we broke up because of him.

Or maybe he never gave it a second thought. And honestly…I don't really care.

I haven't told her I know she's bidding on the same project, and I can't decide whether that's a mistake or the right thing to do. I didn't see any of her plans, and I suppose it wouldn't hurt to be honest about it. But at this point, so much time has passed and so many things have happened between us that it might be more out of left field to say something now than to just let it be.

It's not like it gives me any advantages knowing she's bidding on the same project as me.

Part of me wants to see her win it…but the other part of me, the competitor that lives inside me, wants it for Bradley Group.

It's in these moments that I realize maybe I always *have* wanted the company…but I just wanted it on my own terms rather than on my father's.

It's sort of entertaining, even, to focus on these projects knowing who one of my competitors is so intimately well. And not for the first time, I wonder how we can combine resources to really rock both this town and Chicago—and Vegas, New York, and wherever the hell else we want to bring our business.

And *that* is the sort of thinking that actually has me excited for the future.

But then I remember the discovery we made this weekend, and my father's shady shenanigans, and his words that hurt Kennedy.

It feels like she trusts me, and when it's just the two of us, everything feels good and right.

But it won't be just the two of us forever. It'd be so much simpler if it was.

Now we have even bigger issues to deal with. The illegal, underground casinos, the secrets and lies we uncovered…and now the questions. What else is out there I don't know about?

Will she keep my family's secret? Worse, what will my father do if she doesn't?

I've never seen my father in a vulnerable position. Ever. And it makes sense if he started this operation back before I was even born. He sustained his injury, healed as well as he could, and started down this road long before I was ever even a gleam in his eye.

It still begs the question about how much of my life he's orchestrated, though. Did he pay off colleges to accept me or my brothers? Did he have the right influences to ensure those of us who had basic talents in football were developed in a way to get us to the pro level? Furthermore, did he have connections there that gave us options that others would never have had?

At thirty-five, though, does any of it even matter at this point? I like to think I'm a strong man who's made his own decisions over the course of his life, but these secrets have me questioning all of it.

And for the first time, I'm grateful for this trade to San Diego. I'm grateful I don't have to stay in Chicago in close proximity to my father and his secrets.

Dex is lucky, too, playing football in Vegas, and Ford in Tampa Bay and Liam in Pittsburgh. Archer is lucky to be playing baseball for the Vegas Heat. My sisters, though…Everleigh and Ivy are out of luck in Chicago, close to home.

I should warn them. They're my little sisters, after all.

But this thing with the casinos…it feels like a secret I need to take to my grave. If our father wanted us to know, he would've told us. I wonder if my mother knows about them. I assume she does. She certainly spends the money from them on whatever whim befalls her at any given moment.

"You're quiet," Kennedy says beside me. We're up in first class, and the plane is going to touch down soon. She reaches for my hand, and she threads her fingers through mine and sort of plays with our hands together as we talk.

"Lost in thought," I mutter.

"About?"

I clear my throat and glance around. "Saturday morning's discovery."

"What about it?"

I lift a shoulder. "I was just wondering if my mother knows." I keep my voice low. "Or any of my siblings."

"Did you ask your dad that?"

I shake my head.

"You never said what you two talked about after he asked me to leave." It's a clear prompt for me to share, but I'm not comfortable discussing this at all, least of all on an airplane, to be honest.

I shake my head a little. "He told me a bit about why he got into it, but that was as far as we got. He asked if I can ensure your silence." I say the last part a little meaningfully, hoping she'll catch the point that I don't want to be talking about this.

"I won't tell anyone anything. Why'd he get into it?"

"Let's talk about it later," I suggest.

She nods, and she pulls her hand from mine. It feels a little symbolic, and I'm sure I don't like it.

When we walk through my front door, I'm expecting to feel relaxed. We're back in California now. This is our safe haven.

Only…it doesn't feel that way at all.

"Can we talk about it now?" she asks.

I blow out a breath. "Can we just…I don't know. *Not* talk about it?" I walk over and take her in my arms as I do my best to sound apologetic. "I just don't want to ruin our safe space here with talk about my father."

She looks disappointed, and I hate that he's coming between us. I blow out a breath and relent, but I let go of her first.

"He got his ass kicked when he was a senior in college for unpaid debts, and long story short, he decided he'd never be the one getting his ass beat again."

Her eyes are wide. "What does that mean?"

I run my hand through my hair. "I don't really know. That's about as much as he told me, and I don't really want to think about what it means." I turn away from her and walk over toward the window where I can look out at my view and don't have to stare at her prying eyes as I admit some pretty fucking hard truths. "He kept going on about everything he's done for this family, and I don't know what he meant by that, either. My entire life and those of my siblings may have been orchestrated by him, and maybe I don't even know who the fuck I am anymore. And most importantly, I still don't fucking know if he was *ever* planning to tell me about his money laundering schemes or if I was going to take over the company and be on the hook for his sins."

That's the brunt of it, and the problem is that while I was never particularly close with my father, the last two days have told me that I actually never knew anything about him at all.

I don't know what I expect her to say to all of that. Nothing, maybe. I don't think I'd be surprised if she just walked out. How can she love me when I don't even know who the fuck I am anymore?

Instead of responding to my ramblings, she doesn't say anything at all. I spot some movement in the window beside me, and then I feel her fingertips on my shoulder.

"None of it matters, Madden." She reaches around me and hugs me from behind, and then her hand moves to rest on my chest. "I've gotten to know who you are in here, and that's all that matters to me."

I set my hand over hers as I feel a bit of the anxiety that I didn't realize I was carrying for the last two days melt away.

She's here. Despite everything, she's not going anywhere.

And, for now, anyway, that's all I need.

CHAPTER 43

KENNEDY VAN BUREN

Luxury, Grandeur, and Sustainability

I've spent every second of my working hours—plus overtime—this week on this bid, and I'm nervous as I get ready on Thursday morning. I haven't said a word to Madden about it because despite how close we are, when it comes to business, he's still the competition.

I wouldn't expect him to say anything to me about it, though in my research, I discovered that there's a player on his team associated with this particular vineyard. Apparently the teammate married into it, which is why I worked even harder to keep it quiet. If he knew about it, he'd have a better shot at winning the bid because of his connections, but I *need* this project.

For one thing, wine is in my heart. Aside from that, I have a particular passion for winning this project for VBC. It's my ticket to credibility, to proving to not just my father but to the entire company exactly what I'm capable of. That my father didn't choose me because of nepotism but because of my strengths…even if nepotism is still the biggest reason that landed me here.

MAD RIVALS

Let's face it. I've worked part-time for this company for the last ten or fifteen years, yet I'm in line to take it over. That's nepotism at its core, which is why it's even more important to prove myself. I can't let my life spin out of control again the way I did when I was clamoring for independence. This time, what I want is right within my reach. I just have to get my ass out there and win this fucking bid.

I'm charging myself up this morning, obviously. I stayed at Madden's, but I left early to go to my own place to get ready for this meeting. It's taking place at the winery itself at ten, so I need to get a move on and get out there. It's over an hour to Temecula from my place in San Clemente, only slightly longer than from Madden's place in Carlsbad, but I needed to pump myself up at home without him staring at me wondering what I'm getting pumped up for.

He said he had a busy day at the office, too, so we kissed goodbye, and I headed home.

I recite my speech to myself over and over as I make the drive, and I'm as prepared as I can possibly be as I pull into the parking lot of the vineyard. We're meeting in the tasting room, and the signs on this gorgeous property point me right toward it.

I feel a rush of excitement as I get out of the car and start walking toward the door. This could be *my project*. I could be expanding this beautiful land in the sunshine into an entirely new space complete with luxury tourism amenities, and the ideas I've put together are absolute perfection for my own demographic, which is the exact target demographic of this place.

The focus is on luxury accommodations, of course, with an on-site resort offering unparalleled vineyard views, but I also put a big focus on the tourism aspect, offering wellness, dining, and shopping experiences along with the sort of ambiance a woman in her thirties might turn into Instagram-worthy photographs to share this place with the world on social media.

I draw in a deep breath. This is it. This is within my grasp. I deserve this. I am going to win this.

I tell myself that over and over, praying that the power of my mindset is enough to actually attract this win.

I head into the tasting room with a confident bounce in my step, and I find a woman with her head bent close to an older man's as they look at something on a tablet behind the counter. They both glance up when I walk in.

"You must be Kennedy," the woman says, and she walks out from behind the counter toward me, extending a hand for me to shake. "I'm Grace Nash, the owner of Newman Vineyards, and this is Theodore Monroe, my uncle, who is currently running production here at Newman."

"Kennedy Van Buren," I say as I shake her hand. "It's so lovely to meet you."

"And you. We have two other developers who are submitting bids, so we'll get started in just a few minutes once they arrive. In the meantime, how about a taste?" she asks.

I grin. "How could I possibly say no to that?"

She smiles back. "What's your preference?"

"White and not too sweet."

She nods and tips a bottle over a glass, and I can't help but think that this job really isn't half bad. Before she hands it over and I get to drink while I'm on the job, the door opens. The beam of light from behind the open door blocks my view of whoever's walking through it, and Grace pushes the glass across the counter to me as she greets the person at the door.

"You must be Jason," Grace says, and she walks around the counter toward the man who just walked in. "Grace Nash, owner of Newman."

"Jason Cartwright of Cal-Wright Construction," he says. "A pleasure."

I've heard of Cal-Wright. It's some combo of their last name and California, and what I know about them is that they're incredibly pretentious. I hardly know Grace, but she seems so sweet, and I just don't see Cal-Wright as a good fit.

"Come on in," Grace says, shaking his hand. "We're just waiting for one more, and then we can get started."

The door opens again, and the light creates another silhouette around the person walking in.

But I don't need the brightness to dim in order to immediately recognize the figure standing there.

My heart pounds in my chest.

"Madden," I murmur at the same time Grace says, "Madden, welcome."

He glances at Jason first and then me, and he tilts his head as we each play dumb—like we didn't wake up in each other's arms a few hours ago.

Well, this just got a whole lot more complicated.

I should've known he would know about this project. As soon as I spotted the connection between the vineyard and his own career, it shouldn't have come as a surprise.

All I can do is hold out hope that my bid outshines his and that they choose based on which feel they want for their vineyard rather than who they know personally.

"Everyone's here, and Theo is happy to get you each a glass of wine," Grace says. "White or red?"

"Merlot," Jason says first.

Madden follows with, "Whichever is your favorite."

Theo gets to pouring while she begins.

"Thank you all for meeting us here today. We've kept this project largely under wraps, and we were purposely vague about what we're looking for. For that reason, I can't wait to see what sort of visions you've each come up with. I'd like to hear from Kennedy first."

I nod, and I take one more fortifying sip of wine before I present my vision. I pull out a tablet that will complement my speech as I launch into it.

"Thank you, Grace. As a woman in your target demographic, I started this project by thinking about a luxury space that I personally would want to visit, and I didn't limit the possibilities from there." I open my tablet and flip through the first few slides to show Grace some of my ideas. "In my plans, I have everything from a resort to unparalleled dining and shopping experiences with wellness, relaxation, and luxury at the core of every experience here while keeping the vineyard at the center of everything."

She raises her brows in approval as she looks at the preliminary renders of some of my ideas.

"I love that," she says. "Jason, hit me with it."

"While luxury is, of course, essential, we want our visitors to be hit with the grandeur of the vineyard. To that end, we're redefining luxury here with amenities not available in the vicinity. We're focusing on lavish and exclusive craftsmanship for all buildings to create an icon here in Temecula."

He shows some of his renderings, too, all of which don't really seem to fit with what's currently here. It's almost as if he just jumped in with his ideas without having done any market research first, or at all, and if I can tell, then surely Grace can, too.

Once he wraps up his presentation, it's Madden's turn.

"Thank you for having me." He glances over at me, and then he draws in a breath. "I, uh…" He clears his throat, and then he seems to pull himself together. "I can understand how important this vineyard is to you and your family, and my plan blends the beauty of what you already have here with an eco-friendly approach to expanding into a luxury resort." He talks a bit about sustainability, and he keeps the focus on how the vineyard is central to this project and his job will be to add luxury around what they've already built.

She asks a series of questions that we each answer, and I'm almost ready to admit defeat by the time we're nearing the end.

I put too much focus on the luxury of it, and I can see that now. Madden's plan isn't just the most well-rounded, but it's truly the best for this vineyard as they look toward a future. His plans don't take all the new land and just build on it. Instead, his plans allow for the expansion of the current vineyards along with options for updating the production facilities to be able to handle additional crops.

It feels like I'm going to lose this project.

"Thank you all for coming today," Grace says at the end. "You've certainly given us a lot to consider, and we're going to take the next few days to discuss what vision we see for the future of our vineyard."

We all shake hands and exchange goodbyes, and I follow Madden out to the parking lot.

Jason gets into his Porsche and speeds away, kicking up dust in the parking lot as he's the first one out.

"You did great in there, tiger," Madden says.

I turn to look at him, and I tilt my head as realization dawns. "You didn't seem surprised to see me there."

He shrugs. "Why would I have been? They're only interested in working with the best."

"You got it in the bag, Madden. Your focus on the current land was smart." I tap my temple. "Plus, you know...you're teammates with her husband."

"It's why I didn't tell you I would be here."

"You knew I would be?" I ask, and a slice of anger bolts through me.

He nods. "I saw you working on it when we were in Chicago."

"And you didn't say anything?" I ask.

"What good would it have done?"

"Oh, uh, I don't know. Maybe I wouldn't have been blindsided when you walked in?" I say it like a question as irrational anger that he knew plows into me.

"You held your own just fine." His phone starts to ring, and he glances at his watch. "Shit, I need to take this. See you tonight?"

I fold my arms across my chest, and I stare at him with pursed lips. "Are you kidding me?"

He sighs. "Kennedy, I don't have time for this right now. Just…tell me everything is fine so we can both go on with our days."

I shake my head as I get into my car. "Take your call." I don't tell him everything's fine. I don't speed away and kick up dust the way that asshole Jason just did, but I do manage to get out of the parking lot before Madden does.

And then I spend the next hour as I drive toward the Aliso Viejo office positively fuming that he knew and didn't say a damn word.

CHAPTER 44
MADDEN BRADLEY

We're a Family

I blow out a breath as I answer the call, glancing in my rearview to see her pulling out of the parking lot.
"Hey, Coach," I answer.
"Madden, I need you in my office in one hour."
I glance at the clock. I can be there, but it'll be tight. I don't tell him that. I guess I'll just speed. When Coach calls, you show the fuck up. "I'll be there."
I have no idea what this might possibly be about, but I had to answer. It's not like I could've stood in the parking lot arguing with Kennedy when I saw Grace walking out the front door and around the side of the tasting room. She didn't need to see Kennedy glaring at me with all that fire in her eyes, and she didn't need to hear our argument, least of all when this bid is clearly going to come down to the two of us.
I hate that we're competing here in California. This was supposed to be our safe space, and it's turning into something else.
Not for the first time, I wonder at the possibility of us working together. We're going to run into a problem here if Newman wants us to draft new bids with their notes. I only have a month of the offseason left before training camp begins, and I

won't be able to dedicate the sort of time to this project that this vineyard deserves.

Kennedy, however, can.

Her ideas were genius and on point for the demographics, but it just depends what Newman is looking for. If it's luxury, they'll choose VBC. If it's sustainability with a focus on the vineyards, they'll go with mine.

One thing I know for sure is that Cal-Wright is out of the picture. He didn't bother to do any market research first or he would've known that Newman Winery is a bit more reserved than the plans of splendor Jason presented this morning. Lavish and exclusive craftsmanship? Hand-laid Venetian mosaics? Is he fucking nuts?

I dial Kennedy after I hang up with Coach, and she doesn't answer. I leave a voice message anyway.

"Sorry, my coach was calling me, and I had to take that. I'm sorry I didn't tell you that I knew. I didn't want it to feel like we're competing here in California. This was supposed to be our haven, you know? But I should've told you, and I get that now. Can I see you tonight?"

I leave it at that and hang up, and then I spend the rest of the drive toward Coach's office pondering how things feel like they're going up in smoke right now and trying to figure out how to salvage what felt like the most important thing in my life.

I arrive at the practice facility that houses Coach Brian Dell's office, and I make my way to his secretary. Coach Clark, the wide receiver's coach, is waiting outside Coach Dell's office, and so are Spencer, Clay, and DJ. Trey and Zach are absent, but this was an emergency meeting, and it's possible they're not in town.

I glance around at everyone, my brows pushed together. "What's going on?"

"Did you just come from a funeral?" Clay asks, his eyes moving along my suit as I glance at his athletic shorts and sleeveless Storm shirt that tells me he came here from workouts.

He's putting in the work to be better, faster, and stronger ahead of this season. I, on the other hand, am spending my time chasing after a woman and trying to manage a company that will eventually become mine when I really don't have the time for it. Maybe my priorities are in the wrong place. Or maybe his are.

"A business meeting," I murmur.

"You can all head in," Coach's assistant says.

We do, and we find Trey already sitting in Coach's office. There aren't enough chairs around the desk for us all to sit, so the four of us receivers stand near the back of the room while Coach Clark takes a seat next to Trey, who isn't looking up from the fixed spot he's staring at on the floor in front of him.

"As you all know," Coach begins, "here at the Storm, we're a family. We celebrate each other's victories and mourn each other's losses. And when one family member makes a mistake, together we all pay the consequences. Trey, I'll hand it over to you."

Trey looks despondent as he glances up at the rest of the receivers gathered here in the office today. "Last night, I was taken into custody on suspicion of drunk driving."

Silence meets his confession.

"I made a mistake, and I shouldn't have gotten behind the wheel. I'm so sorry," he says, and he truly does sound horrified by his own actions. "I was very lucky that nobody was injured, and I have made a promise to serve whatever punishment the team and league decide upon."

"The league will suspend you for one game, and the team has already decided that they will hand down a mandatory substance abuse program," Coach Dell says. He studies the rest of us standing in the back of his office. "In addition, we'd like all six receivers to band together with some community outreach specific to at-risk youth and local charity events sponsoring addiction recovery. We have several opportunities in mind that Deb will distribute on your way out, and you will be required to sign up for a minimum of two, while Trey will be present at all six events. Zach was unable to make it here today, but he will be expected to attend as well. Any questions?"

Nobody says a word, and in a different setting, I could see these men here grumbling about how it's not fair that we have extra responsibilities on our plates because one of us fucked up. But this is a team. When one member fucks up, we all pay the price just as we all celebrate our victories as a family.

Besides, I've been meaning to get more involved in the community, and this feels like one place to start.

It's as I'm heading out to my car that Spencer stops me. "How'd the bid go this morning?"

I'm glad he brought it up instead of me. It feels like mixing business with…well, business, and something about it feels off.

"It went well. I haven't heard back from Grace just yet, but she seemed to like our focus on sustainability."

"Her great uncle has taken quite the interest in eco-friendly construction lately, so I'm guessing he'll be pressing for your bid."

"And Grace?" I ask.

He shrugs. "She envisions this resort where she can get away for the weekend with friends or take a romantic trip for two…you get the picture. A one-stop shop where she can stay all weekend and have everything she could possibly want right at her fingertips."

That's exactly what Kennedy delivered, and it probably would have done me well to have this conversation with Spencer ahead of the bid meeting. I couldn't take that advantage over Kennedy, though.

I don't have a call back yet from Kennedy after I sign up for my two events and head out, but I need to get back to the office, brief John on today's bid, button up a few other projects, and then get to the gym since I slept in with Kennedy and didn't get a workout in before the meeting this morning.

I'm just pulling into the office when my phone starts to ring, and the number flashes as Newman Winery.

"Madden Bradley," I answer.

"Madden, hi. It's Grace Nash from Newman Winery. I'm calling to let you know that we were very impressed with two of the three presentations today, and I have just a few notes that I'll send over your way with the request for new bids by Monday the sixth."

Monday the sixth. It's over two weeks away.

The Monday after a holiday weekend.

Two Mondays until I need to be at training camp.

It felt like I had so much time spread out in front of me just a few weeks ago, and suddenly everything feels like it's teetering on a very tight timeline.

"I'll get it to you before the holiday," I say confidently, and as soon as the words are out of my mouth, I regret them. The woman I love is mad at me, I have new service activities added to my already full plate, I have two weeks to get into the best shape of my life, and I'm in a new place trying to build an image of myself that appeals to both my sports world and my business world.

I don't have time to get it to her before then, but I suppose if I pull late nights and early mornings, I can get everything done.

"I know the season is starting for you shortly thereafter, and if you need to pull someone else to work on this project, I understand," Grace says.

"This one's important to me," I say. And it is. It's a chance for me to prove how worthwhile I am to this company. I have connections in this world, and that could be quite advantageous for Bradley Group. "John, the man running the California branch of Bradley Group, is fully invested in all aspects of the bid, and he'll be able to take my place in the event of my absence, but I truly don't believe that will be a problem."

"Madden, it's okay," she says. "I get it, right? My husband is your teammate, and he was new to the Storm not so long ago. I know what it takes to build a reputation in a new town, so if you need to pass this off—"

"I won't be passing it off. I want you to know that I will be here every step of the way."

"Okay," she says, but the way she says it tells me she's pretty damn skeptical about that...which she has every right to be considering she knows what the next half a year will bring.

I head inside, brief John on how it went, and open the files Grace sent over to start editing our original plans. As predicted after my conversation with Spencer, she liked my sustainability ideas and Kennedy's luxury resort ideas, and she's looking to sort of combine the two into one perfect project.

It hits me once again how much easier this would be if I could just work on it with Kennedy instead of against her...but the longer my phone call goes unreturned, the less likely that seems to be.

CHAPTER 45
MADDEN BRADLEY

We're a Family

"I need your help."

They're four words my father has never spoken to me before. Maybe he's never spoken them to anybody before. I can't imagine him saying it to my mother, or to a business partner, or to a sibling or a client.

"We're a family, and family comes together when one member needs help." It's wild to me how when my coach spoke those exact same words earlier—*we're a family*—they meant something to me. And now my father is speaking them, and I'm not sure they mean anything at all.

"What?" I mutter.

"I need you to come home to Chicago. I need you in the office here for a few days to make it look like we're working on a big project together."

"Why would I need to be there for that?" I ask. "I can work from here."

"I may be facing an investigation, and if it comes to that, I'll need you to potentially gather bail and liquidate the shell companies."

"I don't want anything to do with the illegal activities," I say firmly.

"You should've thought of that when you started sniffing around." His voice is firm and to the point, and it pulses a shudder of fear through my spine as I think about how Kennedy was with me when I was sniffing around. She knows, too, and for the first time, I wonder what sort of danger that puts her in. "You have a legacy to protect, and if I'm hauled off because I was trying to provide for my family, it's you who will need to step into my place."

"I have a season starting in a few weeks," I say, and I hear the fatigue in my own voice over all this. "I can't just drop everything and come to Chicago."

"You can, and you will."

"What are they investigating you for?" I ask.

He sighs. "It's complicated."

"No shit," I mutter. What the fuck *isn't* complicated these days? "If you want me there, I need to know what's going on."

"I gave someone on the zoning commission a little nudge to push one of my permits to the top of the list, and his boss found out."

"What do you mean by a little nudge?" I ask. "Is this wrapped up in your gambling operations?"

"I can't talk about this over the phone." His firm words tell me that yes, that is exactly the issue here. "Just another reason why I'd like you in town."

Right. Because I'm sure he's planning to spill all the details to me once we're together. I clench my jaw. He's not giving me much choice here. "I can't."

"Look, I've dealt with this guy before, and I know what works with him. Okay? He's a big Bears fan. I just need you here to smooth things over with him for me."

I think back to other times he's used me for tickets to games or merchandise or whatever it is that he wants at any given time from me or any of my siblings.

He's been doing this our whole lives…but I was too naïve or too trusting to realize that he was just using us for his benefit.

"Think of the legacy, Madden," he says quietly, as if *that* will be the thing that kicks my ass into gear.

"The legacy! The fucking legacy! I'm so goddamn tired of hearing about the legacy!" I yell into the phone. I hang up on him and slam the stupid phone down on the counter, cracking the screen.

What choice do I really have here? Let my father go to prison for bribing a government worker? Let his underground casinos be discovered? Let him serve his time no matter what it does to tarnish the Bradley name?

Let him drag *me* into this now that I know about his illegal activities?

I'm too tied up in this company now to let that happen. If it's supposed to be my future after my playing days are over, I can't let it all blow up, and I can't let investigations happen that would reveal how he's been laundering money through the real estate development business.

Maybe I'm the only one who can save this family. This company.

The legacy.

And maybe I'm the only one who can protect Kennedy from the fallout.

I know what I have to do, and once my mind is made up, there's little that will change it.

I move to action.

I start by picking up the phone with the cracked screen and giving her a call.

She doesn't answer. She's mad. I get that.

But she's going to be even angrier after I say what I have to say to her.

I hang up and text her instead.

Me: *I'm on my way over. We need to talk.*

And then I pack my small suitcase and head for her place.

She doesn't text me back, but she does open her door once I ring the bell.

"What do you want?" she asks tiredly.

"I'm sorry I didn't tell you. I made the wrong call, okay? But I need to talk to you."

She opens the door a little wider to let me in, and I storm past her.

I don't want to do this. Everything inside me is screaming that I'm making the wrong decision.

But I have to. It's the only way I can protect her from whatever investigation might come next.

She folds her arms as she leans against the front door, and when she sees me pacing like a caged tiger, she asks, "What's going on?"

I finally stop and face her. "I need to get to Chicago tonight, and I just stopped by to let you know I'll be out of town for a few days."

Her brows dip together. "Is everything okay?"

I shake my head. Fuck, what a day it's been. First the bid, which went well. Then the emergency wide receiver's meeting. Then the call from my father.

And now…this.

"No. It's not. There's too much bad blood between our families for us to do this." My chest feels like it's cracking in half as I say the words I rehearsed on my way over here.

"To do what?" she asks.

"You know too much, Kennedy. It's too dangerous. I can't be with you, and I need you to keep your mouth shut for your own safety."

Her brows crease together as anger steps its way back in—as it should, considering the words I just spoke to her. "Keep my mouth shut?" she demands. "But I'm on the video footage of you breaking into the warehouse."

"I can easily say you were someone else and let it die there," I say.

"Where is this coming from?" She hasn't moved from her spot where she's leaning against her front door, but now it almost looks like she's slumping against it, like it's holding her up now instead of just being a place to lean, and I feel it, too.

I feel like my legs could buckle beneath me at my words to her. I can't believe I'm really doing this.

"My father may be under investigation, and I need to make sure you're not involved in any way," I finally say. "I need to protect you and your family." The last part comes out much more gently than any of my prior words.

Her hand moves to cover her mouth. "An investigation?"

"I can't get into particulars, Kennedy. I need to catch a flight to Chicago."

"Let me come with you," she says, and there's a low, begging quality to her tone.

I shake my head. "You can't."

"Don't do this," she says, and her voice is edged with desperation as tears start to fall. "You know how right we are for each other."

"I know. And that's why I have to end this now. It's the only way to keep you safe." I press my lips together as an unfamiliar heat pools behind my eyes.

I won't break down here. Not in front of her. Not when I'm the one ending this.

I manage to hold it together for the moment. "I need to go."

"I wish you wouldn't." She steps aside from where she stands by the front door.

"I wish that, too. And in another life, maybe this was meant to be. But in this life, I have to say goodbye." I leave those words behind me as I open the front door, walk through it, and shut it behind me, the click reverberating through my whole chest as I make my way to the car.

CHAPTER 46
KENNEDY VAN BUREN

Girl Time with Clem

I should've known. I should've felt it coming.
I crumple to the floor as grief plows into me.
He really did it. He really just broke this thing between us off.

I bet the call he *had to take* this morning was his dad beckoning him back home. I don't know if he's doing this because he thinks I'll betray him or what, but telling me to keep my mouth shut was about the most hurtful thing he said to me, as if I'd ever betray him after everything we went through.

Aside, of course, from his words actually *ending* this thing between us.

Maybe he's right. Maybe it's better this way. It's too complicated working against each other, and maybe I should just swallow my pride and move back to Chicago. It was a bad idea for me to come out here, chasing some man who was never meant to be mine.

Except it's not like I can go to Chicago *right now*. For one thing, that's where he's headed. I don't know how long he'll be there, but I can't make it look like I'm chasing him even though every instinct in my body is telling me to do exactly that—to save what we have because it's the first time I've ever felt something so meaningful in my life.

It's why it hurts so much. It felt like forever, and I know it did to him, too. I could see the way he was affected as he brushed past me to leave.

He doesn't want this anymore than I do, but for some reason, he feels like this is what he needs to do.

I hate it. I hate him.

I don't hate him. I could never *hate* him.

But I'm angry and disappointed. I'm mad and sad. I'm heartbroken.

I truly didn't think this was how today was going to go, but here we are.

I call the only person I can think to call at a time like this…the one person who has always been there for me even though I haven't been a very good friend lately.

"Kenny Van Benny!" she answers cheerfully, and a broken sob falls out of my mouth. "Oh my God, babe, what's going on?"

"Madden ended it," I manage to choke out.

"Oh, shit. Why? Hang on, I'll grab a flight out there to kick his ass," she says, and *this* is why I called her. The solidarity.

I gasp for a breath, and I manage to find one. I gulp in some air, and then I say, "He's on his way to Chicago."

"Then I'm on my way to Los Angeles. Where are my shoes? Where's my fucking suitcase?" she says to herself as she starts gathering her things to toss them into a suitcase.

I'd tell her not to, but the truth is, I need her here. I don't bother to put up a protest she'll ignore anyway.

"I'll book you a flight," I say instead. I wander over to my laptop to look up flights. "Tell me something good while you pack."

"Work is going really well. I'm living with Lainie from marketing, and we're having fun." She lowers her voice. "Not as much fun as I had with you, though."

It prompts a small chuckle from me. "How are things with Lance?"

"You don't want to hear about Lance," she says.

"That good?"

"Better."

"I'm happy you're happy, Clem."

"I know you are. And that's why I love you. Even when you're down in the dumps, you're still cheering me on. And vice versa. Did you find me a flight yet?"

"I did." I book it on the spot and give her the details.

"I'll be there in a few hours, and then we can get wasted and numb this bullshit, okay?" she says.

"Deal," I say, and we hang up.

I spend the next few hours crying, lamenting, and wondering if my ex and my best friend are crossing paths in the sky as he heads to Chicago and she heads to Los Angeles.

It's late, and I'm dozing on my couch by the time there's a knock at my door. I feel a surge of relief that my best friend is here. It feels like I'm not alone, and while the pain from losing Madden is still incredibly fresh and deeply dark, Clem manages to bring brightness wherever she goes.

"I missed you so much," I say, hugging her tightly.

"Back at you, babe," she says. "So what happened?"

And then I spill everything.

Well...*almost* everything.

I leave out the bit about the casinos, which really is the underlying cause of why he broke it off. I realize it's pretty hard to explain why he ended things out of the blue without that piece of the puzzle, so I blame a lot of it on the events from today.

"He must've realized how hard it is to compete with each other in a business setting, and that's why he did it." That's what I tell her, anyway.

Because I wasn't lying to him when I said I wouldn't tell anyone his family's secrets. Even though he just broke my heart, he can still trust me—whether or not he deserves that privilege.

"I'm so sorry, Kenny. What can I do?" she asks.

I shake my head. "Nothing. You're here, and that's all I need."

It's a lie. All I need is Madden, but I can't have him.

She reaches over and grabs my hand. "Do you think this is permanent? Or do you think it's a blip and he'll realize what he lost and come crawling back?"

"The better question is whether I'll take him back when he does." I press my lips together, and they're big words from someone who's fairly certain she would take him back in less than the space of a single heartbeat.

We spend the next day getting massages and pedicures and watching our favorite movies while vegging out on the couch with popcorn and Twizzlers, and then she has to fly back home since she can't miss too many days of work. Girl time with Clem was exactly what I needed, though. And now, I guess it's time to start focusing forward.

I dive into edits on the bid for Newman. I throw myself into other projects, too.

None of it really helps. Before I know it, a week has dragged its way by, and I haven't heard a word from Madden. The Fourth of July comes and goes, and the new bids for Newman are due on Monday morning. I slip into my favorite dress and spend a little extra time on my hair and makeup since I know I'll be seeing Madden at today's meeting.

I'm not trying to impress him. Instead, I just want to feel overly prepared and confident as I walk in to face the man who just broke my heart.

I pull into the parking lot first—just like last time.

I get out of the car and head toward the tasting room.

And when I walk inside, I'm hit with a surprise I never saw coming.

CHAPTER 47
MADDEN BRADLEY

An Epic Disappointment

"You did *what?*" my father asks.

"I backed out of Newman."

"Why in God's name would you possibly do that?" he demands.

"Because I took enough away from her, okay?" I hiss. "I need to go. I have workouts this morning." I'm about to hang up when he stops me with a reminder.

"You're forgetting about the legacy, Madden. I'm so disappointed in you."

"Enough about the legacy!" I yell over the phone. "I am so goddamn tired of this legacy. It isn't worth giving up everything that ever mattered to me."

"Your family isn't worth it?" he sneers. "Every damn thing I've done for you, and this is how you repay me?"

"You keep saying that. Tell me exactly what you did for me." My voice is low as I wait for it.

"Don't you think it fell into place a little too easily? You playing most of your career in Chicago where you always dreamed, your brothers each in the cities of their choosing. It doesn't work that way, son."

"So you engineered it?" I spit.

"I used the connections I had to get you what you wanted. And when I needed you in San Diego, I used those connections again."

I suck in a sharp breath at his confession. I should have known. He orchestrated my trade. He needed me here for whatever reasons he had, and here I am giving away projects that should have been ours.

What an epic disappointment I must be.

Well, truth be told, I'm fairly epically disappointed by my own father, so I guess we're even.

"But even I couldn't have predicted you'd be so stupid as to give away a project you had in the bag," he says.

"Sorry to disappoint you. I have to go." This time I really do cut the call, and even though he's disappointed, I feel good about my decision.

I wanted Kennedy to have the vineyard. I put work into changing around my bid to give Newman exactly what she wanted, but in the end, it was my conversation with Spencer during workouts last week that sealed the deal.

I didn't want Grace to choose Bradley Group because I'm teammates with her husband. I wanted her to choose us because we had the best plan to move forward.

But we didn't. As it turns out, Spencer confessed that his wife loved Kennedy's vision for the place. And knowing that she could easily add in the sustainability features to her plans while also knowing I wouldn't really be around to handle the project with the attention it deserves...it was a no-brainer.

And honestly, what went down last week was a small part of it, too. I hated the look in her eyes when I broke things off. I didn't want to go in today and face her, so in some ways, I took the easier way out.

I was in Chicago for three nights before I came back here.

I stayed out of it but stayed close in case my father needed me, and I instructed him to get his shell companies the fuck away from Bradley Group if he expected me to take over the company.

As far as I know, he either liquidated the companies or transferred ownership, and when I checked the financial records this morning, all traces of Vivicorp Commercial Ventures, Peoria Property Group, and Geneva Holdings were gone.

That's not to say he isn't doing something else illegal. For all I know, there are more companies. He might've transferred funds to offshore accounts or altered the records to delete these companies, but at least the books look clean now for those three accounts.

And that's why I'm surprised when my phone rings after I hang up with my father and I see it's my sister Everleigh calling.

She never calls. We aren't really all that close. She's closer to Dex and Ford than me, the two she falls in between in age, and on the rare occasion we communicate, she texts.

I pick up right away. "Everleigh?"

"Hey. I know this is weird for me to be calling, but I was just talking to Dex, and he said you were in Chicago last week because Dad's being investigated. What's going on?"

I blow out a breath. "It's a long story."

"So it's true? Dad's being investigated?"

"It's complicated," I say, not sure how much to confess to here. Does Dex know about the casinos? Does Everleigh? "He, uh, got himself into some trouble and asked for my help."

"What trouble?" she presses.

"He tried to bribe a zoning commissioner. I got the guy tickets to a Bears game, and he walked away." I'm going to leave it at that when she asks me a question that tells me she knows something she probably shouldn't.

"Does this have anything to do with Vivicorp?"

"What do you know about Vivicorp?" I ask.

"Dad asked if he could name me as the CEO for one of his smaller companies. Vivicorp."

"What did you tell him?" I demand.

She clears her throat. "I said it was fine. It's in name only, and he's giving me a paycheck from it. Why wouldn't I?"

Fuck! He's dragging my sister into this now?

"Tell him no," I say. "Revoke your permission or whatever you have to do. You don't want to get involved with this."

"Why, Madden? What's going on?"

"It's a shell company, okay? He's been laundering money through Bradley Group, and it sounds like he wants to get Mom's name off it and put yours on it."

"But why?" she asks. "His wife legally doesn't have to testify against him, but his kids don't have the same protections. If he trusts you with the family wealth, that could be why he'd want your name on it." Unless there's something else going on that we don't know about. A divorce on the horizon, perhaps, or maybe he's trying to layer ownership to confuse authorities. Or maybe he knows that an investigation would freeze assets in both their names, and he doesn't want this particular account frozen.

I guess there are any number of reasons.

"Get out of it," I tell her, and we say our goodbyes.

But one thing she said sticks in my mind. Something I hadn't considered before.

Something big and important.

His wife legally doesn't have to testify against him.

If my father is investigated and I'm called into question, my wife wouldn't legally have to testify against me, either.

Maybe I went the wrong route with ending things with Kennedy to keep her safe. Maybe there's another way…one I hadn't thought about and, at the same time, one that I thought about constantly.

Time is short. Too short. The season is creeping up on me, and I barely have time to focus on Bradley Group at all right now, let alone on my personal relationships.

In just two weeks, I have to report for training camp. In the meantime, the trainer for the Storm has gotten in touch, and he's built a stacked program for me to get season ready. It means long hours at the gym with my teammates, and it means my focus needs to be on the game.

And so rather than give in to the idea that just pulsed through my mind, I turn my focus back to where it has been for the better part of the last two decades, and I get the fuck to work.

CHAPTER 48
MADDEN BRADLEY

Doesn't Have to End with a Hookup

"I have an appearance tonight. Come with me," Clay says at the end of workouts.

Clay has tried to get me to go out, but the mere thought of a hookup feels like something some past version of me might've participated in. Current me wants nothing to do with it. I only want her, but I've convinced myself that being with her is too dangerous for her.

I guess that whole Clay Mack and Mad Brad taking San Diego by storm is an idea of the past—at least off the field, anyway.

"Thanks for the offer, but I'm out."

"Out? Why? What happened to Mad Brad and Clay Mack taking over this town?" he asks, mirroring my thoughts. Maybe the two of us have grown closer than I've given us credit for in the short space of time we've gotten to know one another.

I huff out a chuckle. "I'm not in the same place."

"What place? San Diego?"

I give him a pointed look, and he nods.

"Ohhhh," he says, exaggeratedly drawing out the word. "The woman." He nods knowingly.

"Yeah. The one who really fucked me up without my permission."

He laughs. "Don't they all?"

I raise a brow without a comment.

"We've all got one." He says it in a way that tells me he thinks everyone has skeletons in their past. "She's moved on now, though. Married. Kid. The whole shot. And I'm here in San Diego playing like that was my plan all along."

"So you're saying you have regrets?"

"I don't know about that. I'm in an okay place now, you know? Commitment isn't for everybody."

I press my lips together. "But it was for you once upon a time."

"Yeah. I guess. I put my focus on football, and it ruined that relationship. But what am I still doing now?" He glances out at the practice field. "Not her."

"Football," I say flatly.

He nods.

"But how much longer?"

"I think I've got a few more years in me than you do," he says, and I chuckle at the jab.

"I don't know, man. I've seen your sprints. Could take a lesson or two from this old man."

He laughs. "Come with me tonight. Some of the other guys will be there, too. Spencer, Tanner, Miller. Maybe a few of the other receivers."

I think of the guys he just named. All three are in relationships, somehow figuring out how to balance personal and work life, and all three happen to be related, too. Tanner is back at quarterback after a season-ending injury last year. Miller, his twin brother, is our star running back, and I'm already growing closer to Spencer.

Going out tonight doesn't have to end with a hookup. It can simply be friends getting together for drinks and then going home.

"Fine," I finally say. "I'll go. But to be clear, you're not wing-manning for me tonight."

"Man, she must've really fucked you up. Do you want to talk about it? Or, you know…find a hookup to help you forget about it?"

I press my lips together. "It's complicated. Her father and mine are business rivals, and she was with me when I found out my dad's been doing some shady shit for a few years. If he comes under fire for that, I don't want it to be her ass on the line because she was in the wrong place at the wrong time."

"So let me guess…you're being the hero by writing her off so she doesn't get caught in the crossfire if something happens."

"I wouldn't say I'm writing her off," I protest. Is that what I'm doing? I'm no hero. I'm just trying to protect her. That's all.

What if there's another way?

It's not the first time the thought has entered my brain. What if there's some other way to solve this problem? What if there's another way where we can still be together and she won't be fucked by something that doesn't really involve her?

How do I protect *myself* in all this, too?

That's a question I hadn't really considered yet. I don't want to get called in for questioning when I had nothing to do with my father's choices.

And that leads me to one simple conclusion.

I need to cut my father and all his suspicious activities out of Bradley Group. He may have cut those three companies out, but that's just because those were the ones I found.

I won't work there another second if it's risking my reputation or Kennedy's.

"The wheels are turning," Clay says, interrupting my thoughts.

"Yeah," I grunt. And then I stand. "Thanks, man." I slap him on the shoulder, and then I head out.

"Wait! What about tonight?" he asks.

"Text me where and when. I'll be there." And maybe after I call the Bradley Group lawyer, I'll have some semblance of what comes next.

After speaking with my lawyer, as it turns out, I don't. Not really. I have an idea, but it's just the first glimmer of it. It needs work, but I don't have a lot of time here.

But I do have a lot of decisions to make in a relatively short amount of time.

I handle what I can for today, and then I head to meet my teammates at the nightclub where they're already waiting for me. I spot Tanner first, and he holds out a hand for a fist bump.

"How's it going, man?" he asks.

I shrug. "I'm at a paid appearance not getting paid if that tells you anything."

He laughs. "That good, huh? I heard there's a woman involved."

"Clay has a big mouth."

"Nah. I heard you in the weight room earlier." He holds up his glass for a second, but I don't have one to toast back with, so I nod at the bartender, who nods back that he'll be right over. "Look, for what it's worth, I've been where you are. If you want my advice, you do whatever it takes to get her back. Clay may say something different since he's single, but I've been with her, and I've been without her. I know which side of that coin I want to end up on."

It's good advice, I think. They're words that will stick in my mind for a while, anyway.

After I order, I congratulate him on his upcoming wedding. He shares a few details, and his brother saunters over with a glass of his own to make a toast to his twin's upcoming nuptials.

We take a few pictures, have a few drinks on the house, and put in our time before Clay finds some girl to leave with and the rest of us head our separate ways.

I head home to my empty house. It's better this way. I don't want some meaningless hookup.

I just want Kennedy.

And I've got a fire in my veins now to figure out how the hell I'm going to win her back.

CHAPTER 49

KENNEDY VAN BUREN

Nothing Keeping Me in San Diego

Zero part of me thought I would walk into this meeting today with my new bid and walk out of it with a signed contract, but here we are.

I thought Madden had it in the bag. Turns out he's too much of a coward to face me…or something like that. I'm letting my bitter anger toward him win when the truth is that I think he might have done something nice for me.

Grace didn't say what happened, just that I was the only one coming in with an edited bid today. She loved my new plans. I took everything she gave me in her notes and implemented it into my strategy, and then I crossed my fingers and hoped for the best.

But when I crossed my fingers and hoped for the best, I still thought I had some competition. I still thought Madden would show up today—that I'd get to see him, at least. That I'd get to judge the look in his eye and determine if he's already moved on or if he's sitting around sulking the way I'm trying not to.

Grace told me she loved my plans from the start and that she had to compromise with her uncle to be sure we had the right number of sustainability features to keep him happy.

I guess it worked. Newman Winery is mine, and in two to three years, I'll get to stay in the luxury resort that I planned and executed for this land.

I wish I felt more excited about the prospect. It doesn't feel like I won it the way I wanted to. It feels like Madden backed out because he didn't want to face me.

I wish I felt anything other than numb, but numb about sums up how I've been feeling for the last week or so.

I've had to numb myself. If I didn't, I'd spend the better part of every day with the heavy grief that the best thing in my life has ended, and that's no way to live. So I've numbed myself with work. And vodka.

I've started taking daily walks along the beach. I find the water to be calming and tranquil in the rush of chaos my thoughts have become.

I miss Madden.

I miss the dynamic we shared together even though it was short-lived. Maybe we didn't have all the answers, but it sure felt like we did when we were together. It felt magical anyway.

I'll move on. It just sucks that I'm moving on in a new place where I really don't know anyone. It makes it harder not to focus on the heartbreak.

I decide to fly to Chicago to spend the weekend with Clem. I debate going home to see my parents or not, and eventually I decide to stay with them.

Even though my parents don't really know me all that well, they can immediately tell something is wrong.

"Darling, you know they make fillers to help with those dark eye circles," my mother tells me.

I try my hardest not to roll said eyes with dark circles, but it's impossible.

My mother is offended anyway. "I'm just trying to help."

"Ruth, give the girl a break," my father says, nudging me like we're old pals. "She's been partying it up in California."

Partying it up. Yeah, right. More like sulking and crying.

"I'm meeting Clem for dinner in a bit, so I better go get changed," I say. "But thanks for the advice."

Everything feels dark and heavy until I get to the bar where I'm meeting my best friend, and her wide smile immediately puts me in a better mood, but her warm hug is what I needed even more.

We each order a drink and some appetizers, and she asks me all about life in California. I don't really have a whole lot to say. "Mostly I've just been busy with work."

"Liar. You've been busy pouting."

She knows me well. "So what do I do?"

"Give yourself some time to get over it, and then you move forward. Have you thought about coming back to Chicago?" she asks. She stirs the cherries around her glass with the little straw.

"I've thought about it, but I know how it would look to my father. I just scored a big client out there, and there are responsibilities for me there now that he rearranged things here for me." I shrug and make a face.

She makes a face back. "Then he can rearrange them back. I miss you." She reaches over and squeezes my hand.

"I miss you too. Move out there with me."

She laughs. "You know I'm a city girl, though I can't pretend like the beach doesn't call to me. It's why I spend all my time at North Avenue Beach."

"I wonder whether my dad will want me here or there once I'm CEO," I muse, stirring my cherries, too.

"I'd imagine you'd get to decide that when you're in charge. What will you do?"

I take a sip of the drink. "No clue. There's nothing keeping me in San Diego now that Madden and I are over."

"Are you, though?"

"Are we what?" I ask.

"Over. Is this a break, or is it the end?"

I lift a shoulder. "It feels pretty damn permanent, and the fact that he hasn't bothered to call in weeks combined with the fact that he gave Newman to me tells me he's done with me."

She tilts her head. "Babe, when it's as strong as it was between you two, is it ever really over?"

She makes a good point.

I stare into my drink. "I don't want to talk about him. Tell me something good."

"Lainie started getting serious with some guy, so I have the apartment to myself almost every weekend," she says. "Why don't you spend the night? It'll be like old times. We can make popcorn and drink ourselves silly."

"It's a tempting offer, but I don't want to take you away from Lance," I say.

She reaches across the table and squeezes my hand. "You're here, and it's been weeks since we've had time together. You're not taking me away from anything."

She really is a good friend.

I nod. "Okay. Let's have a sleepover."

And we do. It really is like old times. We both fall asleep on the couch watching sappy rom-coms, and when I wake in the morning, despite a slight headache from drinking more vodka than I have in weeks, I feel a little better. We go out again later that evening, and she introduces me to Lance, who really does seem perfect for her.

I need more weekends with Clem and less weekends by myself focusing on everything I've lost.

Maybe it's time to put myself out there. Maybe it's time to build a network of friends in my new city.

Maybe it's time to face reality and start moving on from what I thought was supposed to be my happy ending.

CHAPTER 50
MADDEN BRADLEY

You're Out. I'm in.

I'm back in Chicago on Monday morning, and after a quick check-in with SCS, I officially delegate the project to Margot until the end of this season. She came with me to the SCS offices this morning, and she's been briefed on everything she needs to know for the next phase of the project.

It feels like the final nail in the coffin of my relationship with Kennedy. It was the last loose end that I needed to tie up to really extract myself from having to work with her.

I didn't have the heart to email her to let her know who I assigned to the project in my place. Instead I gave Margot her details and told her to take care of introducing herself.

It shouldn't feel as shitty as it does. It's been four weeks now since I ended things with her. We were only together a couple months. I figured by now I would've moved forward, only…I haven't.

At all. Not even a little.

And it's why I find myself at the Bradley Group headquarters after my meeting with SCS, waiting outside my father's office for a quick meeting. If I get targeted because of my father's investigations, that's one thing. But if *she* does, I could never forgive myself. So I'm here to ensure that won't happen.

I thought I would be nervous to hold a meeting like this, but the truth is that there's really nothing to be nervous about. I already lost everything. What's the worst that could happen now?

I'm trying something new. I'm making an attempt.

Four weeks and no healing tells me I have to fight for her. I feel like I always knew that deep down, but I allowed the pressures of timelines and deadlines and legacies to get in my head.

No more excuses now. It's time to fight, and it's time to win.

If she'll even take me back at this point. Maybe she's already moved on. Maybe she's dating someone new. Maybe it didn't mean to her what it grew to mean to me.

Maybe she's clutching her sheets as some other man makes her come.

"You can head in, Madden." Darla's voice helps snap that image out of my head.

I stand and walk into my father's office, and I slide into the chair opposite him. I casually cross my leg and rest my ankle on the opposite knee so I'm in a figure-four position.

"Trying to give off confidence?" my father guesses as he glances at my casual seating arrangement.

I shrug. "Don't really care what I'm giving off."

"What do you need, Madden? I have a lot on my schedule today."

"Yeah, fighting off authorities, hiding illegal activities. I imagine it's taxing."

He sighs. "Was there something you wanted?"

"Yes." I nod and press my lips together, and then I give him what I came here for. I uncross my leg and lean forward, elbows on my knees now. "I want you to finish extracting all traces of your illegal activities from this company today. Once you finish that, I want you to sign Bradley Group over to me, and then I want you to resign."

"Your new season starts in a week, son. Don't be ridiculous."

"I'm not being ridiculous, and I'm not joking. I have plans for this company, and I want to get started on them immediately."

"What plans?" he demands.

"As if you're in a position to ask," I mutter.

"Excuse me, but I'm still your father, and I'm also still your boss." He gives me a pointed look, but it doesn't much matter.

Like I said, I've already lost everything, and a relationship with my father was never on the table anyway.

"And I'm the son who was able to fairly easily uncover your underground casinos. I'm the son who knows your secrets. I'm the son who the other siblings call when something's going on. Did you think I wouldn't find out you're trying to sign Vivicorp over to Everleigh? And Peoria and Geneva to Liam and Ivy?" I shake my head as I settle back into the figure-four. "Leave them out of this. I don't know what other illegal things you're doing, but it stops where Bradley Group is concerned. Now."

"It's their inheritance, Madden," he says. "It's my way of setting them up for the rest of their lives."

"So you randomly choose three out of the seven of us? That doesn't even make sense. And if it's obvious to me that you're extracting Mother from the shell companies, it'll be obvious to the authorities, too. Find another way to set up the inheritance without involving three of my siblings in your crimes, and get your name off everything to do with this company before you hand it over to me. I won't take it if it's not squeaky clean."

"Then I'll ask Dex. If he doesn't want it, Everleigh. Ford. Archer. Liam. Ivy." He shrugs as if he doesn't give a fuck because he probably doesn't. "One of them will surely want it."

"Unless one of the girls wants it, which they've expressly said they do not, then you're going to be waiting more than another year to retire."

"So you're done at the end of this year, then?" he asks.

The truth is…I don't know.

I want to get a feel for San Diego. I want to play. I want to get back on the field and away from all this exterior noise that's proving to be nothing more than a distraction.

And I want to do all that with Kennedy by my side.

I have a plan, and I'm not leaving here without executing the first part of it.

I lean back a little and fold my hands behind my head. I guess maybe I *am* trying to give off casual confidence now. "Maybe, maybe not. But you'll do what I'm asking, or I'll go to the authorities with what I know. And if you're paying them off, I'll go higher. I won't stop until it's all uncovered."

"You wouldn't dare," he hisses.

"Wouldn't I? Tell me, *Father*, what have you done to ensure I wouldn't?"

He rises to his feet to move to a power position from behind his desk before he explodes at me. "I've done everything for you!"

"You manipulated every aspect of my life to be what you wanted." My voice is eerily calm, a contrast to his. "That stops now."

"I gave you advantages you wouldn't have otherwise had," he hisses.

"I guess we'll never truly know, will we?" We'll never know if I was good enough to play football without his assistance, but the truth is that if I wasn't, I never would've made it in the league for the last thirteen years. I wouldn't still be playing today if I hadn't proven myself on the field.

I mean...I don't think I would be, anyway. Coach would've sat me. I wouldn't have been a starter.

Unless my father paid for that, too.

I feel like there are some things money just can't buy, though. At least I haven't become so jaded that I can still believe that to be true.

He sighs. "You wouldn't turn me in. Think of the legacy, Madden. The house always wins, and it's your inheritance, too. Bradleys always win."

"I swear to Christ, Father, if you mention the legacy one more goddamn time to me, I will turn you in so fast your head will spin. You made that whole thing up so you could lord it over me, over all seven of us, and I refuse to sit back and take it any longer. You want a legacy? How's this: you're out. I'm in. Get the hell out of my office by the end of the day."

"I didn't sign anything over to you yet," he sniffs, raising his chin self-importantly.

"No, you didn't. But you will. I have the non-emergency line pulled up. Dare me to make the call," I say, flashing my phone at him for proof.

"Where did I go wrong with you? Dex would never treat me like this."

I can't help a snort at that. "No, Dex would definitely support your illegal activities, but we both know the right person to lead this company is me. I'm the one who will treat it honestly and with integrity, even if you never did."

He studies me, tilting his head a little as he contemplates that. "I suppose you're right about that. But what good is it to vote me out when you won't even be here? At least let me close out my current contracts and tie up loose ends."

That's not going to work with the plan I have in mind, so I shake my head. "No can do, Pops. You can stay to finish out your contracts and loose ends, but you'll be demoted from CEO. Like I said, you're out. I'm in. Sign it over today, or I call my friends over at the police station."

He presses his lips together. "It's not that simple, son. It's going to take me a few days to get things sorted."

"I don't have a few days," I mutter.

He presses his intercom button for his assistant. When she answers, he says, "I need Paul in here."

The Bradley Group lawyer appears in my father's doorway a few moments later.

"Close the door," my father says, and Paul does it before he sits in the chair beside mine.

My father's eyes are on me when he says to Paul, "I'm signing over the company to Madden as soon as possible. I need to erase all the shell companies first, and I'll need your help. We need to get this done before training camp begins."

"When is that?" Paul asks.

"Six days," I grunt.

"Six days? That's impossible," he says.

"It needs to be done *before* six days." I raise my brows at my father, whose eyes are still on me.

He sighs. "Get it done in five," he says to Paul, and then he turns away from both of us back to his computer.

"Three," I demand.

Both men turn to look at me.

"Five, Madden. It's the best we can do," my father says.

I huff out a breath. It's not enough, but I guess it's my only shot.

Paul sits silently for a few seconds before he heads off to do whatever it is he has to do to make this company mine.

My father's right about one thing.

Bradleys always win. Maybe the younger generation has some advantages there, but I count this as my first win.

Now to figure out how the hell to win back Kennedy.

CHAPTER 51
MADDEN BRADLEY

Golfing

I remember Kennedy saying how taxing it is to go back and forth between two cities, and now I'm experiencing the same thing.

I'm back in San Diego after leveraging what I know against my father, and it feels like I'm battling between those two sides of my personality again.

I had to get back here. With training camp starting next week, this is the last week where I'm free for a while. That means workouts, meetings, endorsements, and sponsorships.

Take today, for example. I'm in my jersey, standing to the side while Clay films his part in the local anti-bullying spot we agreed to.

"Respect the game." That's my line.

"Respect the team." That's Clay's line.

There are other local celebrities, too, and the final one ends with, "Respect each other."

It's a great message for kids, especially in today's atmosphere. I'm really trying to be present in the moment, but I'm waiting on that call from Paul letting me know it's done.

I haven't gotten it yet.

I have a feeling they'll wait until the very last possible second, and then I'll be scrambling to get everything done, get back to San Diego, execute the next part of my plan, and be ready in time for training camp.

It's cutting it down to the wire, and I'm waiting on other calls, too. I'm distracted.

As shown by the fact that I need to say my line twelve times before the crew is happy with it.

I'm all over the place. A hot mess, as my youngest sister might call me. But I'm doing all this for a reason. I have a bigger purpose in mind.

Tonight Clay and I have an appearance at a bar, and tomorrow I'm running a 5K for charity.

There's little time to accomplish my other tasks, in particular any tasks related to Bradley Group, which is why I've started moving people around and getting people into place. The company won't be mine until the ink is on the paperwork, but we're close enough, and I have enough authority where I sit now to start shifting things around—like, for example, bringing a few employees from Chicago out to San Diego to start training them on how things work out here.

I'm putting a lot of trust in John to run this office, and I'm not sure whether that'll be for one year, five, or more.

I head back to Chicago on Saturday in anticipation of what to expect on Sunday, and sure enough, it's around noon on Sunday when I get the call from Paul.

"The company is yours when you're ready to sign the paperwork."

It took the full five days for them to extract whatever traces my father had left of illegal activity in the company, and maybe I'll never fully trust that it's all gone…which is why one of my first orders of business is to have a separate law company go over everything to ensure we're squeaky clean.

And once the ink is dry, I'm the official president and CEO of Bradley Group.

I need to get back to San Diego. Stat.

Training camp starts tomorrow, and I can't miss a second of that. I have things to do to prepare for it, too. Life is kind of crazy right now…yet nothing eclipses the priority of the current task at hand.

I push the button of the doorbell as nerves crawl up my spine.

I've faced three-hundred-pound linebackers who I was less nervous to go up against.

The fact that I'm the CEO now won't be announced for a while, but I don't care. I just needed the credentials to get started on executing the next part of my plan.

The door opens, and a woman with a face that looks too smooth for her age stares at me. I see traces of Kennedy in her. She looks like she may be trying to pinch her brows, but the Botox is preventing the movement. Hell, she looks like she'd be best friends with my own mother if there wasn't a huge feud between our families. "Can I help you?"

"I'm looking for Mr. Van Buren. I'm Madden Bradley of Bradley Group."

"He's golfing." She purses her lips. "We don't do business with the Bradley Group any longer. Have a nice day." She moves to shut the door, but I refuse to be deterred.

"Ma'am, if I could just have a moment of your time—"

"I'm sorry."

Just before the door clicks shut, I yell out, "I'm in love with your daughter."

The door doesn't close quite all the way, and after a few seconds that feel like the longest in history, it inches open just a bit.

"What did you just say?" she asks.

"I'm in love with your daughter. Kennedy. We met and started working together on a project, and I know Walter told her that she needs to stay away from me, but the connection was too strong. And now it's been four weeks that we've been apart, but I have a plan, and I need to talk with you and your husband because I will stop at nothing to win her back."

"Win her back?" Her hand flies to her chest. "I'm sure if you're apart, there's a good reason. Now if you'll excuse me."

She moves to shut the door, but I set my hand on it before she can close it.

"We're apart because I was trying to protect her. But I fixed the issue, and now the best way I know how to protect her is to keep her close."

"Protect her from what?" she asks. "Is she in trouble?"

"No. I was protecting her from the investigations my father may be facing."

"Oh." She purses her lips again. "Why is he being investigated, and how was my daughter involved?"

"I assume you know about his casino," I say carefully, and she purses her lips. "Well, I didn't know about them. Kennedy was with me when I discovered them. I kept her at a distance to protect her, did what I had to do, and this morning, Bradley Group was signed over to me. And now I'm here with an opportunity I'd like to discuss."

"An opportunity?" she asks.

"Ruth, who was at the door?" Walter asks as he walks into the foyer behind his wife.

I glance at Kennedy's mother. "Golfing?"

She has the grace to look a little sheepish at the lie.

"Madden Bradley," Walter says.

"Mr. Van Buren," I say. I stick out a hand to shake his. I'm still standing in the doorway.

"What are you doing here?"

"He says he's in love with Kennedy, and he's the new CEO of Bradley Group," Ruth says, basically summarizing our interaction so far.

"What?" Walter asks.

I lift a shoulder. "It's complicated. But my father has erased all traces of illegal activity from Bradley Group, and this morning, I became the new president. And I'm here today to talk about a merger."

"A merger?" Walter repeats. "Absolutely not."

"Sir, let me begin by saying that your daughter and I have been secretly seeing each other for months. I'm going to ask her to marry me, and I'd love to do that with your blessing, but I'm going to do it either way. We're a great team, and we've found that we really actually enjoy working together. What was something we both thought we never wanted has become something I want more than anything if it means I get to do it with her, and I know she feels the same way. She never wanted VBC until she got to compete against me. But imagine how great it could be if we were working together instead of against each other. And once we're married, I plan to merge VBC with Bradley Group to create a new super development company that we can run as co-CEOs. I know it's a lot to ask, especially given how little you trust my father, but my season is starting tomorrow and I have nothing to lose by coming here to present this idea to you to get the ball rolling while I get my ass back to San Diego for camp."

Both Walter and Ruth stare at me like I've lost my mind, and maybe I have.

But honestly, I just think that's what love does to you.

Walter raises his brows. "I can't agree to any of it, son. I'm sorry. Your father betrayed me one too many times, and the apple doesn't fall far from the tree."

"Then you put whatever conditions you want on the merger. You may not trust me, but I trust Kennedy." I shrug. It's as simple as that to me.

I realize it's much more complicated than all that. I realize there's a long road we need to travel down and a merger won't happen overnight. There's a lot to be considered between negotiations, legal considerations and reviews, and integrating the two companies.

But all of that *could* happen over the next year or so while I'm playing football. I have people in place to help me with the things I can't be present for, and I'm putting a lot of trust in them to help me the way they've said they will.

"Look, I had to throw the idea out to you before I presented it to her, but ultimately, you're signing the company over to her, and it's going to be her decision. Maybe you just sign it over now and we can move forward with our future," I suggest.

"You're a cocky son of a bitch, aren't you?" Walter asks me.

"No, not cocky. I'm confident, sir." I press my lips into a grim smile. Whatever happens, I'll still have that confidence.

And *that* isn't something my dad just bought for me the way he claims he bought everything in my life.

I know we're at an impasse, but I also know that ultimately this isn't his decision.

It's Kennedy's.

And I'm going to present this idea to her next…and let her decide what our future together is going to look like.

CHAPTER 52
KENNEDY VAN BUREN

I'm Caught

"Is it true that you were seeing Madden Bradley?" my father asks.

I'm caught.

There's no sense in lying about it now, though. "Yes, but it's over now."

"I told you to stay away from him."

"I know you did, and I tried. I really tried. But ultimately I also realized a few things. For one, your feud with his father has nothing to do with me or with him. And for another, I'm an adult who's pretty darn capable, and you still see me as a little girl. I'm not."

"I know you're not, Kennedy. I just wish you would've been honest with me. I'm disappointed that you were in an important relationship that you chose not to tell us about."

I sigh. "You never set up the kind of relationship with me that would've allowed for that. You were adamant that I couldn't go near him, and we didn't have a choice but to be together when we were each given half of SCS. The more we got to know each other, the more we knew it was useless to try to fight it."

"You're right," he says quietly.

"Excuse me?"

"You're right. He's our top rival, and I never gave you the chance to be honest with us. You're not a kid anymore, and I think I can finally see that. And that's why I'm flying out this week. My lawyer is sending over the paperwork today to name you the CEO of Van Buren Construction, and I'll be there on Tuesday to celebrate with you."

I gasp. "What?"

"You heard me, Kennedy. You knew this was coming, and I trust you to take VBC to the next level. You're smart, and you're intuitive. You get to decide what that looks like."

"Wow, Dad," I say as I jump up from my chair and start pacing around the room. "I wasn't expecting this. I mean…I *was*. Eventually. I thought you'd be there a while longer."

"I will be for a little. I'm at a point where today's technology has surpassed what I want to learn, and I'm ready to retire—or, for now, to cut back to part-time. Get out on the green a bit more. And even when I officially retire, I'll still be around if you ever need anything."

Tears spring behind my eyes at his words. I'm sort of shocked, at least in the sense that it's all happening so soon.

"Thanks, Dad."

I hang up, and the email from his lawyer is already waiting for me.

I print out the paperwork, read through it, and sign it before I scan it and send it right back.

Holy shit.

I'm officially a CEO. At twenty-seven. It's sort of unbelievable, and there are a whole lot of ideas I want to implement. Probably. Eventually. It's a lot of decision-making, and I'm honestly sort of glad my father will be around to help with the transition.

I stare at the screen in front of me, a little confused as I try to will some ideas into my head. What was I working on again?

I have plenty of work to do—especially *now*. I have plenty of things that have gone unattended to over the last couple weeks as my mood swings from high to low at the drop of a hat.

But I need to pull myself together. Especially now.

The truth is that I thought he'd be here by now.

I thought he'd realize we belong together.

I thought he'd come back to me to fight for me. For us. For our future.

But training camp starts tomorrow, and as the clock ticks to eight o'clock on a Sunday night, it's time for me to face the truth.

He's moved on. Or he's moved toward the season. Whatever. Same difference, or it may as well be. He's not here with me, and he's not coming.

Maybe I'll never be *okay* with that fact, but it's a fact that it's time to face.

I need to move on, too. Or at least throw myself into work and try to figure out how to focus on all the new tasks that are suddenly on my plate.

I may be just the tiniest bit overwhelmed, and that's why I'm not even thinking when my doorbell rings at nine o'clock on Sunday night and I throw the door open.

I guess deep down I assumed it was food that I don't ever actually remember ordering, but it's not.

Instead, it's Madden Bradley.

In a suit and holding a bouquet of flowers.

Looking fine as hell, and also…wait. What is he doing here?

"Did you do something different with your hair?" he asks with a grin.

I can't be moved to laugh in my total confusion and shock that he's actually standing on my front porch. "What are you doing here?" I ask. "Don't you need to be at camp?"

He nods. "Yeah. Tomorrow. I should be home packing. But this was more important."

"What was?"

"Being here with you." His dark eyes are so sincere as they pin me to my place. "I missed you, Ken."

I sigh. "I missed you, too. But I just convinced myself that I need to face facts that it's over literally like five minutes ago, so let me ask again, what are you doing here? Is this like some final goodbye? Or like a maybe we'll see each other sometime once the season ends since you'll be gone until then?"

"It's none of that." He shakes his head. "And for the record, I have Tuesdays off. Sometimes Mondays, too. And if we move in together, I'll be there as much as I can."

"If we move in together?" I repeat. I blink, and I glance over at him. "Madden, you broke up with me. You said you had to in order to protect me. You left me. You gave me Newman so you didn't have to face me. And now we're moving in together? I feel like I missed something."

"I was an idiot, Ken. I thought I was doing what was best for you by cutting myself out of your life. I didn't give you Newman because I didn't want to face you. I *couldn't* face you. I was far too broken without you, and the more time I spent apart from you, the more I knew how very wrong I was to let you go. I may not be good for you, but you're good for me. I love you. I want to be with you. I want a future with you. I want to work with you. I want to play with you and laugh with you and live fucking life with you. I want it all, and I want it with you."

I sniffle, not sure how to respond to all that.

He clears his throat. "I came here to tell you that and some other things."

"What other things?"

He chuckles. "I realized pretty quickly how much I need you in my life, but I needed to find a way to get you back while still keeping you safe. And so I told my father about us. I also told him that he needed to extract all traces of illegal activity from Bradley Group and then he needed to sign the company over to me."

I gasp.

"Once that was done, which was just this morning, I went to talk to your father. I asked him for his blessing for the two of us to be together, and then I proposed another idea."

I gasp again. "Did he give you his blessing?"

He shakes his head and hands the flowers to me, and I take them in my hands.

"No. But I told him it didn't matter." He bends down onto a knee right in front of me, right there on my front porch in my doorway, since I still haven't invited him in. "I told him I was going to ask you to marry me either way."

His words prompt my third gasp in the last thirty seconds.

"This may not be the most romantic time or place to ask you this, but I can't wait another second. I love you, Kennedy. I thought I could keep you safe by pushing you away, but it turns out I just needed to pull you closer. The last month has been the worst in my life, and I realized it was because I didn't have you by my side. I want to spend the rest of my life with you. I've never had anything so powerful and incredible, and I never want to let you go. Will you marry me?" He pulls a box out of his pocket and flips it open, and my eyes fall to a ring with a huge round-cut diamond inside.

My hands fly to my mouth.

I haven't spoken to him in a month, and he shows up here today out of the blue to ask me to marry him.

I'm not sure how I feel about that.

I'm equal parts confused and giddy and unsure and positive.

"This is all so fast," I say, and it sounds very much like a *no*.

"I know it is, and I'm not expecting you to answer right this second. Take your time. Think about it. I'm just running short on time, and I had to ask before it was too late."

I blow out a breath, reach out to pull him up from the ground, and slip the box back into his pocket before I slide my arms around his waist. "I feel like I need some time to be sure I can trust you after you walked out on me."

He pulls me close as he wraps his arms around me. "I'm back, Ken."

He's back.

But I don't know if *we* are back quite yet.

"Come on in," I say, and we walk inside my house and over toward my couch. "What was the other thing you proposed to my father?" I ask softly once we're sitting.

"I asked him to sign VBC over to you today," he says, and I school my reaction to his words carefully. "I had this idea that we could work *together* instead of against each other, that we could merge Bradley with VBC and run this supergroup together. You know…make actual billions together the *legal* way. I've thought about little else since I had the idea months ago. I thought someday we'd get married, and once we merged our lives, we'd merge our companies." He shrugs with a bit of sheepishness. "Maybe it was only ever a pipe dream, but I loved the idea of working with you ever since I saw you working on SCS. If I'm the CEO of a development company, I'd rather work with my top competitor than against her."

Heat pinches behind my eyes again at his words, but that call I got earlier today is enough to give me the confidence that what he's saying is genuine.

"Say something," he urges.

"My father called me earlier today. He forwarded the paperwork to me to officially name me CEO, and I signed it earlier today." I duck my head a little. "I think it might be his way of giving us his blessing, not that either of us really needed it."

He looks surprised by that.

"He made it sound to me like he was just ready to retire, but he specifically said that he knows I'm ready to take VBC to the next level. I think this might be what he meant by that." I press my lips together as a tear escapes and rushes down my cheek. He thumbs it away.

"I know it might take time for you to trust me again, and I deserve that. I never should have left. But I hope you can see that I was just trying to protect you from the illegal things my father was doing. You deserve so much better than getting tangled up with that. Just tell me what it'll take. I'll do anything to prove to you that this is genuine."

I chew my bottom lip as I think quickly. I mean…he *has* sort of proven that, hasn't he?

First by trying to protect me from getting involved with his father's illegal activities, then by basically handing over Newman, and now by getting the ball rolling by talking to my father and extracting his own father from Bradley Group.

It feels like he's doing what he can to take care of me in the way he will for the rest of our lives together.

All that feels like enough, but the feeling like I'm finally *home* again after floundering for weeks seems to be the most overpowering thing right now.

"VanBrad Construction Group. VBC Group. You make me fifty-one percent owner to your forty-nine, and we're co-presidents. I want full financial transparency from both sides as well as an exit strategy in place before I sign anything, and I will demand a prenup that protects my family business in the event this goes south. We'll also need a conflict resolution plan as well as a plan to separate work and personal life." I give him my most intimidating pointed gaze.

He doesn't even blink at my intimidation techniques. "God, you're hot when you go full-business mode on me. Now when you say prenup…am I hearing a yes?"

I laugh, and it's one of those deep belly laughs—a truly light and happy feeling that I haven't felt in far too long. Probably since the last time we were together. Once I take a breath and can use my voice again, I say, "It's still not a no. I just need some time."

"I understand, and I will wait forever if I have to." He reaches over and takes my hand in his, and it's this display of patience right here that tells me we're going to be okay.

CHAPTER 53
MADDEN BRADLEY

Secrets

I came here today to win her back. Does not having her answer scare me? Fuck yeah it does.

But so much of life is fearfully walking through it, totally unsure of what could be waiting on the other side. If we let the fear win, well, that's not really living life at all. And so I'll live for her, sure of us even if she's not, ready to give her whatever she needs to prove to her that this is the future we both deserve.

"When I said fifty-one and forty-nine, I was kind of just testing you," she says.

I glance over at her with a laugh. "I know. But honestly, if that's what it takes to prove to you that I'm in this, then I'll agree to it."

She presses her lips together.

"We don't need to decide anything tonight, Kennedy. But I do need to get home. I have to be at the training facility in the morning by six. We're here in town this week, but next week we'll head to SDSU for camp with the rest of the team. Will you come back to my place with me tonight?"

She nods. "Of course."

She packs a quick overnight bag and follows me in her car to my place. I decide to check in with Dex on my way home, and his voice comes through the Bluetooth speaker in my car a moment later.

"Mad Brad," he answers. "Don't you have camp tomorrow?"

"Yeah, but I figured I could check on my little brother first."

He laughs at the technicality. He's my younger brother, sure, by two years—a far cry from our youngest brother, Liam, who's nine years younger than me.

"Did you get everything ironed out with your situation?" I ask. I realize now he never really told me much about what was going on. Or maybe I didn't ask. I was a little busy with Kennedy at the time as we started building the foundation that carried us to where we are now.

"No, actually. I, uh…I recently got some news, and I'm not really sure what to do with it. Actually, a couple pieces of news."

"I take it you were planning to pick up the phone and call your older brother?" I ask.

"I called Ev instead," he says.

"Did you want to talk about whatever it is?" I ask.

"No," he says vaguely. "What about you? Anything new?"

Aside from the fact that I discovered our father's illegal underground casinos, signed the paperwork to become Bradley Group's CEO, and proposed marriage to a woman? "Yeah. Life's been a little crazy lately."

"When isn't it?"

Ain't that the damn truth?

As if the gods can tell I'm holding back some news, I swear I hear a baby cry in the background.

"I gotta go," he says, and he hangs up without so much as a goodbye.

So Dex has some news, he talked to Everleigh about it, and there may or may not be something wherever he was that makes the same sounds as a baby crying?

What the hell is going on?

I guess we're all keeping some secrets, and like most secrets, the only thing that will reveal them is time. Now that I'm wondering what Dex is hiding, I can't help but wonder when the rest of the family's secrets will come out.

And I also can't help but wonder what any of it will mean for the Bradley legacy.

We get back to my place, and I just finished packing my clothes as she watched from my bed when I head into the bathroom to pack up my toiletries.

She follows me in, and I'm suddenly voracious for her.

It's been far too long without her.

I pull her into my arms and press my lips to hers. We immediately fall back into each other. She sinks into me and kisses me with the hunger I knew was there after being apart for a month, the same hunger I feel after having been away from her. Our tongues tangle languidly and luxuriously, and the need to be inside her roars over me.

I pull back. "Take off your pants and bend over the sink."

She looks up at me with this demure, sweet look in her eyes that is hiding the depth of need we both feel. And in a split second, she scrambles to do what I just demanded.

Her ass is up in the air for me a moment later, and I stare at the creamy skin first before running my palm along it. I give her a little smack, and a small gasp escapes her.

"Do you want me to wear a condom?" I ask.

"I got on the pill," she admits.

Oh, fuck yes.

Our timeline is short, so rather than take my time the way I want to, I reach down and sink two fingers into her wet pussy. I'm met with a throaty moan that tells me to keep going, so I pull back and push in again, fingering her first to make sure she's ready for my cock.

"Fuck, you're so wet for me," I murmur. She responds with a moan, and I slip my fingers out and rub her clit. I want her tits in my mouth, but it's going to have to wait. Instead, I slide the zipper of my jeans down, pop the button, and pull my cock out. It's hard and heavy, ready for her, and I pump my fist along it a few times. I've been inside her bare exactly the one time, and I pulled out that time.

This time, I won't. This time, I'll feed her greedy pussy every last drop I have.

I use my cock to tease her clit as she widens her legs for me, and then I slide right into her. Her cunt clings onto my cock immediately, holding me in a tight, hot vise. She's eager as she shifts her hips back toward me, and I'm eager, too—so eager that if I move too quickly, it'll all be over.

Instead, I pump slow, long strokes into her, watching her in the mirror as she claws at the countertop, bites her lip, and squeezes her eyes shut. She's moaning as she gives into the pleasure between us, and I'm growling and grunting too as I try to hold onto my release even though just a dip into her for a few seconds feels like enough to make me come.

It's futile to try to make it last. It's too goddamn good. "Eyes on me," I demand, and her eyes fly open to meet mine in the mirror. I watch as her gaze clouds over with lust, and that's it. Her one single look is enough to send me over the edge into bliss.

"Fuck, Ken. I'm about to come. Do it with me."

She squeaks out a moan, and I let out a mighty roar as I tip my neck back, my eyes still down on hers in the mirror as I start to spill into her.

Her pussy contracts around me, and she cries out, "Yes! Oh God, Madden, yes!"

My eyes are on her in the mirror as I watch her fall apart because of what I'm doing to her. My memory flashes me back to the first time I fucked her in a bathroom at a charity event, when I got to watch her fall apart in a mirror similar to how I'm watching her right now. How very far we've come since that moment when we sort of hated each other but could no longer fight against the carnal attraction we shared. I know now that it wasn't just carnal. It was the way our souls seemed to engage with one another before we ever had a chance to fight against it.

And now, months later, I'm coming inside her for the first time, and it feels quite unlike anything I've experienced before. I pull out of her once both our bodies have calmed, and I immediately reach down to catch my cum as gravity does its thing and it starts to leak out of her cunt. I trace it around her clit, and there's something so goddamn hot about it all.

Eventually I remove my hand and offer her a tissue to clean up as I tuck my cock back into my pants, and I give her a moment of privacy before I use the restroom next.

I finish packing and join her in bed. I wish we had more time. I wish I had an answer.

And I will, eventually. I just need to exercise a little patience.

CHAPTER 54
KENNEDY VAN BUREN

Champagne Toast

I'm still in bed when Madden kisses my forehead and bids me goodbye. Part of me thinks maybe I just dreamed it, but the other part of me is pretty sure he left. He said something about how he loves me and I should just stay here, I think.

I just got him back, and now he's gone. And who knows what changes are in store for us this season? Time will tell, and that's really all we have to go on right now. He'll be back tonight, and I plan to be here waiting for him.

But then what? I don't have much out here. No friends since I've spent a large portion of the last month wallowing in self-pity instead of making new connections as one does in a new city.

I force myself up and take a shower in Madden's wonderful shower with that shower gel that smells deliciously of him. I head downstairs and find a note with a key beside it.

I glance at Madden's rather neat penmanship as I read his note.

K-
Here's my key. I hope you'll stay here tonight with me again.

All my love,
M.

This isn't how I saw today going—at all. In fact, I figured I'd be crying as I stared into my Cheerios without eating them. Instead, I'm standing in Madden's pantry as I try to find something to eat that isn't simply protein powder or a protein bar.

Does he eat anything that isn't packed full of protein?

When I think of those gorgeous abs…yeah, probably not. I text Oliver to let him know I'm running late, and then I head toward the office.

My phone rings as I'm commuting, already wondering-slash-daydreaming how exactly merging our two companies is possibly going to work. I glance at my car's screen and see it's Grace Nash calling me.

"Good morning, this is Kennedy Van Buren," I answer.

"Hi, Kennedy! It's Grace Nash. I was wondering if you were available to grab lunch this week to chat about the plans."

"I'd love to," I say. "And it'll be nice to talk to someone who is used to their significant other heading off to camp as a grown adult."

The words are out before I even realize that Grace has no idea that I'm with Madden.

"Training camp?" she asks, clearly confused.

"Oh, I'm sorry. I didn't even think twice about saying that, but I'm actually seeing a player on the Storm."

"I didn't know that! Who is it?" she squeals.

"Madden Bradley."

"Oh my God! I had no idea! Even with you two working for competing companies?"

"Yeah. Actually, that's how we met," I admit. It's not really the full truth as I think about our actual meet-cute at Starbucks, but it's close enough.

"I love that. Let's talk more over lunch. Are you free today?"

I confirm that I am, and we set up a time and a place to meet.

Once I get to the office, I'm shocked to find both my parents standing there with champagne and flowers along with Oliver. He's been wonderful here, and I look forward to continuing to work with him in this office.

Wait a minute…did I really just think that?

Maybe I *do* have a friend in San Diego. And I'm meeting another one for lunch.

And I definitely have something keeping me here now that Madden and I are back together.

"To the new CEO!" my dad says as he holds up the bottle.

I burst into tears.

This is really happening.

The four of us toast to my new title.

"Can we take you to lunch?" my mother asks.

"I actually have lunch plans with a client," I say apologetically, not mentioning that Grace feels like a friend in some ways already. "But I'd love to do dinner if you're free. Maybe with Madden, too?"

"I think that would be nice," my father says, and I'm shocked that he says it genuinely and not begrudgingly.

Shortly after that, I head to lunch with Grace, who's already waiting in a booth for me when I arrive. She gets up to greet me with a hug, and we chat a bit about her vineyard. Once the food arrives, I say, "So as a football wife, tell me everything I need to know."

She laughs. "Honestly? Patience and understanding go a long way, and so does having something of your own to focus on when he's in season. I lucked out with Spencer, though. He's my other half, truly. He helps me with the vineyards, and he's kind and logical and so, so smart." She shrugs. "He makes sure to call me every day when we're apart, and he prioritizes us over everything else. And we love building Lego sets together."

"That's so sweet," I say, leaning back into the booth.

She pulls her phone out. "You have to meet my sister-in-law, too. She's married to the quarterback, and it's her first season with a player."

My brows dip. "She's married to him, and it's her first season?"

"He was out all last season with a knee injury, but he's back. She's so excited."

"I'd love to meet her. I'd love to meet everyone. I guess I'm diving headfirst into this new world."

"Hell yeah, you are!" she says, and we both laugh as we high-five.

I feel like I made my first genuine friend in this town. I'm starting to find my own way, and it really feels like everything is falling into place.

When Madden gets home, I attack him with a kiss the second he walks through the door, and he laughs.

"This is sure a nice way to arrive home," he says, sliding his arm around my waist and pulling me close.

"How was training camp today?" I ask.

"Great, actually. It felt incredible being back on the field, and it wasn't as intense as next week will be. It was more meeting the rookies and meetings with the coaches. I feel energized."

"Good. I'm glad you feel that way because I sort of agreed to dinner with my parents tonight."

"Oh," he says. "No worries, I'll find something."

"No. It's a celebration dinner, and I want you to come with."

He wrinkles his nose. "Won't that be awkward?"

"Yes. Awkward as fuck. But if we're really considering a future together, we better get started on smoothing out that path now." I shrug and twist my lips.

He grins. "Touché. Let's go."

I love how he's up for anything, and we slip into the car and head toward the restaurant my mother made reservations at.

And when I get to the table, I'm shocked to see Clem and Lance sitting there. "Ahh! Clem!" I scream, and she laughs as she jumps out of her chair and tackles me with a hug.

Thanks to having my best friend there with her boyfriend, the meal turns out not to be awkward at all. I'm not sure why my dad made such a quick turnaround, but he pulls me aside as everyone else walks out of the restaurant, and it all sort of clicks together.

"Madden seems like a good guy," he says quietly.

"He's the best."

"When I saw him back out of Newman for you, I had a good feeling about him. But when he came by the house and said he stayed away because of his father's activities, I knew he was a good man. I know it feels like this was a quick turnaround on my part, but it wasn't. It took me a long time to come around. I see how he has so much potential, and I think you and him working together and merging the two companies could be incredible for your future."

I give my father a hug. That's as much a blessing as I'll ever get from him, and even though I didn't need it, it still means a lot.

CHAPTER 55

MADDEN BRADLEY

A Brand-New Legacy

I run the slant route for a third time, and Tanner quickly throws the ball to me after I make my forty-five-degree cut inside.

"Good, Madden," Coach Clark praises. "Great quick release, and that cut was pristine. Starting material, really. Going to be a tough call for us coaches deciding who we'll play, but you're already a force against our starters."

I feel good about the plays I've learned today, but there's still a long way to go. I haven't studied a full playbook in years since I was with the same team for so long and only had to learn a few new plays each season. But this is different. I *want* to succeed. I want to prove that I deserve to be here. And the bitter, mad part of me down low wants to show my former team what a mistake it was to let me go…especially when we go up against them later this season.

I'm even excited to get to what's beyond the game now that I know the direction the company is taking next.

And that's why I'm so torn about whether I want to keep playing. I know it isn't a decision I need to make right now, but just stepping out onto the field, feeling the grass beneath my spikes, cutting routes that confuse defenders because I can read this game so fucking well…it fuels me. It gets my heart pumping and my blood roaring to life. I'm Mad Brad out here. I'm quite sure I'm not ready to give that up, and the thought of seeing my girl in the crowd cheering me on as she wears my name on her shirt gives me next-level energy.

I'm lucky enough to get to go home this week, and she's there every night when I arrive. On Wednesday, it's after eight when I arrive home, and I was at the practice facility at six this morning. I'm exhausted, but seeing Kennedy sitting on my couch with a book fills me with the sort of energy I didn't know I could dredge up right now.

God, I love her. And she's mine. Eventually she'll answer my question, and then we'll be working together, making choices for a company that belongs to us both.

And that's when the next phase of our life together will begin.

The hours are slow, but the week is fast as I find myself packing on Sunday night for a week away with my team while my girl watches my every move from the bed, where she's relaxing.

"Are you going to be okay with me gone?" I tease as I walk over toward her and climb on the bed.

"I'm getting to know my community here. Especially Grace, who's quickly becoming my best friend here in San Diego."

I hover over her, and then I narrow my eyes at her and thrust my hips at the same time. "I thought I was your best friend."

She laughs. "Yes. You and your cock are my best friends. I meant to say that Grace is becoming my best *girl*friend here in town. Clem will always be my number one girl, though."

I finish packing, and I make love to my girl, and the next morning I'm heading to the team bus at the practice facility to head to our home away from home for the week at San Diego State University. We're assigned dorm rooms and roommates, and I guess when you go pro, you expect luxury accommodations from there on out.

Yeah, that's not real life.

But it's my life.

I'm sharing a room with Clay Mack, who has somehow become one of my best friends, and it's on the first night of camp when the lights are out and we're aching after a painful day trying to prove ourselves on the field when he says, "Why do we put ourselves through this?"

It's a great question. We bunk up in college dorm rooms for a week and put our bodies through the kind of wear and tear that's been compared to getting into a car accident day after day for the entire week, and then we return back home to continue the pain.

"Because we love the game?" I say, and it comes out like a question.

He laughs. "We do."

We're both quiet for a minute, and then I ask, "Can I tell you something?"

"Yeah, man. Anything."

"I proposed to Kennedy."

"Dude! I thought you were going to say this is your last year. I wasn't expecting that. Congrats, man."

I chuckle. "She didn't say yes."

"Oh, shit. Well, then I'm sorry, I guess."

"She didn't say no, either."

"Did she give you an answer?" he asks.

"Yeah. She said she needs time, but we both know this is right. We both know she's going to say yes. She's just playing it safe while we work on rebuilding some trust."

"Back to congrats."

I laugh. "What about you? Any future Mrs. Mack on the horizon?"

"Fuck no. It'll take some mighty magical pussy to get this guy thinking serious again."

"Could be a brand-new legacy, Clay. Little Clay Macks running around with little Mad Brads," I muse.

"Jesus," he mutters. "You propose to one woman, and you're already dreaming of having kids?"

"Nah. I'm just kidding around. I still don't know if I want that. If it happens, it happens."

"Don't put that out into the universe for me. I'm staying single."

"Yeah, that's what I said, too. And then I met the one woman who knew just how to take me down," I admit.

"I'm not as weak as you, old man," he teases.

We both laugh, and it must be a little too loud because we hear a pound on the wall from Spencer and DJ's room next door.

We take that as our cue to go to sleep, and I need it after the way I worked today.

Instead of going to sleep, though, I text Kennedy.

Me: *I miss you.*

I think back to our early text conversations where I'd stare at my phone like an idiot, smiling down at what she was saying.

That still holds true to this day. I smile as I see her text come through.

Kennedy: *I miss you more.*

Everything about life right now feels pretty damn sweet as I'm back to playing the game I love, I'm CEO of Bradley Group, and I'm positive that the woman who was once my rival is eventually going to say yes.

EPILOGUE: KENNEDY VAN BUREN

He Grins, and I Swoon

One Month Later

A year ago, you couldn't have paid me enough to don a Bradley jersey, in particular one that wasn't for my home team from Chicago, but here we are. I'm proudly wearing my man's San Diego Storm jersey as I sit beside Clem in the front row right in the middle of the field on opening day on the Storm's side of the field. I spot Cassie, the quarterback's wife, sitting with Sophie, her soon-to-be sister-in-law, in the end zone, and I text her to let her know where we are. She waves wildly at me, and we already have plans to go out after the game to celebrate since we're all feeling a victory down to our bones today.

Grace is here, too, up in the suites, I think, maybe with Spencer's mom. These women—the football wives—have become my little local family as I've started to dig into life in San Diego. I realize they can come and go at any minute. Trades or retirement or injuries—it's all possible in this ever-changing world, but for now, I feel like I'm part of something big and exciting. It feels like we've started bonding in ways that will take us far beyond this game.

I floundered a while as I worked out whether I really wanted to be here. I'm a Chicago girl at heart, and I always will be. But sometimes the heart can grow to love something else even more, and for me, that's Madden. Home is wherever we make it, wherever we are together, and right now, we're making it pretty damn sweet just outside of the San Diego city limits.

I haven't told him yes yet, but it feels like today's the day.

I'm nervous as I watch our boys take the field. I say a quick little meditation in my own mind: *stay safe, have fun, and play your heart out.*

I know he's got three-hundred-pound defenders ready to plow into him to stop him from moving the ball up the field, and I don't know how he's so damn brave to face them. Something about this game is in his blood, though—even though his father couldn't play, he and his brothers can.

I never in my life thought I'd cheer for anybody other than the Bears, but now that the man I love is a player on the San Diego Storm, my allegiance seems to have shifted to a new city. *I'll never cheer for anyone else* has become an adage of the past. If the Storm plays the Bears, I might tease Madden that I have some issues with who to cheer for, but my allegiance will always fall to the man who holds my heart in his hand.

Clem and I are both eating popcorn and drinking beer, and even she showed up in a Storm shirt today.

Our team receives the ball first, and Tanner hands it off a few times to running backs. He passes to Spencer, and then Madden has a catch before the Cowboys take offense, and Madden stands on the sidelines while the Storm's defense takes the field.

I watch the back of his head from where I sit, and he's watching the game carefully. He's dialed in and focused as he watches every play with an analytical eye, something he's been trained to do for the last thirteen years that he's played in this league. Will that number tick to fourteen? Time will tell, but we've talked fairly extensively about it, and I think I know what he wants to do.

He wants to play through some of this season before he focuses on what comes next.

He may not even get an offer to stay, but if he does, it'll be a decision we'll make together. That much I know. And I also know that I'll support whatever it is he wants to do. We're a team now, and teams run more smoothly when everyone on it is doing what they love.

It's my first time experiencing game day with him. He was quiet this morning as if he was already focused on today's game, but he also kissed me like his life depended on it before he headed out the door this morning. He told me he's always a little quiet on game day morning, so I knew what to expect.

He turns around during a commercial break, and I give him a small wave when I think he's looking at me. He grins and waves back, and my heart absolutely melts. And then his eyes shift down to the number eighty on the front of my shirt, and I spot the heat in his eyes as they move back to mine. He raises a brow, and it's one simple look that speaks volumes to me as if we share our own language now. That's the look that means we'll both be going to bed with smiles on our lips tonight.

And I can't wait for him to make me smile.

Near the end of the first half, Tanner hands the ball off to his twin, who's taken down by a defender almost immediately. But on the next play, Madden cuts downfield and is wide open. Tanner spots him and throws him the ball. It sails easily into his arms, and he runs it into the end zone for a touchdown.

I scream as I jump out of my seat, spilling popcorn everywhere without a care in the world, and Clem screams next to me, too, as we celebrate Madden's touchdown.

After the play, he runs over toward me, and I bend down to slap his back. "Oh my God!" I scream at him. "Great play!"

He grins, and I swoon, and it's pretty much the most perfect moment in history as he celebrates his big play with me.

He pulls his helmet off, and I kiss him.

When I pull back, I say, "Yes. I want to marry you."

"Yes?" he repeats.

"I want to marry you."

His smile widens, and he kisses me again, and it's all a blur since he has to get back to the sidelines. I stare at him from where I am with a huge smile on my face for the rest of the game. Clem is next to me screaming and cheering at my yes, and everyone around us must think we're nuts, but I'm getting married.

That man right there wearing number eighty on the sidelines? He might've started as my enemy back when we were mad rivals, but now he's something else entirely to me. He's my fiancé. He's my entire future, and whether we're here celebrating victories on the field or in an office building or at home, I can't wait for every single second of what's coming next.

THE END

Want more Madden and Kennedy?
Scan this QR code to download a bonus epilogue!

Scan this code to join Lisa on Facebook at Team LS: Lisa Suzanne's Reader Group!

ACKNOWLEDGMENTS

Big thanks first as always to my family. Thank you to Matt for the love and support and to our kids who all this is for.

Thank you to Valentine PR for your incredible work on the launch of this book.

Thank you to Valentine Grinstead, Christine Yates, Billie DeSchalit, Serena Cracchiolo, and Patricia Rohrs for beta and proofreading. I value your insight and comments so much.

Big thanks to my ride or die bestie, Julie Saman. We'll always push each other to hit those deadlines no matter how impossible they may seem!

Thank you to my ARC Team for loving this sports world that is so real to us. Thank you to the members of the Vegas Aces Spoiler Room and Team LS, and all the influencers and bloggers for reading, reviewing, posting, and sharing.

Thank you to my ARC Team for loving this sports world that is so real to us. Thank you to the members of the Vegas Aces and Vegas Heat Recovery Room and Team LS, and all the influencers and bloggers for reading, reviewing, posting, and sharing.

And finally, thank YOU for reading. I can't wait to bring you more sports romances where swoony superstar heroes ride emotional roller coasters to their happily ever afters.

Cheers until next season!

xoxo,
Lisa Suzanne

ABOUT THE AUTHOR

Lisa Suzanne is an Amazon Top Ten Bestselling author of swoon-worthy superstar heroes, emotional roller coasters, and all the angst. She resides in Arizona with her husband and two kids. When she's not chasing her kids, she can be found working on her latest romance book or watching reruns of *Friends*.

ALSO BY LISA SUZANNE

Grayson & Ava

Spencer & Grace

Asher & Desi

Tanner & Cassie

Miller & Sophie

Made in United States
North Haven, CT
15 August 2025